Many straight men are down on having a secret relationship with someone like Stash Burcell, but not out in the open. Living in such a close-minded society makes it hard for him to find someone he can trust, let alone surrender his heart to.

Anthony Charles Eisemann has only ever been out with women, though secretly he'd always been drawn to androgynous femme men who looked and dressed like women.

When Anthony meets Stash, their lives take a sudden turn from complicated to dangerous.

It's Not That Complicated
Copyright © 2020 Jo Tannah
ISBN: 978-1-4874-3003-0
Cover art by Martine Jardin

Published by eXtasy Books Inc or
Devine Destinies, an imprint of eXtasy Books Inc

Look for us online at:
www.eXtasybooks.com or www.devinedestinies.com

It's Not That Complicated
CyNapse, Inc. Book 2

By

Jo Tannah

Chapter One

The moment Anthony Charles Eisemann saw the figure of the woman standing waist-deep in the pool, he knew his life was going to get complicated. Not that it already wasn't, it was just going to get even more so than usual.

There was something about how the wet tips of the long, silky, flame-red hair brushing the small of the woman's bikini-clad back made him crave someone like he never had before. Where the water lapped beneath the tresses, it teased the plump curves of what appeared to be smooth butt cheeks. At the thought of stroking between those curves, the tips of his fingers began to tingle. Already he could imagine how that skin was going to feel and taste against his tongue.

When it came to sex, smooth silky skin was Anthony's main weakness. The one that never failed to make his knees buckle beneath him—the touch and taste of soft, smooth skin over firm, hard muscles. In his opinion, women who worked out had the best skin, and this one obviously did.

He narrowed his eyes behind the sunglasses he wore and leaned further against the balcony railings, hoping for a better view. At that very moment, the woman hauled herself out of the pool revealing strong, lean muscles on equally long legs. And that butt. It didn't even jiggle.

Anthony licked his lips when he belatedly realized the woman was nude. Well, almost, for he caught sight of the strip of fabric tucked between those gorgeous globes, and his initial disapproval disappeared. For some reason, the sight of the thong eased him. It was an irrational and totally unexpected reaction from him. Normally, he didn't mind in the least what a woman chose to wear in or out of a pool, but somehow, this stranger was making him feel things he couldn't explain.

Oh yes, Anthony considered himself a connoisseur, and that woman was definitely to his taste. Pale smooth skin peeked between red tresses, making his mouth water. The woman still had her back turned to him when she raised an elegant hand to gather and then twist her hair, bringing it off to one side and revealing the rest of her flawless back.

Anthony couldn't suppress a gasp escaping his lips. *Oh wow.* The thought of touching that unmarked skin made his cock tighten in his pants. The woman wrapped her arms around herself and then started jumping up and down where she stood. The move made her butt cheeks jiggle. He really needed to know who she was.

Turning his head slightly over his shoulder, keeping his gaze on the vision by the pool, he called for his personal assistant. "Gregory, do you know who that woman is down there?"

From behind him came sounds of a chair scraping on the floor, and Gregory Morgan stepped up beside him.

"Hmm, I'm not sure. I wasn't aware of anyone else joining us here other than Mr. Burcell and his people." Gregory stepped away from the railings. "I'll go and find out."

"Thank you, Gregory."

Gregory left, and Anthony turned his attention back to the pool area. Another woman had approached, dressed in a black tracksuit. Her long black hair was combed in a severe high ponytail that hung to the middle of her back. She helped the mystery woman into a thick white robe she was holding up. The two women began to speak in low voices, so Anthony couldn't really hear what they were saying. The second woman threw back her head and laughed out loud just as

Gregory stepped out from beneath the awning to his right.

A movement from the sidelines distracted Anthony's attention. He straightened as a brawny bearded man stepped into Gregory's path. The man was dressed in a gray tracksuit and black running shoes, the complete opposite of Gregory's navy-blue woolen suit, silk tie, and highly polish loafers. Gregory might appear to be weaker and pretentious in his attire, but he didn't flinch under the bodyguard's fierce glower. Instead, he said something beyond Anthony's hearing and handed over what Anthony knew was a calling card.

The guard took the proffered card without breaking eye contact from Gregory before handing it over to another bodyguard who walked over to join him. Both men stood shoulder to shoulder, effectively dwarfing Gregory with their height and breadth. That was no mean feat, as Gregory was well above average height. It was a clear display of intimidation. Anthony frowned at the realization that these were highly trained men. Who was the woman to need security of their caliber as guards?

The second guard glanced at the card before walking toward the black-haired woman, who had begun picking up stuff off the lounge chairs. She didn't even glance at it but pointed to someone out of Anthony's line of sight. A third man came into view. This one was bearded, lean, and moved quite gracefully. To Anthony's observation, the third guard was most likely more dangerous than the previous two. The third man said something to the mystery woman, who then shook her head before glancing over her shoulder to speak to the other female.

The breeze must have shifted, for Anthony could suddenly hear her voice, but just barely. He frowned and leaned further over the decorative wrought iron.

"Meggie, I'm freezing. I'm going inside. The pool temperature is too cold. Can you talk to the maintenance crew, and ask them to increase the heat?" The woman snapped her fingers, and somewhere in the distance came an answering yip. "Come on, Flossy, time to get back inside, baby."

"What did you expect?" the woman called Meggie countered. She shook her head. "You're crazy wanting to swim in this weather."

Anthony jerked away from the railings. Not from the sight of the tiny fluffy cream-and-caramel-colored dog that came running toward the woman. It wasn't even because the dog had long bouncy hair sweeping the tiled floor, which completely hid its short legs.

No. It was because the woman he had been admiring and lusting over had a voice that didn't sound like it belonged to a woman. For one, it was too low to belong to any female. That was unless said woman pretended to have a baritone voice.

She—no, not a *she*, definitely a *he*—looked up just as Anthony was about to turn and walk away. Something must have caught his attention. Maybe he heard Anthony's startled exclamation. Or it could have been because he'd noticed Anthony leaning over the rails, making them creak and groan in protest. Whatever it was, Anthony froze when their gazes met and held him bound. If he hadn't been experiencing it, he would have thought the scene straight out of a movie. It was so cliché, but he was truly and completely trapped.

Even from across the distance, Anthony could clearly see light-colored eyes. He didn't know exactly what color they were, but they dazzled under the morning sun, and he was hooked. Time stood still, and for a moment, he couldn't breathe. That was definitely no woman he was lusting over.

Anthony could never mistake the sharp, contoured facial features as belonging to any female. The man was certainly androgynous, beautiful with a strong feminine aura, but he was undeniably male. Also, his Adam's apple was hard to miss. Whoever he was, he had to be the most stunning creature Anthony had ever seen in his life.

His life wasn't going to be complicated at all. It was going to explode.

The beautiful man continued to stare up at him. The longer their gazes remained locked, the more his expression morphed from one of curiosity into that of outright sexual interest. The slight upturn of one corner of his mouth, the lick on the lower lip, the heavy lids — there was no denying that whoever that man was down there, he found Anthony attractive.

There was no way on Earth Anthony could deny the lust he felt gripping his cock. He didn't want to refute the open invitation, but he stood frozen and unwisely continued to stare back at the man, unable to look away. Definitely *unwilling* to look away.

Too shocked about his body's sexual excitement, Anthony peeled away from the railing, gritted his teeth, and forced himself to step back. The moment he lost sight of the man, the need to know more about him became harder to resist. So he took a hesitant step forward and looked down. That was when he realized he'd made a major mistake.

The man's expression had turned from lustful interest to one of disappointed resignation before sadness took over. His shoulders drooped slightly. Not enough to ruin his posture, but enough that if Anthony hadn't been staring so intently, he would have missed it completely.

But then, the beautiful man broke their eye contact and turned away. Wide-rimmed sunglasses, which successfully hid most of his face, were slid on before he began speaking inaudibly to the third man, who was now standing beside him. There was a look of concern on the guard's face, but the beautiful man shook his head. Back held straight, he walked away and disappeared under the awning, the furry dog following closely on his heels.

The three guards followed while the woman had paused

from her conversation with Gregory to look toward the beautiful man and dog. Her expression briefly tightened, and she turned back to say something to Gregory. Anthony couldn't hear what she said, but after she finished speaking, she looked up and narrowed her eyes at him. He didn't know what to think when she slapped on her own pair of sunglasses and walked off. Her quick, jerky movements were telling of her emotions and what she thought of him.

Normally, Anthony would have dismissed such reactions to his presence, but for some reason, what had just transpired made him feel dirty. That he had somehow managed to disappoint both that beautiful man and the woman within seconds of each other was something of a record for him. He didn't know why he was feeling that way, but he knew he was, and he didn't like it.

For the first time ever, Anthony didn't like himself. That was another huge surprise. He was arrogant and self-aware enough to know that he never worried about disappointing others, especially when it came to business dealings. This, however, was no business deal. He'd crossed a line.

He didn't know what would happen next, but the pressing need to apologize and make up for his mistake was hard to shake off.

Anthony mentally berated himself. He could have waved at the beautiful man, or maybe given him a smile. Instead, he'd looked on like a lustful teenager and cowered like an idiot when the favor had been returned.

Confused over his warring and confusing emotions, he didn't realize minutes had passed. A sudden movement brought his gaze up to find Christian Adams, the head of his personal security, standing beside him. It took most of his pride to keep from yelling out in surprise.

He pretended to clear his throat and faced his guard. "What is it?"

"I was wondering if you ever read the report I sent over last week," Christian said in a quiet voice.

Anthony frowned in annoyance. He didn't know how long Christian had been standing there, looking down at the scene below. There was no doubt in Anthony's mind that his guard had witnessed his embarrassing reaction.

Once more, he cleared his throat. "Which report was that?"

"The one about Stash Burcell, sir." Christian tilted his head with a concerned look. "Are you unwell, sir? Do you want me to call a doctor?"

Anthony covered his embarrassment by raising a brow at Christian before slowly turning back and looking down at the pool area. Two men were standing in front of one of the walls and appeared to be checking a control panel partially hidden by ivy.

"No, I don't need a doctor. And no, I never received the report. Who's Stash Burcell? I'm not familiar with that name."

"Gregory's coming back upstairs. I'll return with a copy of the report. Excuse me, sir." Christian dipped his head and left the room.

Anthony gritted his teeth. Christian could be quite cryptic, but that was just the way he worked.

A soft knock on the door had him looking over his shoulder to check who was coming in. The door opened, and Gregory stepped inside. Not for the first time in the past six months since he'd hired Gregory, Anthony wondered what other things Gregory had kept hidden from him. Was the file about the unknown Burcell the only one, or was he withholding other information?

"What did you find out?"

Gregory scoffed. "That woman was no woman—that was Stash Burcell, CEO of the fashion house, Anastasia Beauty. Heir to the Burcell Group of Companies."

Anthony breathed through his nose as he tried to control

his rising irritation. Why hadn't Gregory briefed him about such important information? Could it be that Gregory hadn't read Christian's report either?

"Is he Adrien Burcell's son?"

Gregory smirked. "It appears that way. According to the young Burcell's assistant—her name's Meggie—Stash is here to represent his father. He's the one you'll be meeting with tomorrow."

Anthony shook his head at Gregory's lack of knowledge. Knowing the name of one's counterpart was essential for his position. His personal assistant should have known this basic information and shared it with him before now.

"I always thought Adrien had a daughter. Anastasia," Anthony wondered out loud. "Why am I just learning about this, Gregory?"

"I'm not sure who Anastasia is, but according to my file, Adrien Burcell has a son. There's no mention of a daughter anywhere online." Gregory shrugged.

Anthony's brows furrowed as Gregory's lack of care and apparent incompetence became more and more obvious, but he decided to play the inept fool.

"I swear Adrien had a daughter. I remember my father mentioning it once. I think I even went to a birthday party one time." Anthony scratched at his chin. "That was a long time ago, though. I think I was seven or eight. What about Adrien—why can't he meet me tomorrow? He was the one who called me and asked for this meeting. Do you know why he changed plans on us?"

"According to Meggie, there was some sort of situation that had developed. The older Mr. Burcell said he needed to personally handle it and flew back to the States last night. Meggie didn't really explain, but she did say that the older Mr. Burcell is going to be delayed two or three days. She suggested that if you're willing to wait, your meeting with him can be postponed until such time he can make it. Otherwise, he's sent Stash over in his place. She claims that Stash is more than ready to meet with you tomorrow night."

"Why am I just finding this out now? Why didn't you investigate fully?"

Anthony barely reined in his anger when Gregory merely shrugged nonchalantly.

"According to Meggie, they *did* inform us. I told her we never received any notification. She apologized and said there was no excuse for the miscommunication, but that we'll just have to take her word for it."

"I see," Anthony turned his back on Gregory as the need to wring the man's neck was getting more and more impossible to control. He studied the pool area, wondering again about Gregory's ineptness. *Or is he doing this on purpose?*

The mental image of Stash's red hair brushing against his back made Anthony's cock jerk beneath his trousers, and all thoughts of violence faded away. He walked back into his suite, trying his best to hide his arousal from Gregory, but his imagination refused to give him rest. Those light-colored eyes, the lust turning to disappointment . . .

Anthony knew why he felt this way, but his secret was something he was unwilling to make known to anyone, especially Gregory. But he *could* do something about his other issues with his personal assistant.

Behind him, Gregory began to snigger, and once more, the need to punch him came back in full force.

"Seriously. Did you see what that guy was wearing?" Gregory chuckled. "Jesus. What a freak show."

Anthony's vision blurred, he clenched his fists, and he slowly placed one foot parallel to its mate. He took off his sunglasses, then slowly turned around to face his assistant, barely able to contain his displeasure at hearing first-hand Gregory's scorn and disrespectful attitude.

"Kindly repeat what you just said, Gregory."

Gregory was still laughing over his own comments as he walked toward the desk he'd set up as his temporary office. Perhaps that was why he failed to notice Anthony's rising anger. He picked up his tablet and began to type something on it, all the while laughing at whatever else he was thinking about.

"Burcell's swimsuit. Did you see that red wig? He looked so bizarre." Gregory shook his head, still oblivious to Anthony's irritated silence. "I don't know what he was thinking of, wearing women's clothing, putting on that makeup. He's obviously gay—"

"Gregory, this is the only warning you're ever going to get from me on the subject of Stash Burcell," Anthony said through gritted teeth.

Only then did Gregory look up, the smile frozen on his lips.

He stared directly into his assistant's eyes. "I never, ever want to hear from you or hear about you making your personal opinions known regarding his choice of clothes or sexual orientation."

Gregory slowly straightened his expression. He swallowed loudly before lowering his gaze and dropping his arms to his sides. "I apologize for giving you offense, Mr. Eisemann. I won't disappoint you again," he said in a voice so low, it could barely be heard.

"See to it you don't." Anthony sat at his desk in front of a picture window. He pulled sharply at the handle of the middle drawer, snapping it open.

"Yes, sir."

Annoyance made Anthony avoid looking at his assistant. He could hear the regret in Gregory's voice, but he suspected it was more because he had been reprimanded, not because he was sorry for his words.

Anthony set aside his laptop before taking out a pad of

elegantly embossed stationery from the drawer. He slapped the pad hard on his desk before reaching out for a pen. "Tell Christian to see me. Now, gather your things and get out. That will be all, Gregory."

"Yes, sir."

Anthony kept silent but quietly observed from his periphery as Gregory picked up his things before finally leaving the room. He knew his angry silence had probably made Gregory nervous, but it was either that or make the man physically feel the sting of his fist.

Anthony was a patient man, never one to take out his anger on anyone, but there were a few things that set him off. Open bigotry was one of them.

He took his time, thinking over what he wanted to say in a note to the younger Burcell. Finally he took a deep, calming breath and began to write. When he was done, he read over what he'd written before signing his initials and folding the paper in half.

There was a brief knock on his door before it opened. Christian stepped inside and quietly placed a folder on top of the desk. Even though Anthony was tempted to read what the file would reveal, he decided to wait. He opened the drawer once more to pull out an envelope that matched the stationery he'd used, placed the note inside, and sealed it before handing it over to Christian.

"Take this to Mr. Burcell's room. When you hand it over, tell them it's private and for his eyes only. Don't leave without a reply, and don't come back until you get it in your hands. That's all, Christian."

"Yes, sir," Christian said before leaving.

Alone in the suite, Anthony looked out the window and breathed in the clean, cool mountain breeze before pulling his laptop closer. He browsed for Stash's name, tapping his fingers on the desk as he waited for the results to load up.

Seconds later, the results were in.

"Thank you, Howell," he murmured under his breath. If there was one thing he could rely on, it was CyNapse technology. Even on top of a mountain surrounded by endless forest, the internet signal still came on strong.

When Adrien had first called about the impromptu business meeting, he'd told Anthony that he'd reached out to Paul Howell, CEO of CyNapse Inc., for somewhere private and out of view from the media. Although it had been the older Burcell who had reached out to him, Anthony wouldn't waste the chance to talk to the man. The annual general meeting wasn't scheduled until the beginning of the fourth quarter, but Anthony could not pass up the opportunity for a one-on-one meeting.

Adrien Burcell was a director on the board for Eisemann Industries, and his vote carried a lot of weight. Anthony knew it was important to get the man on his side. He'd personally thanked Burcell for the quick arrangements for their meeting. It was his way of letting Burcell know that their meeting would be advantageous for both of them.

Anthony was surprised when he learned that their meeting was to take place in the Rhône-Alpes. He'd known about the property but had never been, so he had been looking forward to getting away from the hustle and bustle of New York. He loved the city, and that was where his offices were based, but there was nothing like breathing in fresh, unpolluted air and waking up to the trill of birds and the scent of the woods. A major plus was that even at this secluded location, he could continue to work.

Howell was well known for owning out of the way and technologically enhanced properties all over the world. This particular estate was a ten-bedroom French chateau in Saint-Pierre-d'Albigny within Savoie, which Anthony learned Howell had bought only three years before. It was a stunning fortress located atop a mountain, overlooking a panoramic countryside with pristine forested peaks behind it. From what Gregory had discovered, there were three floors, ten bedrooms, and more rooms that could be counted as living and recreation spaces. Anthony's suite was on the second floor overlooking a mountainside.

Images began to quickly load on the screen of the laptop. There were hundreds of pixilated pictures of what appeared to be a thin figure of a man taken from afar by the predatory lenses of paparazzi. There were more pictures, if the search numbers were to be believed. Most were candid shots that showed a man wearing signature high fashion Italian and French men's suits. There were closer images of accessories, some of which Anthony recognized were more expensive than regular homes on the current market. He smiled when a particular handbag was featured. It was one of his products, and he concluded that Stash Burcell knew the difference between quality and luxury items.

What truly fascinated Anthony most were the marketing images of the world-famous brand Stash had created. According to the reports, not only was the man the brains behind the billion-dollar cosmetic and fashion company, but his was also the face that sold the products. Now that he was looking at the overall view, he realized that he'd been familiar with the brand all along. He'd just failed to connect it to Adrien. He should have known about this, made the connection. A mistake like this was something he could not afford to do, not with his position, status, and power. Gregory should have updated him on this, kept him at the top of the game.

Anthony tapped a finger on the keyboard and focused once more on the information before him. He found it curious that there were no actual full-face images of Stash in any of the photos. If they were not blurry ones taken from several hundred meters away, they were close-in marketing images of specific body parts. One that grabbed Anthony's attention was of an overly made-up eye complete with Swarovski crystal accents. One eye. Others were of lips, and there were a few shared images of a dog that Anthony recognized as the one he'd seen earlier.

He clicked on a link and found himself directed to a social media fan page devoted to everything Stash Burcell. After browsing for several minutes, he decided that no one really knew what Stash looked like other than a generalized conclusion that he was male. What could one get from one eye, lips, a dog, and expensive bags?

Anthony's stomach clenched as he stared unseeing at the screen. With or without makeup, the Stash he'd seen was simply stunning to behold. As he stretched his arms to the ceiling, one thought kept repeating in his mind. He was in serious trouble.

Taking a deep breath, he finally took up the folder Christian had left earlier and read through the report. The more he read, the more intrigued he became, and the more he wanted to meet the mysterious Stash Burcell.

After he was done reading, he set the file aside and went back out to the balcony. For a long time, he stared down at the now-empty pool area and thought about what his next move would be. When he finally reached a decision, he was not shocked. It was a scenario that had been a long time coming. What was surprising was how quickly and decisively he'd reached it. He knew there would be repercussions. But he didn't feel there was anything that would make him hesitate or be afraid.

Anthony knew a man of his position and wealth had clear responsibilities. Whatever decision he made in his personal life would be deemed a reflection on his family and businesses. Should he act on his desires, it was sure to give rise to many questions about his capabilities as a leader. Succeed or fail, there would be no going back.

On the other hand, he would be free. There would be no more need for denials or suppression of the media. No more secrets to agonize over. His family, his company, the whole world would soon know that he, Anthony Charles Eisemann, CEO, multi-billionaire, and a man publicly known to only date beautiful women, was, in fact, not quite as straight as people thought.

Chapter Two

Stash slammed the bedroom door behind him. His mood had quickly spiraled into a black hole, and he didn't care if anyone thought his actions childish or not. It was, but at times like these, the sound of a door banging against its hardwood frames and remaining shut was satisfying. He turned to glare at the door with a satisfied nod. Stomping farther into his room, he shrugged off his robe, kicked off his slippers, stripped off his bathing suit, and plopped face down on the plush coverlet.

He was acting like a diva. He knew that, of course. But if he went down the route he really wanted to, he would have no friends left. And friends were all that was left for him, other than his dad. Aunt Irene technically wasn't a blood relation, but really, he considered her the closest thing to one.

Images of his humiliation downstairs chose that moment to flash in his mind's eye.

"Argh," he screamed into the covers. Throat aching, he took deep breaths and began the de-stressing exercises one of his psychiatrists had taught him years ago. One, inhale, two, exhale, three, inhale . . . He had reached twenty and was finally coming down from his rush of angry humiliation when he heard the door open and someone stepping inside.

"Want to talk about it?"

The gentle voice coming from behind him broke through his zone. It belonged to his best friend, Meggie. After his temper tantrum, she would be the only one brave and confident enough to enter a closed door without first knocking. He could feel her cold glare on his bare ass.

"No," he said, shaking his head. He continued the breathing exercise. When the bed beside him slumped, he opened one eye to peek through his tangled mess of red wig.

"Was it really that bad?" Meggie pressed. Her brows scrunched to a frown, and her luscious, matt-finished lips puckered up into a pout.

He didn't answer immediately, his attention distracted by how the lipstick lay on her mouth. The color really looked gorgeous on her.

"Stash!" Meggie's sharp voice snatched him out of his daydreaming.

"What?" He didn't look up from his perusal. He knew it would irritate Meggie, but really, the lipstick she was wearing was quite lovely. One of his better creations, he thought with a satisfied smile.

"Pay attention, geez." She gave him a gentle shove. "What are you thinking about?"

"Your lipstick. It's really nice on you. I should release it."

"No. It's not quite ready yet. You said so yourself." Meggie grinned. "And thank you. I like it, too." She flashed a quick frown. "Don't be in a rush. We don't want to ruin this release with a half-baked product."

Stash returned her smile. He rolled over on his back only to giggle when Meggie cursed and threw a pillow over his crotch.

"Jesus, Stash. Cover yourself up."

"You don't mind it," he said. Another giggle escaped his lips. "Remember when I didn't have a penis?"

"Oh, my God! Don't remind me, please!" Meggie snort-snickered into her hand.

When their giggles subsided, Meggie's face turned serious. "You know you can talk to me, right?"

Stash rolled on to his side so he could fully face his friend.

He and Meggie had grown up together in his father's house and had been born only months apart. While Magda Lacierda, Meggie's mother, had been his father's housekeeper, she had also acted as Stash's wet nurse. She had continued to work for them until her retirement five years before. Magda was like a mother to him, since his own mother had abandoned him. When he'd asked about why his mother had left, Magda told him that right after he had been born, the doctors of the time couldn't truly diagnose whether he were a girl or a boy. Shocked and upset, Samantha Burcell nee Stalinski packed her bags and left Adrien Burcell. She told everyone who listened that she couldn't accept she'd given birth to a thing like Stash. After the divorce came through within weeks of her leaving, his mother had never once contacted them. Magda had told Stash later that his father was a good man and rich enough to have made sure his mother would leave them alone.

"Stop thinking about your mother, and stick to the present. What she did had nothing to do with you at all. That's all on her. It isn't your fault you were born that way. In any case, she wouldn't have liked you if she'd stayed. You're more beautiful than she is."

Stash shook his head, leaned sideways, and kissed Meggie on her cheek. "You always know what I'm thinking."

Meggie let out a derisive snort. "Of course I do. We're practically twins."

"We're breast mates," Stash said with a huge grin.

"That we are. I'm your sister of the breast," she said as she dramatically flung an arm up toward the ceiling.

Stash sobered. Meggie was not just his best friend and confidant—she truly was his sister in spirit. "Yes, you are."

A knock on the door made Stash quickly get off the bed and escape into the bathroom, although he left the door slightly ajar. Inside the bedroom, he heard Ian speak. Ian was one of his personal bodyguards who also happened to be Meggie's younger brother.

"Someone called Christian, from the second floor, handed over this note and is waiting outside. He said he was instructed by his boss to give this to Stash, and that he was not to leave until he got a reply."

"His boss being Eisemann?" Meggie asked.

Stash's eyes widened. So that was who the man was. His embarrassment grew a little more unbearable, and he scrunched up his nose. Of all the people to flirt and crash with, it had to be the man he was scheduled to meet the next day — a straight man. Stash pulled on the door so he could peer through the gap he'd made.

"I guess." Ian shrugged.

"Okay, just wait a sec," Meggie said.

Stash hurriedly wrapped a towel around his waist and walked out of the bathroom. "What is it?"

"Eisemann. He sent you a note," Meggie said. "Do you want me to take care of it for you?"

"No. Let me see that," he said, nodding to Ian as he gave a small salute before closing the door.

Meggie shrugged, handed him the note, and left him to read it while she picked up his suit and robe from the floor.

"Do you want me to give your dad a call?"

"Not yet," Stash said cocking one hip as he opened the envelope and unhurriedly took out the note. The script was neatly done, but one he assumed was written in a hurry. His curiosity raised a notch at the words he saw written there.

Can we meet? Hang out? Businessman to businessman or simply as two ordinary men who are staying in the same private residence? Say yes. ACE

"Oh, okay. Wow."

He hadn't quite expected what he'd just read. It didn't sound like a rejection of his earlier flirting or even a placating excuse. Stash twisted his lips and tapped a long fingernail on his chin as he considered the request. It was quite an interesting note. Very interesting indeed.

For one thing, it had been written on actual stationery. Stash had received tons of text messages before, but never anything painstakingly handwritten on real paper. With genuine ink, not printer ink. It wasn't much of a difference, but for some reason, it made Stash want to meet Eisemann despite his earlier embarrassment. From how it had been written to the tone of the words, it seemed like Eisemann truly wanted to meet him. He could still remember how his mouth had watered simply from watching the man standing on the balcony.

"Stash?"

"Hmm?" He raised his head and looked at Meggie.

"Where were you? I was like, calling your name for about a minute there."

"Oh." Stash straightened up. "Uhm, do you have a pen?"

"Yes," she said, lengthening the word. "You want me to take down something?"

"No." He bit his lip and gripped the note close to his chest. "I want to write down a reply. To this note."

"Okay," Meggie said, hanging his soiled clothes on the crook of her arm. "Give me a sec."

Stash tapped his foot on the carpeted floor. When Meggie came back, he couldn't help feeling excited and curious. He quickly scrawled the word *Yes* below Eisemann's initials, folded the note, and pushed it back into the envelope. He gasped when a part of the envelope tore, but he smoothed it down. Humming under his breath, he carefully eased the frayed edges.

"Meggie? Can you go and get Ian, please?"

"Sure," Meggie said in a bewildered tone, but she did as he requested.

When Ian reappeared at the door, Stash went over and pressed the envelope into his hand. "Take this to what's his name outside. Now, please."

"Okay, boss. You want me to go with him, so I can wait for the reply?"

Bless Ian. To anyone else, Ian was a bearded, mean-looking man, but among Stash's personal bodyguards, Ian was also the one who was the gentlest and understood him best. He'd also served longest as a protector. Stash loved Ian and Meggie. Both were his friends and part of his chosen family.

"Yes, please. Thank you again, Ian."

"Anytime, boss." Ian gave him a sweet smile and closed the door behind him.

"Stash? What's going on?"

"Hush." Stash held up a well-manicured hand. "I don't want to talk about it." He made a zipping motion over his lips.

"Are we going to start passing notes like we used to in school?"

"Hush, I said. I want to see where this goes." He narrowed his eyes at Meggie and tapped a finger over his lower lip. "And I don't want Dad knowing about this. We cool?"

"Cool?" At his determined nod, Meggie rolled her eyes and turned to leave the room. "Yeah, yeah, yeah, we're cool. Can we call your dad now? You know he's waiting for you to give him an update and is probably getting impatient."

"Shh, he can wait another five or twenty minutes. I want to know what Eisemann wants from me."

Meggie released a heavy sigh as she left the room. Stash ignored her and went back inside the bathroom, where he took off his wig and placed it carefully over a Styrofoam head. He looked at his reflection in the mirror and grimaced at his flattened blond hair. He'd have to wash it and make sure to use conditioner before meeting with Eisemann.

Stash smiled at his reflection as he thought about Eisemann. There had been something about that note that had gotten him feeling energized. Sure, he'd been upset earlier at seeing the shock on Eisemann's face when he realized he was looking at a man rather than a woman. Even from afar, his facial expression had been quite obvious.

Stash was more than familiar with reactions like that, as he'd seen it so many times over the years. For that was how it always was. Men, and women, always thought of him as a woman at first glance. It was an honest mistake. His features were androgynous enough to be confusing, especially when he was in his femme mode, wearing wigs and makeup. Then again, even when he wasn't, he'd seen too many people do a double take as if they were trying to figure out whether he was a man or a woman dressed up like a man.

The hot spray of the shower felt good against his skin, and he was scrubbing away at his legs when he heard Meggie clear her throat.

"I got back a reply," she said.

Stash slid open the glass door and peered out. "Leave the note on the counter."

"Ooh, but I wanted to read it," Meggie said with a disappointed pout.

"No, you can't. Get out." Stash stuck out his tongue at her before turning to shut off the shower.

"So rude!" Meggie said, but she did it with grace and a giggle to let him know she was teasing as she walked out.

After the door closed, he stepped out of the shower and grabbed the towel hanging on the heated rack. When his hands were dry enough, he hurriedly opened the note.

Thank you for giving me another chance. I promise I'll make it up to you. I'll see you at seven? Tell me where, and I'll be there. ACE

Stash didn't know why he felt so giddy over a silly note, but he didn't care. He grinned so broadly it felt as though his cheeks were going to split. After hurriedly toweling himself dry, he put on a fresh robe and walked out of the bathroom. Meggie was waiting for him, wearing a frustrated expression.

He ignored her and walked over to the desk, where he had left the pen she'd given him earlier, and hurriedly wrote his reply under Eisemann's second message. With a flourish, he turned and held out the note to Meggie.

She rolled her eyes once again. "No need to say anything, I know what to do."

"Thank you, Meggie!"

"I love you too, Stash."

Chapter Three

Anthony automatically took the can of soda Meggie handed him as soon as he stepped into the room.

"Take a seat. Stash's call is going on a little longer than expected, but he should join you soon." Meggie clapped her hands twice in quick succession. "Okay. There's food on the coffee table that way." She pointed a thumb over her shoulder. "And there's drinks in the fridge over thataway." She pointed a finger to somewhere behind Anthony.

He glanced over his shoulder and easily spotted said appliance. When he turned back around, Meggie had left his side and was shrugging into a coat.

"All ready. I'm out of here. Just in case Stash forgets and looks for me, please remind him that I'm going down to the village to visit the pubs. Or whatever they call it here. Chino, the guard who met you outside the door? He's staying. Anyways, I'm off. See ya. Oh, wait, good night, Mr. Eisemann."

Before Anthony could think of a response, Meggie disappeared out the door. He was left standing in the middle of the room, looking around for somewhere to set down the can of soda. He finally settled on the fridge. He didn't really drink soda, finding them too sweet, and he much preferred juices. Unsweetened. Sugar additives made his stomach act up, and he couldn't afford to have a stomach screaming insults at him. Not tonight. He was nervous enough as it was.

The room, he discovered, was very different from the one he'd been given. First of all, this one was a floor above his, which he had suspected contained more exclusive suites. The hallway on this floor was decorated more luxuriously, yet homier than on the second floor, which he could only describe as basic. Second, this room was twice the size of his. His accommodations didn't have a cozy feeling, not like this one did.

He didn't really know how to react to that. Should he feel slighted? Probably, if he were to act entitled. He'd known from the start that this was one of Paul Howell's private homes, so if he were given a smaller guest room at a moment's notice, he shouldn't complain.

According to the write-up Gregory had given him on the flight over, there were ten private suites in this chateau. There was probably a reason why he was placed on the second floor and not the third, but he couldn't think of what he was missing.

When he opened the fridge, he grunted in appreciation for the selection of canned drinks he found there. Depositing the can of soda inside, he reached for his preferred favorite, unsweetened pineapple juice.

"Yes, he's here. I've kept him waiting long enough. I'll talk to you tomorrow, Dad. Good night."

Anthony jerked at the sound of the voice. He turned around and froze, still holding the unopened juice in front of him. A very different looking Stash was walking toward him.

"Hey. Sorry for keeping you waiting, Ace." Stash was all smiles, wearing a blue tracksuit splattered with a whole lot of orange and intertwined double Gs.

Anthony recognized the luxury brand. Anyone else would have looked ridiculous wearing the outlandish design, but somehow, Stash pulled off the style with aplomb. Not only did he look like he belonged in it, but he also wore it like it defined him. Sassy and self-assured. Anthony felt his attraction for Stash rise a notch. It didn't help that the man's sultry, husky, and very male voice felt like a soft caress down the length of his spine.

"Oh, you got yourself a drink? Good idea," Stash said as he approached.

Stash's clear brown eyes flashed curiously as his gaze drifted down to Anthony's hand that held the can of juice. Somehow, that one unconscious move managed to amplify the already uncontrollable urges Anthony felt toward Stash.

All right, Stash wasn't even flirting with him, but Anthony still couldn't find his voice. How could he? The creature walking toward him was stunning in the sexiest way. How did one describe a person like Stash?

Stash appeared freshly showered, and by the look of his damp, strawberry blond hair, it must have been recent. Anthony did a double take. The color must be his natural hair color, not the red of earlier. As Stash came closer, Anthony found it harder and harder to comprehend what he was seeing.

Had he ever even seen skin like that on a woman before? Or a man, for that matter? With his obsession for skin, he mustn't have, for his cock had never jerked so hard inside his trousers like it was doing that very second. He didn't realize how tightly he was gripping the can of juice until it exploded in his hand.

"Oh shit!" Anthony's face heated as he helplessly watched the yellow liquid bubble up from the ruined tab and dripped down his hand.

"Are you all right? Here, let me get some towels." Stash grabbed a roll of paper towels from the counter beside the fridge and ripped several segments. "There you go. It's only juice, so it shouldn't stain your jacket. Why don't you take that off so I can rinse it?"

Like an automaton, Anthony placed the ruined can on the counter and took off his jacket. Stash made quick work of running cold water over it in a small sink before setting it to one side.

"There, that should take care of it. I can have the maid take it to laundry tomorrow."

"Uhm, thanks for that. It should really be dry cleaned, though." Anthony cringed inwardly. Why was he talking about laundry, for God's sake? What was it about Stash that made him forget that he was supposed to be an experienced man . . . Lover? Whatever. What the hell? He wasn't here for any of that.

"I'll make sure it gets cleaned properly. Now. Are you hungry?" Stash linked his arm through Anthony's, who didn't resist the move or move away.

Anthony looked down at their intertwined arms. Stash's arm looked just as smooth as his face. The temptation to reach out and touch the skin was hard to ignore, but he had to if he were to save himself from complete embarrassment. He focused on his breathing, and thankfully, the need subsided.

Damn. This was worse than he'd previously thought. He just knew he was going to make more of a fool of himself.

"Paul usually hires a chef whenever he has guests, and I can't wait to taste what they have to offer," Stash continued. "The last time I was here was last year. I hope it's the same chef. He was incredible."

Anthony shook himself. Food was easy, a topic he was more comfortable with.

"You mean Paul Howell? I know he's always hired the best. So you've been here before?" Good. That was a good start. Anthony cringed and did a mental facepalm. At least he was recovering from his lust-filled fugue.

"Yes, I've been here several times. I came with Aunt Irene the first time. This is my regular room whenever I'm visiting."

"Aunt Irene?"

"Wattenberg. She was my father's cousin's wife before he died."

"I see." Anthony erased the frown that rose between his brows. He had a feeling he was missing something, but there was no coyness to Stash's explanation, he was just stating facts.

"She's also Paul's aunt. His mother's sister," Stash said with a smile. "Come, sit with me."

Anthony nodded in understanding. Things were clearer now. So Stash and Paul were not just connected, they were related in a roundabout way. Among their circles, connections were everything.

Anthony met Stash's gaze. A hint of a smile played over the plump lips, but Antony couldn't read whether Stash were secretly amused with him or something else. Stash was a beauty, but Anthony could see he was one who didn't easily betray his thoughts. He made a mental note to ask Christian to dig deeper into Stash's background.

Anthony sat on the plush sofa Stash had led him to, finding himself facing a large TV. On the coffee table before him were several covered dishes and two pitchers off to one side. Stash began removing the covers to reveal cold cuts, cheeses, choice breads, and some fruit. It all looked homegrown and organic — even the meats.

"Ooh, have you had this? Its iced tea infused with herbs and fresh fruit."

Ice tinkled as Stash poured out two glasses of the tea. After handing one to Anthony, he took a long sip from a metal straw. Anthony gaped at the sight of Stash pursing his plump pink lips around the straw. The way he closed his eyes as he sipped the liquid was suggestively erotic. With his thick, sweeping lashes, Anthony could already imagine how Stash would look when in an orgasm.

"Oh my God, this is utterly delicious," Stash said with a dramatic roll of his eyes. He held up the glass and tapped a nail at the fresh berries there.

Anthony's gaze focused on the pointed and elegantly decorated fingernail. It was painted bright neon yellow, with what looked to be Swarovski crystals pasted on it. It should have looked garish, and it was a style Anthony never really admired. However, on Stash, it managed to enhance his elegance.

"Wow," Anthony said, unable to stop himself.

What level of luxury was Stash at? Even Anthony's mother couldn't have come close to him, and she had been considered one of the best dressed and accessorized socialites in the world when she had been alive. His throat felt dry, so he reached for his tea and took a long drink.

"Look at these, Ace. They look so delicious and cute and so pretty. Just drinking this makes me even gayer."

Anthony gasped and coughed when liquid went down the wrong pipe. After regaining his breath, he stared at Stash with watery eyes.

"I'm sorry. I seem to be making a mess of things," Stash said, his brown eyes darkened, filled with regret, and something else.

The longer Anthony didn't speak, the more Stash's air of despondency deepened. The realization obliterated the conclusion Anthony had reached earlier. Stash wasn't poker-faced at all. Far from it. Stash was self-conscious and insecure.

Anthony shook his head. "No, no. You're doing fine. Why are you saying you're messing things up?"

"I'm sorry if I'm embarrassing you." Stash appeared disappointed and distant. His face shuttered once more. "If you want to leave, it's okay. I understand."

"Now why would you think that?" Anthony placed the tea on the table and leaned his elbows on his knees.

"I can be a bit overwhelming at times," Stash said, placing his own drink beside Anthony's before scooting over to the opposite end of the sofa.

Anthony considered how Stash had quickly lost his previous liveliness, and he didn't like what he saw one bit. He might not know this man, but he seemed quite sensitive regarding his sexuality. That realization didn't sit right with him. Time for a serious talk.

Anthony caught Stash's gaze and held it. "What if I told you that, yes, you're a bit of a surprise? Outrageous, even. I also think you're incredibly beautiful and would like to get to know you better . . . on a personal level. No business involved. What would you say about that?"

Stash was apparently pleased with that idea, for his bright smile returned, as did the sparkle in his eyes. "I like that. We can be friends. Thank you. You mean it, right?"

Anthony fought the frown that wanted to form between his brows at the hopeful tone in Stash's voice. In that minute, it became crystal clear to him that Stash had been hurt in the past. Seriously hurt.

"Of course, I mean it. Why wouldn't you believe me?

"Because I don't know you," Stash said, inching a little closer.

"That's why I'm here. I mean it. I really would like to get to know you better."

Stash tilted his head to the side, his gaze taking on an analytical light. "You don't mind that I'm femme or fabulously gay?"

Anthony bit down on his laughter. "What's to mind? So no, I don't care about that at all. You're who you are."

"You're so nice." Stash's smile broadened.

"Not all the time." Anthony grinned and relaxed into the sofa. "I just really, *really* like what I'm seeing. And you may not believe this, but I'm attracted to you. Very much so. I'm not going to apologize for being blunt about it, either."

"Oh." Stash's cheeks pinkened, and he turned away.

Anthony thought he looked adorable.

Stash picked up two small plates, placed them next to each other on the table, and began filling each with choice pieces of cold cuts. Anthony easily saw through the façade. Stash was nervous and most likely anxious about what Anthony would think of him. Once more, that curious feeling of wanting to put Stash at ease made Anthony act in ways he'd never done before.

"Can I be upfront?"

"Even more than you already are?" Stash flashed a quick smile as he continued to pile food onto the plates. "Go ahead."

Anthony waited until Stash handed him a plate. "I've never been with a man before. I mean dated. But I've always been attracted to men like you." Anthony nodded his thanks when Stash handed him a fork on a cloth napkin.

Stash stiffened for a quick second before visibly relaxing. He licked the bottom of his lip. "What kind of man am I?"

"Beautiful."

"You've said that before," Stash said in a low voice. His cheeks flushed again with that rosy hue beneath his creamy, flawless skin.

"I mean it. You are incredibly stunning."

Stash took a piece of bread and broke it over his plate. "I'm also a man."

There it was again. Anthony couldn't miss noting the lack of confidence. How many men had hurt Stash? Anthony wanted to meet and destroy them all. Gregory's list of faults was getting longer.

"I'm fully aware of that," Anthony said.

When Stash didn't immediately respond, Anthony reached out for a piece of bread and began to eat. They didn't speak for several minutes, but Anthony saw through Stash's silence. He looked to be deep in thought, considering what to say as he meticulously arranged meat and cheese on sliced bread. Anthony didn't mind. He was used to people taking their time before making a decision. He was the same and decided to give Stash whatever time he needed.

When Stash finally spoke, it was with a bit more confidence. "Yesterday, after my dad asked me to take his place to meet with you, I had Meggie look you up. You're straight."

"So they say," Anthony said, keeping his expression blank.

Stash threw him a quick glance before turning back to his meal and sipping at his straw. "I also have a confession to make. I'm into straight guys. Straight acting guys, I mean."

Anthony blinked. He didn't know how to respond to that one.

"So yes, I like you," Stash continued, pausing a moment before looking up.

They gazed at each other, unmoving for a long second, then they both chuckled.

"Can I ask you something? I hope you don't mind or get mad at me," Anthony hedged.

The smile fell from Stash's lips. "Are you asking if I'm transgender?"

Anthony found himself treading in uncharted waters. He opened his mouth several times, only to close it as soon as a question came to mind. This was a tricky situation, and there was no way he could know how his questions would be met. Was he going to get the answers he desperately needed, or was he going to get punched in the face? His gaze drifted over to Stash's fingernails and he reconsidered the options. Suddenly, getting punched sounded better than getting his eyes scratched out of their sockets.

"Relax, Ace." Stash chuckled, patting Anthony's hand. "Ask away. I won't get mad. I promise."

"Thank you." Anthony sighed his relief. He cracked his neck as he considered which question to ask first. "Before we get into that, can you tell me why you keep calling me Ace?"

Stash grinned around the metal straw, his white, even teeth

too perfect to be real. Most likely they were fake, but somehow, it only made him more real in Anthony's eyes.

"You signed your note A-C-E."

"Oh, those are my initials." Anthony tried to fight off his smile, but his lips had a mind of their own, and soon he was beaming.

"I know," Stash said, giving Anthony a slow wink.

Anthony's cock throbbed in response, and he had to shake his head to regain focus. "Jesus. Stop doing that. You're outrageously sexy when you do that."

Stash's eyes twinkled. "Keep going."

"Okay, don't kill me, but are you a guy? Are you a girl? Are you trying to transition? What are you?" The second the words were out of his mouth, Anthony closed his eyes and steeled himself. Anytime now, he expected to be slapped or punched.

Anytime . . .

CHAPTER FOUR

Stash snorted into his tea. "Oh, my God. Wow. I wasn't ready for that."

The unexpectedness of Anthony's questions made him chuckle, but as the words began to sink in and he took a moment to analyze them, it quickly turned into full-blown laughter. His mirth went on for a while until finally, in order to not appear as though he'd lost his mind, he took a deep breath and let it out in a whoosh. He turned to Anthony and took his time studying him.

From the very first moment he'd set eyes on Anthony, something about the man had captivated him—a connection he hadn't been expecting. The initial physical attraction had gone further than a simple sexual one. For reasons he still couldn't fathom, this night was taking him somewhere unexpected.

Should he answer truthfully or go for a lie? Anthony sat next to him, looking absolutely horrified. It made Stash realize that there was something more to this guy than he'd previously expected. Reaching a decision, he decided to go with the truth.

"Well, first of all, I was born male, but you need to know that I have a hormonal deficit."

"Deficit?" Anthony's expression changed from horror to curious to one of confusion. He blinked several times before scratching his head. "Can you explain that to me?"

Stash cocked his head to the side and sucked on the metal straw. This was the point where he had to find the right words to explain what he was. From the past, he knew many people, including his own birth mother, had a hard time accepting the truth, but he had decided to be honest. Should things go downhill, at least it would do so before he got hurt emotionally. Of course, he was used to getting hurt, but that didn't mean he wanted to feel it all the time.

"My condition is called five-alpha reductase deficiency. Basically, when I was born, the doctors initially thought me to be a girl. Then, after further examination, they began to have their doubts. My mother abandoned me and my dad soon after because of the doctors' indecision. She didn't like that she'd birthed a *thing* like me. Initially, the doctor decided that I looked more like a girl than a boy. He later told me it had never once occurred to him that I would turn out to be a boy. Anyway, I was raised as a girl, but I remember thinking that things were not right. Then, in the months leading to my thirteenth birthday, my penis started to grow." He stopped talking when Anthony raised a hand.

"Excuse me? Say that again?"

"My penis grew. It was slow on the onset, but the older I got, the bigger it became. At first, I didn't tell anyone, not even Meggie. I was too scared and embarrassed, but at the same time, I thought that it felt right." Stash smiled ruefully when Anthony raised a brow. "You met Meggie earlier. She works for me as my personal assistant, but I see her as my sister."

"Okay, this is really strange but very interesting from a scientific point of view." Anthony relaxed into his seat, fully focused on the conversation.

Stash began to tap his fingers on the side of his glass. He parted his lips, but the words wouldn't come out. Then the unexpected happened. Anthony reached out and gently caressed the top of his head. He couldn't quite contain his relief at the surprising support.

"Please continue," Anthony said.

Feeling the encouragement shook Stash, and he had to look away for a moment to clear his throat.

"I was fourteen when my voice began to crack, and I could no longer hide the truth. That was the day Dad took me to the doctor, and she confirmed that I was actually a boy." He gave a derisive snort. "Shocker."

"Did . . . How . . ." Anthony shook his head, and his brows furrowed. "Did your dad sue the doctors? For misdiagnosing? What did he do when he found out?

"No, he didn't sue them." Stash shook his head. "We knew it wasn't their fault, and they didn't realize what I was at that time. To be honest, no one actually knew what was going on with me. There was just not enough information about people like me. I don't blame anyone. Neither does my dad. And remember, they didn't have the technology then. No research either, I think. I'm not sure."

"That's true," Anthony said. Frowning, he reached out for his iced tea and sipped on it, appearing to be deep in thought.

Stash watched him closely. When Anthony didn't run out of the room or call him names, a glimmer of hope kindled deep in his chest.

At the same time, Stash couldn't help but worry he might have revealed too much and all at once. He'd lost too many friends and even family—like his mother—after they found out. His heart grew cold, and he steeled himself to the inevitable.

When Anthony turned to look at him, Stash met his gaze with all the confidence he could muster. Anthony looked away, blinking several times before straightening in his seat. He looked down and stared at the glass in his hand for a long minute before setting it down on the coffee table.

"I recall something about the condition." Anthony looked up, meeting Stash's gaze. "One of my companies manufactures pharmaceutical products, and I remember someone sending me a write-up, requesting a research grant on that particular subject. Go ahead, please. What happened next? I'm listening." Anthony leaned back, crossed a leg over his knee, and draped his arm on the back of the sofa.

Somehow, his attentiveness made Stash feel more confident in talking about his condition. Maybe Anthony was different. Would he listen with an open mind? There was only one way to find out.

Biting the inside of his cheek, Stash gestured to himself. "Whenever people ask me about *what* I am, I tell them I'm Stash. Being like me — a guy who looks like a woman — people have always wanted to put me under a specific label." Stash turned serious and met Anthony's gaze. "I refuse to be labeled. I am not a category. I was a girl who turned out to be a boy, and I identified as one from the very beginning. I'm also a man who happens to be gay." He raised a finger, not missing the way Anthony's eyes followed its movement. "That confused many, since I grew a penis, and I mean, literally grew one. I have been scorned and hated for what they say is someone who *chose* to be a man and become gay. Anthony, I *never* had a choice. I am me. I am Stash, and that's all I am."

Anthony nodded his head while Stash rambled.

To Stash, it appeared as though Anthony understood what he was talking about. At least, Stash hoped that he did.

"I remember reading that those who have the condition may enjoy certain perks," Anthony said.

"What?" Stash frowned. What was Anthony talking about?

"Listen to me for a second. Correct me if I'm wrong, but from what I remember reading in that study, there are certain things that people like you may enjoy that the rest of us do not." Anthony reached up and drew a finger down Stash's cheek. "Your skin is like silk, it looks airbrushed. That alone is unusual. I should have paid closer attention, for that is one of the signs that you are who you are." Anthony dropped his hand and turned thoughtful. "Answer me this. Do you even have underarm hair?"

It was Stash's turn to gape in surprise. How had he known? Was Anthony a godsend? Had he finally met someone who saw him as a real person and not a *thing*?

"No, I don't sweat there, either," Stash whispered, finding it hard to breathe.

"I thought you didn't." Anthony sat up and cupped his hands on either side Stash's face. "I noticed you don't have facial hair. Shouldn't you have?"

"Not a lot, but I've also had laser hair removal," Stash said, biting his lower lip as he tried to control the bubble of laughter from spilling out.

Anthony stared at him, his expression admiring rather than ridiculing. "You're incredible, do you know that?"

There it was again. The way Anthony looked at him as though he was a treasure. Stash fought for air. His lungs screamed at the lack of oxygen, since he'd forgotten how to breathe. He couldn't look away, and seconds passed before Anthony finally broke the silence.

"Can I kiss you?" Anthony whispered

Stash thought his heart would melt from happiness. *Oh, damn. The man is actually asking permission? Hell, fuck, yes!* He'd be an idiot to say no to a man like Anthony Eisemann. He nodded and murmured, "Yes, please."

The night was taking him for a spin, and somewhere along the wherever-the-hell-it-was way, he'd managed to forget how to think straight. Anthony lowered his head and pressed his lips against Stash's. The world tilted, and he found himself in wonderland. He held onto Anthony, drowning in a whirl of sensations as he was kissed like never before.

It started out slow and inquisitive. Stash had kissed many men in the last seventeen of his thirty years. Almost all of them had taken his mouth, pressing their wills and insecurities onto him as though they were trying to prove something. With Anthony, though, he found himself on an alien world full of desire. Unspoken questions and longing flowed through each swipe of the tongue, as though Anthony needed to discover who Stash was — the real Stash.

Anthony suddenly pulled back, gasping for breath, but he didn't move far. His breathing ragged, he gazed into Stash's eyes as if he'd wanted to look away. He didn't.

"I just want you to know something. I've never kissed a man before," Anthony said in a rushed tone full in wonder. "Tempted, yes. Kissed? Never. I've never . . ." He pressed his forehead against Stash's. "You're my very first. Do you know how incredible this is for me?"

"You keep saying that." Stash smiled as he ran the tips of his fingers down Anthony's cheek, his acrylic nails rasping against the stubble.

Anthony leaned against the touch. "Because it's true. I've never met anyone like you."

Anthony's gaze shifted as he tucked Stash's hair behind his left ear. Then he pulled Stash closer to his chest and dropped his head in the crook of Stash's neck.

"It's as if every single wish I've had since I first became aware of how I wanted to be involved with someone sexually has suddenly been granted." The warmth of Anthony's breath caused a tickling sensation.

Stash brought his arms up and over Anthony's shoulders, closed his eyes, and held on tight.

Chapter Five

For the first time in his life, Anthony wanted to give up control. He couldn't take his gaze off of Stash. It was as though Stash led him on a leash, and all he could do was follow. No way he could turn away, either.

What had just happened between them went against everything he'd been told, was used to, or done. *Fuck.* He'd actually kissed a man, and he'd liked it. Even in his own mind, that sounded cliché and a twist to famous lyrics, but it fit his situation perfectly. Too perfectly, if he were honest about it. There was one thing he was certain about. Stash felt good in his arms . . . like he belonged there.

Stash's body was lean and hard, the opposite of any woman Anthony had ever slept with. There was also a noticeable lack of body odor. It was quite perplexing. Stash didn't smell like anything other than the soap he'd probably used when he'd showered earlier. Still, after several minutes, there should have been some sort of scent that was uniquely Stash. Even with their kiss, there was only the lingering taste and smell of the fruity herbal tea he'd been sipping on and the food he'd just eaten.

Anthony ran dragged his hands down Stash's back, still sniffing at the soft, velvety skin of his neck. The absence of a unique scent was quite disconcerting. Did that have something to do with the perks Stash enjoyed because of his condition? Anthony closed his eyes and breathed in deep.

He would instruct Christian to find the research file on five-alpha reductase deficiency so he could give it a second read. Now that he had a better understanding of what people like Stash experienced in life, it would be prudent to review the proposal. It would be interesting to see what his pharmaceutical had planned for the money they'd requested. It had been almost a year since he'd first gotten the request, but it wouldn't be too late.

"Are you having second thoughts?" Stash whispered.

Anthony frowned and leaned back. He met Stash's gaze and saw the light of doubt had crept back in his brown eyes.

"Your eyes were light-colored earlier. Contacts?"

Stash chuckled. "Yes. I like to use different colors so they coordinate with my mood or the clothes and makeup I'm wearing."

"You like wearing makeup?" Anthony squinted, looking closer to see if Stash was wearing any. It didn't look like he was.

"I do. Meggie and I played with it while we were growing up, and I never outgrew it. It's my safe place." Although Stash flashed a hint of a smile, there was also a note of challenge to his admission.

Anthony didn't take the bait. "I'll make sure to remember that." His gaze fell to Stash's soft, plump lips.

Unable to help himself, he lowered his head and kissed Stash again. This time, he used his tongue. Stash opened his mouth slightly, touching the tip of his tongue against Anthony's. The move, slight and hesitant, only made Anthony pull Stash closer to his body. He pushed his tongue deeper inside Stash's mouth, urging him to open wider.

Anthony pressed into Stash until they tumbled onto the cushions of the couch. Stash held on to his shoulders and widened his legs. Anthony groaned. He aligned their bodies closer together and took the risk of getting punched for real by reaching down and cupping Stash's crotch.

He'd thought himself ready to feel something familiar, but

the feel of a hard, warm cock in his hand made his own cock throb in response. Anthony deepened their kiss. The hunger rising inside of him was confusing and uncontrollable. Yet everything about what they were doing felt so right. Stash groaned into his mouth, and Anthony gentled his kiss.

"Am I hurting you?" Anthony murmured between kisses.

Stash shook his head and leaned back to gaze up at him.

"Is it all right if I touch you?" Anthony had to ask. Frankly, he didn't know what he was doing. Sure, he was an experienced lover, but with women. He'd didn't know a damned thing about how to please men. How to please Stash.

"It's perfectly all right." Stash sounded pleased. "Do you want me to show you what it's like to be with a man?"

Anthony thought his chest would burst, but he nodded and leaned back when Stash pushed away from him. His eyes widened as he watched Stash unzip his jacket to reveal a chiseled, muscular chest. The flat pink nipples were a definite change from what he was used to, but he couldn't hold back the urge to reach out and touch the creamy white skin. Stash was still shrugging out of the jacket when Anthony started running his hand up and down the man's torso.

"Please. Take off your clothes," Anthony begged. He didn't mind when Stash threw him a look of surprise. "I need to touch your skin."

"You have a skin fetish or something?" Stash asked, but he did push his jogging pants down.

Anthony could only nod, his focus locked on the skin bared before him. "Flawless skin. I just love it, and yours feels incredible. I don't think I'll ever get tired looking at it and touching it."

At the sight of the pale white flesh over Stash's hips and the pink red-tipped cock oozing with precum, Anthony knew he had stumbled into heaven. Stash was everything he'd secretly dreamed of. No one, man or woman, had ever made his head turn like Stash was doing at that moment.

"I need," he mumbled. "Please, Stash."

"Go ahead. Touch me," Stash whispered. "I know you want to."

Anthony looked up and met Stash's gaze and saw the welcoming enticement there. Never able to resist a challenge thrown at him, Anthony caressed the tip of Stash's cock with trembling fingers. He almost jumped at the heat he felt there. It shouldn't have surprised him, for he had felt his own when he jerked himself off.

"Go ahead, Ace. Don't be scared," Stash encouraged in a husky voice.

Anthony responded the only way he knew how. He gripped the shaft in his hand and pumped it. It grew harder and hotter under his touch, and precum dripped over his hand. Stash groaned and shifted, widening his legs. Anthony looked up to watch even as he continued to pump and stroke. He looked down at the cock in his hand, and his mouth watered. What would it taste like? Only one way to find out. He didn't hesitate. He lowered his head and drew the cock into his mouth.

"Oh. My. God!" Stash jerked, pushing his cock deeper inside.

Anthony almost gagged, but he remembered one of his lovers describing to him how she did it. He breathed in through his nose and relaxed his throat, much like he did when he needed to take huge vitamin pills. He almost laughed when the maneuver worked.

Stash moaned and groaned under him. Anthony didn't give in when Stash attempted to push him away. He continued to work over the cock, and the more he did, the more he found he was enjoying giving Stash head. Also, he was relishing the flavors that burst across his tongue. It was vastly different from those of women. The taste of Stash's precum was surprisingly delightful.

Who had said it tasted bitter? He didn't care. His current enjoyment was totally being engrossed in deep-throating Stash, who sounded like he could bring the room down on them with his was gasping and shouting out instructions.

Suddenly, Anthony remembered that Stash's bodyguard was sitting outside the door, so he reached up with his right hand and placed it over Stash's mouth. He pulled away, and the popping sound of cock leaving his mouth made him smile. It was truly a vastly different experience, and Anthony was enjoying every minute of it. The grin split over his face.

A grin split his face as he gazed at his lover. "Shh, baby, someone will hear." Without waiting for a reply, he bent and took the delicious cock into his mouth again. He was getting good at this.

"I don't give a shit. I want to come!" Stash mumbled beneath his hand.

Anthony nearly choked from laughing with his mouth full of cock. Stash was certainly different from his previous lovers. Reluctantly, he pulled back again to release Stash.

"All right. How do you want to come?"

"Hard! Now, suck me, and don't you dare stop."

"Okay, baby. You got it." Anthony prepared to take him back into his mouth.

"Like a Hoover, damn it, Ace!"

Anthony barked out a laugh, but he didn't need to be told twice. He started to suck on Stash like his life depended on it. He didn't know how long he was at it, but when Stash began to tremble, he remembered something. Without missing a beat, he put a finger in his mouth to lubricate it and gently pressed it into Stash's opening.

"Yes!" Stash screamed out.

Anthony peered up at Stash to find him gripping the sofa's armrest and hanging on for dear life.

"Oh my God," Stash managed between gasps. "I thought you said you've never been with a man before. Fuck!"

Anthony was not prepared for the come that suddenly exploded in his mouth. His first instinct was to jerk back, but he didn't. He allowed the watery ejaculate to enter his mouth and swallowed, finding he didn't mind the taste at all. Oddly, it didn't taste like what he'd been told it would. That was really weird.

Stash lay spent on the sofa. Anthony caressed his thighs until the tremors ceased. When they did, he stood up, only to grimace at the sticky wetness inside his jocks.

"Hey, baby. Where's the bathroom?"

"To your left," Stash said, raising a limp hand to point.

Anthony leaned down and dropped a kiss on Stash's forehead. "Stay here, I'll go get a washcloth."

Stash didn't open his eyes, but he did manage to nod his head slightly.

Anthony followed the indicated direction and found the bathroom, closing the door behind him. He leaned both hands on the counter and looked at his reflection in the mirror. Long seconds passed until he regained control and grinned. Oh yes, he was definitely feeling pleased with himself. Sucking cock was exactly what he'd thought it would feel and taste like. There was no going back for him, not after that experience. He wanted more.

After cleaning himself up with a hand towel and washing his hands, he grabbed another towel and wet it with the warm running water. When he came back to the room, Stash was where he'd left him. Only now his eyes were open, and he was staring up at the ceiling, his face devoid of expression. When his gaze shifted to Anthony, his eyes shuttered before he turned away.

Anthony immediately noticed Stash's previous insecurity had returned. For the second time that night, he swore to harm whoever had hurt Stash in the past. Quietly, he approached Stash and wiped the towel down his torso. Neither of them said a word, not even when he dropped a kiss on Stash's lips. He took the towel back to the bathroom and threw it into the laundry basket.

Anthony knew Stash would need time to process what had just happened. Hell, he did, too, but he was excited. He'd never felt so confident in himself before and knew he was already to the point of being arrogant about it. The difference was Stash. They might have only just met a little over an hour ago, but he was everything Anthony wanted in a partner.

By the time Anthony got back to the TV room, Stash was putting on his jogging pants. Anthony pretended to ignore him, but deep inside, he wanted to say something. Instead, he decided to show it.

Stash froze when Anthony sat beside him and dropped a casual kiss on the silky cheek. Anthony reached across Stash's legs and picked up the telephone receiver resting on the table next to the sofa. He punched in the code for the kitchen, flung his arm over Stash's shoulders, and leaned against him. Stash sat ramrod straight beside him, but again, Anthony ignored it. It was the only way he knew how to show that he wasn't going anywhere without sounding like he was trying too hard.

A woman's voice answered the call. "Good evening, Mr. Burcell. This is the kitchen. How may we assist you?"

"Good evening, this is Anthony Eisemann. I was wondering, is it too late to order something?"

"Oh, good evening Mr. Eisemann. No, sir, as long as there are guests in the chateau, the kitchen never closes."

"Fantastic. Can I have two triple ham on rye, with two slices of tomato in each, hold the cheese? Have it brought up to Mr. Burcell's rooms." Anthony turned to Stash and ran a finger down his smooth cheek, feeling satisfied when he saw a smile take shape. "Anything in particular, you want to order?"

Stash nodded and inched a little closer. "I'd like a sourdough veggie sub panini. No mayo. Oh, and more of that fruity iced tea we had earlier."

Anthony pulled a more pliant Stash closer to his side as he relayed the order. He thanked the woman when she told him their food would be delivered in half an hour. Stash took the receiver from him and placed it on its cradle. He then scooted back beside Anthony.

"Why were you looking anxious earlier?" Anthony asked.

"I thought you were going to leave," Stash said.

"Nope. Never entered my mind." He dropped a kiss on Stash's head.

"How are you feeling?" Stash leaned away and fixed his gaze on Anthony, looking as though he was holding his breath.

"I'm perfectly fine," Anthony said, and he meant it. "I am a bit worried, though, about what you're thinking of what just happened. I didn't insult you, did I?"

Stash shook with laughter. "I don't think I feel insulted at all. More like, hmm . . . more like . . . flattered." He sat up and leaned in closer. "You said you've only ever been with women, and yet you sucked me like a pro. How'd that happen?"

Anthony's eyes crossed as he focused his gaze Stash's flawless skin and pink, plump lips. Images of how they would look around his cock intruded, and suddenly, he was hungry for more than just a sandwich.

He took a moment to clear his throat. "I remembered how I liked getting sucked, and I just applied the science." He licked his dry lips as Stash leaned closer until their lips were only a breath away.

"Science?" Stash breathed. "Exactly what type of science is

this?" He punctuated each word with a tiny kiss on Anthony's lower lip. Only the lower one.

"Erotic science," Anthony managed to say. He let out a gasp when Stash's hand started to fondle him between his thighs.

"Ooh, so you did come. I thought you didn't. Now. Tell me about this . . . erotic science," Stash murmured. The softly spoken words sounding more like a dare.

Anthony couldn't rise to the challenge. Words failed him. His cock felt too tight, too painful, and he really, really, wanted that mouth around him.

He finally mumbled a few coherent words. "Your mouth . . . around my cock. Sucking me."

Stash continued his attack of tiny kisses against Anthony's mouth, along his jawline, the side of his lips. When he started to nibble on Anthony's earlobe, Anthony's hips jerked against Stash's questing hand.

"Have you ever had a man suck your cock before, Ace?"

Somehow, the pet name made Anthony get even harder, and he began to squirm. He was feeling a little hotter, and his pants were getting tighter.

"No. Only ever women."

"Do you want me to suck you off? Do you want to feel what it's like to have a man take your cock into his mouth? Do you think you can handle it?"

Stash closed his hand around Anthony's cock, making him squirm and almost fly off his seat. Earlier, him sucking Stash had seemed normal. He likened it to sucking a woman's pussy — also normal. Yet somehow, the thought of Stash sucking his cock seemed all too tangible and incredibly exciting. He wrapped his arms around Stash and pulled his lean body in closer for a kiss.

Stash didn't resist. Instead, he shifted his body to sit straddled over Anthony's crotch, never once breaking contact of their lips.

This time around, their kiss no longer held the awkward getting-to-know-you feel, where they explored the new touch and taste of each other. Stash also seemed different. His kiss was much bolder, more confident. More self-assured. Stash ground against Anthony's crotch until Anthony could no longer stand the pressure. It was either come in his pants again, which he didn't want to do, or come inside Stash. The latter option was much more appealing. Reluctantly, he broke their kiss.

"Hmm . . . I like how you kiss. You said you've never kissed a man before?" Stash hummed and licked his lips.

Anthony shook his head, his gaze locked on Stash's mouth. The sight of that pink tongue peeking out from between red-kissed lips made his cock throb painfully. He dropped his hands to Stash's buttocks and squeezed them tight.

"Let's go take this somewhere else, shall we, baby?"

"I love it when you call me *baby*." Stash tightened his hold around Anthony's neck.

Anthony muttered a curse when Stash continued to grind against his increasingly painful erection.

CHAPTER SIX

Stash couldn't keep his hips still. He didn't want to. It felt too good to be caressed and kissed and held by Anthony.

"Fuck," Anthony said, his nostrils flaring as he took in a deep breath. "What is it about you? Why are you making it so hard for me to resist you?"

Stash couldn't hold back his laughter. He threw his head back and let it out, only to yelp in surprise when he felt teeth nip on his collar bone. He looked down to see the evil glint in Anthony's gaze.

"You're so sexy. Do you know that, Ace?"

Anthony growled low in his throat before nibbling at a nipple. "I'm really beginning to like that name."

Stash moaned, pressing his forehead against Anthony's. "Can you be mine?" *Even just for tonight?*

He didn't say the rest of it out loud. Of course he didn't. He couldn't. How could he?

"You'd like that, wouldn't you?" Anthony chuckled when Stash nodded excitedly. "Where's the bedroom?"

"Over there." Stash pointed to his left and let out another surprised yelp when Anthony stood up from the sofa, carrying him. He chortled as he fought to hang on tightly, wrapping his legs around Anthony's waist as he walked them to the bedroom.

Once there, however, fears and doubts resurfaced. He'd had lovers before, and he loved sex. He loved sucking men's dicks even more. What he didn't love was getting ditched after the sex or being treated like a dirty little secret by the not-as-straight-as-they-pretended-to-be men he'd hooked up with. The smile froze on his lips.

Stash had experienced enough hurt from being unaccepted for most of his life. Except for his father, Aunt Irene, Meggie, Ian, and Magda, he'd never felt fully loved by anybody. It was one of the reasons why he hadn't had a boyfriend in the past seven years. He felt old at only thirty-two, and too tired of hearing he'd never be good enough for any man or being laughed at and ridiculed.

Why did he think that Anthony was going to be different? He didn't want to jinx whatever was happening between them, and to him, the connection felt real. He'd learned to rely on his instincts, and it was telling him he wasn't imagining things. There was something he couldn't put his finger on, but it told him to trust Anthony. What Anthony said next validated his thoughts.

"I never thought you'd say yes to meeting me. I'm so sorry about what happened earlier. Back when you were down by the pool." Anthony carefully laid Stash on the bed, then straightened and stared down at him. His brows furrowed, and a look of uncertainty came over his face. "Can I tell you a secret?"

Stash's throat tightened. He didn't know what to expect, but he nodded anyway. Anthony looked vulnerable, and when he took in a harsh breath, Stash knew that despite his previous show of confidence, Anthony was floundering.

"I've only ever dated women, but you already know that. Maybe I told you?"

"Yes, I know." Stash leaned up on his elbows and nodded his head to encourage Anthony to keep talking.

Anthony closed his eyes tight and pinched the bridge of his nose. Stash saw how his hand trembled and felt his heart melting.

"What you don't know is that I've always been attracted to

men who looked like you. Like a woman, but not really."

"You mean androgynous," Stash said quietly.

Anthony nodded. He looked up and met Stash's gaze. "Meeting you . . ." He paused and took in another deep breath. "I don't know why this is happening now, at this point in my life. But you're going to be my salvation. You don't know how long I've struggled to find someone who would understand my needs. I'm not bi-curious. Fuck that. I've always known what I wanted. I'd just never met . . . Am I crazy in thinking you're that man? That individual?"

Stash couldn't breathe. All he could do was stare at the man and wonder if he was dreaming. The connection he'd felt when he'd first locked gazes with this man hit him once again, only this time it was stronger and surer. He hadn't made a mistake.

Anthony's openness was all the proof Stash needed that this man was worthy of the second chance he'd given him. Even though he could probably say many things to help ease Anthony's vulnerability, the words escaped him. The silence that descended between them sounded like thunder in his ears.

Stash raised his arms and motioned for Anthony to join him. "Come here, sweetie," he said in a gentle voice.

Silently, Anthony stripped off what clothes he wore and crawled into bed. When he moved between Stash's legs, Stash wrapped his arms around him and drew him closer.

He gently palmed Anthony's cheek. "Tell me the truth. Have you ever been with a man before or not?" His gaze held onto Anthony's.

"No," Anthony whispered. "I was telling the truth. I've only ever been with women."

"How do you feel about what you just did with me?"

Anthony grinned broadly. "Awesome."

Stash didn't return the smile. "Don't hide behind that sexy

grin, Anthony. I want you to tell me, or we don't go any further than this. I'm not going to be anyone's social experiment. Not anymore."

Anthony's grin faded fast to be replaced by a serious look. Flush rose to his cheeks, and his eyes had a hint of hardness in them.

"I don't think of you as an experiment, and it's kind of insulting you think of me that way," Anthony bit out, his voice low.

If Stash hadn't been close to him at that moment, he would have had a hard time hearing him. "Are you mad at me?"

Anthony shook his head. "No, and I don't blame you for why you'd think that of me. But you're right. We only just met two hours ago, and already we're jumping into bed. On the other hand, I was telling you the truth. I told you how I felt. The decision's yours. Either you believe me or you don't. Which is it?"

Stash studied Anthony's face, and despite the words spoken, there was no anger there or indifference. There was, however, regret.

Stash bowed his head. He didn't like how things had turned suddenly dark between them, but he'd been through too much not to defend himself.

Time for some more honesty. "Do you know how many men I've been with? Hmm? How many of them used my body to satisfy their curiosity? You sucked me off earlier. What's to stop me from thinking that if or when we do have sex, you're not going to be just like those others? Wham, bam, thank you for your asshole."

Anthony's lips thinned, and a strange emotion flashed across his features. "I'm sorry you had to go through that. I don't have those answers for you, Stash. At least, not yet. You should also know that I am not like those men. I know I've only ever been with women, but that was because I never found someone like you to care for. I can't promise to fall in love, either. That's something we'll both need to cross together. You should also know that any relationship I've ever had was never kept as a secret. Should we both decide to have a relationship, I won't hide you from anyone. Well, maybe the media, because I hide everything from them except anything business-related. But I'm not scared of what others would say. Our position in life gives us both that benefit." He chuckled, then sobered. "However, once it's found out—and it will be found out—that we're sleeping together, my reputation will take a bad hit. People won't just target me, though. They will target the company and whatever businesses I'm in collaboration with. I have businesses in Asia, and they're quite famous for rescinding on contracts with just a whiff of scandal. You're not the only one who's taking a risk here."

Stash took a deep breath. He didn't want Anthony to get hurt because of him. Also, he had that business they still needed to talk about. Risking business for pleasure was a basic mistake that could ruin people and jobs.

"I need you to think hard about this, Anthony. Tomorrow we're meeting each other in our official capacities to discuss business matters. Dad's probably going to join us online, but I highly doubt it. Rest assured, if we do decide to have sex, we can have our one-night stand tonight, and in the morning, we can pretend nothing happened. It won't affect our meeting. No one needs to know we had sex. Because I can assure you, Ace, we are going to be sexually involved. Whether it's going to be tonight or some other night, I'm pretty sure it's going to happen. I just don't want either of us to get hurt because of it."

Anthony shifted until he lay fully atop Stash. He took Stash's hands and drew them up until both of his arms were stretched out over his head. Stash didn't say anything, merely watched Anthony's face. He really liked the feel of Anthony's heavy body over his. They were the same height, perfect for parts of their bodies to touch in the most delicious way. Stash squirmed under Anthony, making sure to rub their skin together. He spread his legs wider and lifted them to wrap around Anthony's back. Anthony's eyes darkened, and Stash felt his cock jerk between them.

"I want you too much to even bother to deny what you said, but I think you know that already," Anthony said in a matter-of-fact tone. "And I've no doubt you want me, too. Question is . . ." Anthony stopped and frowned.

"What?" Stash held his breath.

Anthony's face scrunched to one of confusion. "How the hell are we to do this? I don't even know where to begin."

Stash couldn't help it. A snicker bubbled out of his throat, his body shook as he tried to hold back, but eventually, laughter won. He couldn't stop.

"Hey!"

"I'm sorry, but that was too funny." Stash continued to laugh. "Not in the least sexy. Nope. We were being serious, and you drop that."

"Show me how," Anthony said in the barest of whispers.

The hilarity froze in Stash's throat. They stared at each other in silence, mirth replaced by the heat of lust.

Slowly, his gaze never leaving Anthony's, Stash pulled his arms down and wrapped them around Anthony. Lowering his legs, he gently pushed until their positions reversed, and he was looking down at Anthony.

"See that lube on that table? I'm going to reach out for it. I'm also going to put a condom on you before I lube you up. Are you ready?"

"I've done anal, before, baby. I know the drill."

"I'm sure you have. How ready are you for doing it with me?"

"More than," Anthony said. He licked his lips and ran his

hands up and down Stash's back.

Stash was more than ready himself. He reached out for the lube only to stop when the door rang. Somewhere in the suite, Flossy started barking.

"You have got to be—" Anthony bounced his head on the pillow.

Stash looked over his shoulder toward the open door and saw the handle move. A gasp escaped his lips. He quickly swung his right leg over Anthony, lost his balance, and fell on his chest over the side of the bed. Ignoring Anthony's grip on his thigh, Stash leaped toward the door and slammed it shut.

"Oh, fuck," Stash yelped. He shook his hand as he took to his feet and peered at his fingernail.

"What happened? Are you all right?" Anthony said as he reached for Stash's hand and peered at it. "Did you break a nail?"

"Fuck, yeah." Stash held up the ruined nail. Another laugh escaped him. "I completely forgot we'd ordered something from the kitchen."

Anthony rubbed gently on Stash's damaged finger. "It's not a bad break. I think it's just the acrylic tip that snapped. I don't see any damage to your nail bed."

Stash's brows rose. "You know about acrylic nails?"

"Of course I do. My mother used them when we were first developing it. Oh, just so you know, one of the companies I own manufactures the acrylics and other products."

"I didn't know," Stash breathed. He studied the back of Anthony's head while he was still closely examining the broken nail. Before flying to France, he'd done research on Anthony. The man came from a multigenerational business family that focused on pharmaceutical manufacturing. Apparently, Anthony had parlayed capital to diverse businesses. Stash had no idea that the Eisemann's were even involved in nail care products.

Stash held his breath as the tips of his fingers were rubbed gently. In a move that shouldn't have surprised him, Anthony kissed the throbbing finger. Stash bit on his lower lip. He was in so much trouble. Just a couple of hours with the man and he was already getting more and more enamored as time passed. This could get complicated if he were not careful.

"Do you have super glue?"

The question drove all thoughts and doubts from Stash's head.

"What are you talking about?"

"Superglue will fix this for a few days until you can have someone redo your nails again."

Stash gaped. "Are you serious?"

"Yes, I actually am. I helped Mother glue hers several times. It's really quite easy. Now, do you want me to get the glue so we can fix that nail? You know you can accidentally scratch yourself in your sleep if we don't do something about it."

CHAPTER SEVEN

Anthony pulled on the cuffs of his sleeves as he perused his reflection in the full-length mirror. It was early, not even seven in the morning, and he'd had little sleep, but he was wide awake and ready to spend the day with Stash. A movement behind him caught his attention.

"Gregory, were you able to reach Genevieve?"

"Yes, sir. She's on her way and will be arriving sometime before lunch. When do you want to schedule for her services?" Gregory's reflection appeared in the mirror. He was tapping on his tablet and nodding at it. "Also, Jade says that her flight's been canceled. I told her to forget booking another flight. Can I have permission to fly her over in the Lear?"

"Go ahead on the Lear. Genevieve will be tired after her flight. She can start working tomorrow. Same goes for Jade. Also, let Mrs. Louis know I won't be able to join her in the Bahamas next week. My plans have changed."

Gregory's head snapped up, his gaze meeting Anthony's in the mirror. "Changed? How have they changed?"

Anthony smirked and turned away from the mirror. "Don't fret, Gregory. I'll let you know what the changes are as soon as I know them. The only one I'm certain about is — no Bahamas."

Gregory nodded, his gaze returning to the tablet.

Anthony left him to his scheduling and picked up his jacket. "And Gregory?"

"Yes, sir?"

"Get in touch with Bertrand Renault."

"All right, sir. When do you want me to schedule the call?"

"Now would be good. I'm only going to take ten minutes of his time."

"They're going to need a reason why you're calling him this early, sir," Gregory said, lifting his gaze back to Anthony.

Anthony thought about it for a moment. Renault owned over seventy luxury brands, ranging from liquors to makeup. Finally, he decided on one. "Fashion."

"Company business or personal? Also, are you looking into anything in particular?"

Anthony had to smile. Gregory was surely digging. He didn't mind. The man was going to find out soon enough—sooner than any other person on the planet other than himself. "Clothes, accessories, shoes, and bags. Oh, and yes, it's personal, Gregory. Definitely personal."

Gregory didn't reply, but the frown that flitted between his brows betrayed his curiosity. Anthony turned away and began putting on his socks.

Anthony recalled Gregory's words and actions from the day before, how he'd tried so hard to get information from him, how he had talked about Stash, and especially his failure to disclose the report about Stash. His mistrust of the man grew more each day.

Gregory never hid his pride over how he was privy to a lot of information. It wouldn't be farfetched if he used his position for some type of gain. Anthony suspected Gregory wanted to know what had happened between him and Stash. Well, he was in for a disappointment. There had been things Anthony had kept from Gregory, as he had with many of his personal assistants. Quite a few, in fact. However, Gregory had no right to keep things from *him*—things that could potentially put him in an irredeemable situation.

Anthony continued to surreptitiously observe Gregory quietly talking to someone on his phone. After a few minutes, he looked up and met Anthony's gaze.

"Sir? Mr. Renault's ready to speak with you."

"Direct the call into my private number, if you will. Thank you." Anthony stood up from the bed and picked up his phone just as it lit up with an incoming call. Swiping the screen to open the app, he walked out to the veranda overlooking the swimming pool and slid the glass door closed behind him. He kept his expression deadpanned when he saw the flash of shock and frustration flit over Gregory's face. Pasting a smile on his lips, he placed the phone to his ear. After yesterday, he couldn't risk Gregory hearing his conversation with Renault. His decision was made. He would have to do something about Gregory. Soon.

"Bertrand, merci d'avoir répondu à mon appel si tôt. J'ai besoin d'une faveur."

Anthony always enjoyed talking with his long-time friend and thanked him for taking his call so early. Bertrand chuckled at Anthony's request for a favor. Fifteen minutes later, phone call over and plans for a surprise laid out, Anthony went up the stairs to Stash's room, followed closely by Christian.

He'd left a visibly confused Gregory behind in his suite with a stack of research materials and tasks to accomplish by early evening. He wasn't trying to be mean, but after what had happened the day before and what he had observed earlier, he preferred Christian following him around. Not Gregory.

A burly man stood at the door to Stash's suite, older than the one from the night before. Although Anthony had never met the man before, he was greeted with familiarity. The man assessed him briefly and slid his gaze to Christian before shifting back to him and giving him a nod. When Anthony reached his side, the man had already opened the door.

"Hello?" Anthony said into the empty room. The door

closed behind him, leaving him to look about the suite.

A yapping sound answered, followed by the appearance of Flossy. The beribboned long-haired dog came running around the corner only to slide to a stop just a few feet away from him. Black, beady eyes stared up at him, the bark dying in her throat. Her ears twitched as she appeared to study Anthony.

"Hello, Flossy. Where's Stash?" Anthony sank into a crouch and held out his hand.

Flossy dipped her head and took a sniff. Her tail wagged once before she turned around. Tail held high and wagging a mile a minute, Flossy ran back where she'd come from. She paused and looked over her shoulder as though she were making sure that Anthony was still following her. He *was*. She had led him straight into Stash's room.

"Flossy? Who's there?" Stash's voice came from beyond the open door of the bathroom.

Anthony didn't want to disrespect Stash's privacy, so he stopped and leaned against the wall next to the bathroom door. "It's me. Anthony. Little Miss Flossy here kindly let me in."

"She did, did she?" Stash said as he exited the bathroom.

Flossy barked, drawing Anthony's attention. The fluff-dog leaped onto the bed, settled on a pillow, and promptly closed her eyes. She didn't even bother to lower her head over her front paws. Anthony chuckled and turned back to face Stash, only to stop and stare in awe. He swallowed hard at the sight of Stash, tying back his hair. Stash had his arms held up over his head, and the position exposed the smooth, hairless skin of his pits.

What was it about Stash that stole Anthony's breath and made him lose all sense of logic?

It had only been a little over four hours since Anthony had left Stash, sleeping on the sofa. After the rude interruption of the kitchen delivering their snacks, they'd spent the rest of the night talking about all sorts of things. Evening had turned to the wee hours of morning, and they'd found themselves ordering more snacks as the time passed. For a moment, Anthony wondered how Howell would react when he heard about the two of them keeping the kitchen staff busy throughout the night. He hoped Howell wasn't the overprotective type.

Around two in the morning, they had been discussing music preferences, when angry barking had ensued from one of the rooms. Stash introduced Anthony to Candy Floss, or Flossy as she preferred responding to. Anthony had taken one look at the absurdly and highly feminine looking dog and promptly fallen in love with her. Though, technically, that didn't happen until after Flossy had given him one look, followed it up with a sharp bark, then sunk her tiny, sharp teeth into the flesh of his hand. Of course, her having a deep underbite prevented anything serious from happening. Anthony had picked her up and given her a kiss. He'd grown up with pets running around, but since he'd taken over the mantle of CEO to his family's business, he'd been too busy to have one of his own.

Stash was looking at Flossy with a gentle smile on his face, and Anthony thought it was the most beautiful thing he'd ever seen. His heart swelled at the thought that this exotic creature could be his to love and protect.

As soon as the thought entered his mind, he realized that, yes, he *could* easily fall in love and protect Stash. He was quite sure of it. But why was it happening to him now? Why was it affecting him this way?

"Ace? Are we ready to go?"

Taking a moment to settle his growing arousal, Anthony straightened from the wall and held out a hand.

Without saying a word, Stash took it in his.

"Did you have a good sleep?" Anthony asked as they walked out of the room.

"Yes, I did, actually." Stash's grin broadened.

Anthony was about to respond when it dawned on him exactly what it was that made Stash look so beautiful that morning. He stopped and turned to examine Stash's face.

"You're wearing makeup," he said.

The smile on Stash's lips froze. "Yes. I am. Do you like it?"

Anthony didn't respond immediately as he scrutinized the results. "I do, actually." His gaze shifted to the different parts of Stash's face. "It's perfect." He grinned when he met Stash's gaze. "It makes your skin look kind of . . . hmm . . . luminous, I guess is the word I'm thinking. It's doesn't look caked on."

Stash's expression relaxed, and his smile brightened. "It's something that I've been working on. It's not yet out in the market."

"Oh. Well, it works. Your skin looks airbrushed, but . . . real. Yes," he said as he continued to examine Stash's skin. "The finish looks like real skin. When are you releasing it?"

"We're still testing it out on different skin types and in different settings, temperatures, etcetera. We have to make sure that it's as long-lasting as we think it is. If it's not, then we'll have to readjust our claims." A frown appeared between Stash's brows. "You really don't mind my wearing makeup?"

Anthony pulled him closer, wrapped his arms around him, and dropped a kiss on his pink lips. "Why should I mind? Besides, you look stunning. Does it have at least fifty SPF?"

Stash lifted his arms and dropped them over Anthony's shoulders. "Yes, it does. Now, tell me, where are you taking me? You never did say."

"I was thinking of taking a turn around the village."

Stash's eye widened. He stepped back but held on to Anthony's arms. When he started jumping up and down, Anthony thought he'd never seen anyone more adorable.

"Oh, I'd love that. Even though I've been here a couple of times, I'd never really had the chance to look around. Do you think we can go to the local market? It's Wednesday, and I think there's a market day today. Also, I'd love to check out the bakeries. I've heard only good things from Meggie."

"It's a little too cold out, but if that's what you want to do, then that's what we're going to do. You're certainly dressed for it." Anthony admired the long-sleeved tracksuit and furred boots Stash was wearing. "You like to take walks?"

Stash looked at him askance. "Yes, I do."

Anthony brushed his lips over Stash's. "Then that's what we shall do. We'll take a car down and walk around the village."

"We have a meeting tonight, so we need to be back early." Stash sighed. "My father sent word he's calling in so he can join our talks."

Stash pressed his lips to Anthony's, and he, of course, kissed him back. The kiss lasted a moment longer until Anthony broke it off.

"That's good to hear, and no, I haven't forgotten about our meeting. However, it's still early. We can be back around four. That should give us enough time to prepare."

Stash's face crumpled, and he pouted. "I don't know why we need to have such a formal meeting. We can talk along the way if we really want to."

Anthony raised a brow. "Do you *really* want to do that?"

Stash's lips twisted. "No. Let's leave the meeting for tonight. Today, we enjoy the countryside," Stash said.

Anthony let out a sigh of relief and pulled Stash closer. "Sounds good to me. Come on, grab your coat."

"I know it's cold. I was the idiot who went into the pool yesterday. The maintenance crew said it was heated. It wasn't," Stash grumbled under his breath, then walked to a chair that held a long white coat draped over the back.

Anthony took the coat from him. Somehow, helping Stash into the slightly oversized coat made sense. Stash was a man, yeah, but the action felt right to Anthony.

"I'm ready," Stash said. He stood there as though he was waiting for Anthony to make a comment.

Anthony couldn't help the grin spreading over his face. "You look warm and extremely pretty."

"Why, thank you, Mr. Eisemann." Stash beamed and slipped his arm into Anthony's. For some reason, the simple act made Anthony ridiculously happy. With a skip to his step, he walked Stash out of the bedroom, leaving Flossy to her soft snores.

CHAPTER EIGHT

As soon as Stash walked out the door, he immediately knew he was not going to escape as easily as he thought. The guard standing by the door didn't meet his gaze and was focused on something in the distance. Already he could feel the cage doors clang shut, and he was right. Stash turned and immediately spotted Meggie, hurrying toward them. Meggie stopped running and stood blocking their way to the staircase.

"Where do you think you're going, Stash?"

Stash glared at Meggie, still holding on to Anthony's arm. He didn't want to have to deal with her right then. She didn't look bothered and countered his look with a raised brow. He rolled his eyes when she started tapping her foot on the carpeted floor.

"Anthony and I are going out," Stash said, finally conceding to her unspoken demands. He pasted on a grin and pulled on Anthony's arm.

"I asked where you were going?" Meggie took a step forward.

Anthony stiffened beside him. Stash gave him a comforting smile and pulled on his arm once more, but Anthony didn't budge.

"Not that it's any of your business, but we are going to the market down at the village," Anthony said.

"The market?" The way Meggie repeated the words, she wasn't happy.

A wave of indignation swept over Stash, but at Anthony's

indrawn breath, he didn't want to create a confrontation. He tightened his grip on Anthony's arm to draw his attention. Unfortunately, Anthony continued to ignore him.

"Yes. To the market." Anthony enunciated each syllable.

"What about the meeting tonight?" Meggie directed the question at him.

Stash opened his mouth to respond, but Anthony beat him to it.

"I'm not quite sure what the issue is, but that's still hours away," Anthony said.

"There's no issue, is there, Meggie?" Stash said, digging his fingers into Anthony's arm. He hoped Anthony would understand his unvoiced warning.

"Stash, can we talk?" Meggie took another step forward.

Stash closed his eyes and took in a deep breath. He had had enough. Meggie might be his best friend, but he had the right to go out on his own without her tagging along.

"Not right now, no." Stash met Meggie's gaze, held it, and didn't let go.

Meggie bit her bottom lip, her confidence replaced by uncertainty. "Stash, you know you're not supposed to go out on your own without telling us where you're going. Your dad—"

"Shut it, Meggie," he said in a sharp tone. Embarrassment swept through him. There was only so much he would allow, but embarrassing him in front of Anthony was the last straw. He turned his back on Meggie and started to walk toward the stairs, dragging Anthony along. Anthony followed willingly when another voice called out.

"Stash."

Stash stopped in his tracks. Taking a deep breath and licking his suddenly chapped lips, he turned to reluctantly look over his shoulder.

"I've always guarded your back, Stash. I'm going with you.

Please, say yes," Ian said.

Stash bit on his lower lip. He knew Ian meant it—Ian's body language was tense and unmoving. The grim line on his lips brooked no argument. Ian was going with them, whether he got permission or not.

"Oh, for fucks sake," Anthony interjected, shaking his head. "Let's all go out and make a day of it, shall we?"

Stash gaped at him. "Are you sure? I thought we wanted to be alone?"

"That was the plan, but for some reason, your assistant and guards are not willing to let you go out on your own with me without risking an aneurism. I say, let's just all go out." Anthony turned to Ian. "You. What's your name?"

"Ian, sir."

Anthony gave a curt nod. "Ian. Good. Are you comfortable going with us without your men, or do you want them to join you?"

Ian shrugged, but his grim expression didn't wane. "I'm cool."

"Good to know," Anthony said.

Stash hid a smile at the sarcasm leaching through Anthony's words. But to his astonishment, Anthony wasn't quite done.

"Okay, Ian. You're with us. How about you, Meggie. Do you want to come with us, too? Or are you okay with not being able to monitor Stash's every move and word? If you're not, then come along, you're welcome to join us." Anthony didn't wait for a response, he simply turned and began walking away in quick, long strides.

Stash hurried after him. When he reached Anthony's side, he couldn't quite contain his happiness when Anthony grasped his hand and held on to. Together, they descended the stairs in silence. Stash glanced at Anthony, only to grimace at his set expression.

"I'm sorry," Stash said under his breath.

"Don't worry about it. They're only following what, if I presume correctly, are your father's instructions. I can't get angry when they're only doing their jobs."

Anthony smiled at him, but Stash didn't miss the tightness around the corners of his eyes.

When they reached Anthony's floor, a man hailed them from across the corridor and hurried to join them. Stash recognized him as the same man who'd talked with Meggie the day before.

"Sir, Mr. Eisemann, sir!"

Anthony groaned, but he stopped walking. "What now?"

Anthony glared at the man, who braked in his tracks. The man's eyes widened as he slowly lowered his arm, his gaze locked onto their clasped hands. Stash turned away to get his amusement under control. When Anthony began to speak, Stash licked his lips and willed his face free of expression. The morning was turning out to be a spectacle. Who knew so many wanted to go down to the village?

"You want to come, too? Well, get on it, then. You can come along." Anthony looked at the faces surrounding them. "Why not? Let's all make a day of it, Gregory. Let's take everyone with us."

Gregory. So that's the man's name.

"What, sir?" Gregory looked confused as he stared at Anthony.

"It seems like you're getting your wish. If you want to come with us, try to keep up."

Gregory's expression brightened. "Me, sir?"

"Yes. You. Not that you've earned it. Tell all the men they're coming with us. Let's make this a real outing into the unknown countryside, shall we?"

Mortified at the turn of events, Stash was caught between wanting to sink in embarrassment and hiding somewhere so he could cry from frustration. He knew Meggie and Ian were only doing their jobs, but Stash was thirty-two—a grown man. And yet they continued to treat him like a naïve teenager.

Ever since that morning, when he'd woken up alone on the sofa, he'd been unable to quell his excitement. The night before, he and Anthony had made plans to spend the day together—without any bodyguards or personal assistants. They'd even planned on not taking their phones with them.

They'd spoken of their shared curiosity about what Saint-Pierre-d'Albigny had to offer their visitors. If it hadn't been for that, Stash knew he'd have most likely made up another reason just to spend time with Anthony. Now, his day was ruined.

Stash stomped his foot. He knew it was immature of him, but he couldn't help throwing an angry glare in Meggie and Ian's direction. As usual, Ian didn't react, but Meggie raised a perfect brow and met his gaze head-on. He looked away and gritted his teeth. He was so mad.

Although he truly loved the two of them like siblings, they were getting overly protective, and he was beginning to resent their presence.

There were times, like today, that he felt like he was weighed down by their mere presence. Not that he blamed them. Meggie and Ian were through and through their father's children. Although Meggie was the perfect personal assistant, she was, first and foremost, a well-trained personal bodyguard. She had been ever since she'd first showed promise on the firing range.

"Stash?"

At the softly spoken question, Stash looked up to meet Anthony's concerned gaze.

"I've been calling your name. Where were you?"

"Nowhere. I was just thinking." Stash put on a reassuring

smile. "Are we ready to go?"

"Both our security teams are here. There's enough of them to guarantee we're safe from a gust of wind should they deem it necessary to rescue us from one." Despite Anthony's obvious sarcasm, his expression gentled as he hooked a strand of hair behind Stash's ear.

The action made him like Anthony even more.

"Are you okay?"

Stash shivered at the intensity of Anthony's gaze. For a moment, he was too flustered to react, but when Anthony frowned at his silence, he gave himself a mental shake. He also felt everyone staring at them.

"Yes, just a little frustrated. That's all." He plastered on a wide smile, trying to make light of the situation. In the periphery, he could see Meggie's look of incredulity. He truly disliked her at that moment, so he chose to turn his back on her.

"Having bodyguards constantly all over us can be a bit annoying, but I can sense their loyalty to you," Anthony said. He placed two fingers under Stash's chin. "Are you sure you're all right? We can call this whole thing off if you want. Just say the word. We can stay in your rooms and watch cable all day."

Stash wrinkled his nose. "No. We talked about this last night. I want to go out. I'll see to it that Meggie and Ian behave."

"No need. Come on. Let's enjoy the day, okay?" Anthony dropped a kiss on his cheek and took his hand.

Stash chose to ignore the gasp he heard behind them. He'd known Meggie for far too long not to recognize her sounds, so he didn't need to look around to know it had been her.

Anthony led them outside the chateau. Stash expected the weather to be as cold as the previous day and was surprised at the warmth and humidity that greeted them. He looked around in consternation. There was something terribly off with the climate. It was the beginning of January, and the temperature should have been freezing. There should have been snow, but the trees around him were still green.

"Climate change isn't happening. No sir," Anthony muttered as he helped Stash into one of the three white SUVs parked on the driveway.

Stash choked back a snort at the obvious mockery. "Do you think I should go back and give that pool another try?"

"If the weather holds, it'll probably turn to summer in an hour or two," Anthony said with a comical expression.

They were both laughing as they settled inside the vehicle. Stash looked out the window as they drove down from the mountain. He hoped Meggie and Ian would behave themselves. Maybe, for a change, he could relax and live a little.

To his surprise, the day in the village turned out to be more enjoyable than expected, especially after how the morning had started. The weather turned warm enough for Stash to take off his coat. It was certainly an oddity, but that only made their time discovering what the village had to offer more fun.

Meggie offered to guide them around, stating that she'd been to the area several times. When Anthony asked her why she hadn't taken Stash out any of those times, she didn't respond. Stash pretended not to hear the question, and instead, pulled on Anthony's arm and led him in the opposite direction.

They lunched at a café, hunted in an antique bookstore for possible treasures, and visited the local perfumery. There was one particular scent that interested Stash, so he bought a bottle. What intrigued him the most was their next discovery. They'd turned a corner where a quaint pottery shop stood with its doors open. Beside it stood a chalkboard—the style one would see in a bar—with an announcement for pottery lessons. Stash grinned when the owner came out to ask if he wanted to learn, flashing his long acrylic nails. To his surprise, it was Anthony who accepted the offer.

Anthony handed his jacket to Stash before sitting on the stool the shop owner led him to. Stash stood to the side, watching the tutorial. Anthony throwing the clay and laughing out when it flew off the revolving wheel and landed on the floor on his first attempt was an image Stash knew he'd never forget. The lesson lasted one hour, but from the joy on Anthony's face when it was over, Stash knew the time hadn't been wasted.

"I'm totally in love," Anthony said as he shrugged back into his jacket.

"You are?" Stash chuckled. "What are you going to do? Take up pottery for real?"

"Why not? Come to think of it, I remember Mother used to keep a potter's wheel in the shed back at the estate, so I won't have to buy one. That was truly relaxing. Kind of hypnotic. You should take it up."

"With these?" Stash held up his hand.

Anthony squinted and laughed quietly. "Well, maybe after you cut them shorter?"

Stash gasped. "Are you for real? These are very expensive. How dare you?"

"I know, but wouldn't you like to feel the cool, wet clay between your hands? Experience the feel of grasping and pulling and molding it into shape?"

Stash stared at Anthony, and his jaw dropped open. The sight of Anthony looking so free and uninhibited in his enjoyment of such a simple task took his breath away.

"Why do you make it sound so erotic?"

"Because it can be." Anthony dropped a quick kiss on Stash's lips. "Come on, let's get out of here."

Stash couldn't resist kissing Anthony back. The rest of the afternoon, Stash followed Anthony around in a daze. What was it about the man that muddled his brain so?

CHAPTER NINE

Anthony tilted his head at something Stash was pointing to. He took a sip of his coffee and crossed his legs, then watched as Stash examined the variety of mini cakes and pastries. Tiny, delicate, and colorful creations were set on ornate trays over the length of the counter. He couldn't quite contain the feeling of contentment at each bright smile and flying kiss Stash sent his way.

Neither did he care about the surreptitious side glances the guards gave him. They'd probably never seen him have fun before. Or kiss a man. The thought that he'd managed to scandalize his security team warmed his heart. He hadn't felt more relaxed for the longest time. Then again, maybe it was because Stash was enjoying himself despite how their morning had started.

Stash looked calm and happy—a far cry from his downcast look after their initial plans had been disrupted. Thankfully, the day turned out quite pleasant.

Anthony wondered about how Meggie and the rest of Stash's bodyguards had reacted when they'd discovered Stash and Anthony were going off without them. It had been a curious affair. There had to be a story there. He made a mental note to ask them about their intense reactions.

He and Stash had been walking back to their cars to head back to the Howell's chateau when Stash spotted the café patisserie. Anthony hadn't minded. For him, spending barely twenty-four hours with Stash was not enough time to get to know him. The longer he spent time with him, the better.

Throughout the day, Anthony had kept close observation on what Stash liked and disliked. He'd even given Christian instructions to direct their men to take notes in case he missed something.

When they entered the café, Anthony decided he had been right in his assumption that Stash needed a day out when his face lit up at the sight of the delicate pastries. However, Stash didn't point at every delicacy available. Instead, he took his time going over specific creations and discussing their merits with the café's owner. That revealed a thought process familiar to Anthony, because that was how he did things as well. He couldn't wait until he found out more. Strangely, he had a feeling he would like what he discovered.

Knowing he was in for a long wait before Stash made his final decision, he'd settled in his chair and ordered another cup of coffee.

The sound of loud laughter drew his attention outside. Right away, a frown formed between his brows. He noticed Gregory was sitting apart from Meggie and the rest of the guards, who were gathered around mini tables alongside the street. However, what really caught his attention was the way everyone else was enjoying their drinks and chatting with each other, while Gregory was busy talking on his phone. With Stash's voice in the background, acting as a soothing noise, Anthony took another sip of coffee and continued his study of Gregory Morgan.

Gregory had not been his choice for a personal assistant. He'd come in as a temp after Mrs. Jones, his father's PA, had resigned. That was six months ago. After what happened the day before, Anthony had come to realize that maybe he had been a little too complacent or just lazy about his choice of assistants.

He'd only begun to get suspicious of Gregory's actions the week before when a director had dropped a piece of private information at a good friend's wedding. It hadn't exactly been a secret, but he had wanted his gift to have been a surprise. He and only one other had known about the purchase of a private cruise for the newly-weds, and that person was Gregory.

From the way Gregory kept glancing down the street, back at the café, and back to the road again, his conversation was obviously intense. Anthony turned his attention back to Stash and couldn't help smiling. Now was not the time for confrontation, but his suspicions of Gregory were building and needed to be addressed . . . soon.

He looked down at his watch and saw that it was almost six in the evening. Their meeting was set for nine that night, but it looked as though Stash was far from done. Anthony could only hope the end was in sight. Thank God for the wonderful freshly ground coffee the barista had brewed up for him.

Ten minutes later, Stash had made his final choices and was sorting through his fanny pack. One of the women who had been assisting him began placing the items into artsy boxes as an older woman stepped behind the register. Another ten minutes passed before Stash walked away from the counter.

"Are you done?" No matter that Anthony's atypical patience had everything to do with Stash, he was tired and more than ready to get back to the chateau. He stood and took some of the boxes the woman was holding out. "Did you buy out the place?"

"Just about," Stash said, as he struggled with the other boxes. After a while, he let out an exasperated breath and set them on the table. "Hold on. Let me get Meggie." He didn't wait for Anthony to reply. In quick, long strides, he opened the door. "Meggie? Ian? Can you get in here, please?" He closed the door and walked back to the table without waiting for Meggie or Ian's response.

Anthony looked outside the window at the sound of metal chairs scrapping on cobbled stones, then the café door opened. Meggie walked in, followed by Ian and Christian. The rest of the guards stood outside the open door but didn't attempt to enter.

Meggie crossed her arms and tapped a foot on the floor. "You called, princess?"

Anthony choked at the impudence, but Stash didn't take the bait.

"Yes, boo. Can you give us a hand with these, please?"

Meggie's face softened at the endearment. Without a word, she proceeded to take over handing out boxes to the guards standing outside.

Anthony contained his surprise when he counted a total of twenty boxes. "Stash? There's a lot in there. Are we expecting company at the chateau?"

"Oh, no, four of these are gifts to bring home, while the rest are for everyone to enjoy." Stash looked at the two smiling women standing behind the counter and gave them a sweet smile. "Thank you so much for helping me out today. Bye."

The two women waved goodbye as the group left the café. The boxes of pastries were loaded in the back of the car as Anthony and Stash settled in their seats.

"Tell me why you practically bought out that place," Anthony asked.

Stash was still waving at the women who were crowding the door.

"I just wanted to help them out. The woman who was helping me, her name is Louise, and the older woman is her mother. Her name's Patrice. Louise told me that her father died a few months back."

Anthony thought about what Stash said. "Are their pastries really that good?"

"They are, but their sales are not enough to pay for the debts. It would be a pity if they closed shop." Stash looked to the front and then took out his phone. "Meggie, please find out everything you can about the café?" He paused to listen to whatever Meggie said before nodding. "Yes. Get in touch with Paul and tell him I need to speak with him. Thank you." Stash ended the call.

Anthony placed his arm over Stash's shoulders. "Can I ask what you're planning to do?"

"I don't know yet," Stash said, looking thoughtful. "I'll let you know when I think of something."

"You're a good man, Stash," Anthony said. The more he got to know Stash, the more he came to admire him.

"Thank you." Stash practically preened at the compliment.

Anthony couldn't stop himself from dropping a kiss on Stash's shoulder. He was awarded with a caress down his cheek. The touch warmed his heart.

"Excuse me, sir," Christian said from the front of the car.

Anthony turned to Christian and saw his somber expression. He'd known the man long enough to be able to interpret his moods. Christian was clearly alarmed and uneasy.

"What's going on?" When Christian hesitated, Anthony's concern grew. "What's wrong?"

Christian cleared his throat and rolled his eyes in Stash's direction.

"It's all right. Go ahead," Anthony said.

"Mr. Lawrence. He's in France."

All sense of joy from the day turned to a cold, numbing sensation. His gaze locked on the view beyond the windshield, but he didn't see anything. He wasn't blind, but everything turned hazy. Thought eluded him, his mind became a plateau of deadness. The top of his scalp felt like it was being pulled by an unseen hand, tingling as it tried to part from his body.

Finally, Anthony shook his head to clear it of the fog and let out an expletive. "What the hell's he doing here? Who told him where I was? How the hell did he get out without our knowing about it?"

"I don't know, but I'll find out as soon as I can, sir," Christian said. "What I don't understand is why they didn't say anything in advance. They would never release Mr. Lawrence without first telling us about it."

Anthony pinched the bridge of his nose and tried to think through what he knew was anger and growing panic. His brother was here. Things were going to get complicated, really fast . . . complicated and dangerous. He jumped at the feel of a hand on his arm.

"Ace? Are you all right? What's going on?" Stash's voice was laced with concern.

Words failed Anthony as he stared at Stash. Finally, he blinked and found his voice. "My brother. He's here. I'm sorry."

"You're sorry? Why should I be worried?" Stash looked at him, then at Christian, and back to him.

"I'm not sure." Anthony thought quickly. "Christian, let the others know. Call my lawyer."

"Yes, sir," Christian said, quickly turning away.

Anthony took Stash's hand in his and clasped it tightly between his sweaty ones. "Stash, baby, I need you to get in the other car. Don't ask questions. I'll join you as soon as I can."

Stash tilted his head to the side, his gaze searching. "Am I in danger?"

"No. Never." Anthony was lying, and from the raised brow, Stash knew it. "My brother's not supposed to be here. He's not supposed to be anywhere."

"Is this going to affect our meeting tonight?"

"I want to say no, but I'd be lying."

"Will this affect our talks?"

There was steel in Stash's voice that made Anthony rethink his assumption that his man was sweet.

"It can, but not in the way you think. Lawrence is not connected to the company, but he can make noise, and that could affect whatever agreement we reach."

Stash narrowed his gaze. "How noisy are we talking?"

CHAPTER TEN

"He doesn't have a voice in the business. Any of the businesses."

Stash wasn't convinced, even though Anthony sounded confident enough. He had a suspicion there was more to what Anthony was saying, and he needed to find out what it was. There was a lot of money involved, should their discussion result in the collaboration he was about to pitch, and he couldn't afford for their talk to fall apart before it even began.

"Then tell me why you're acting like this?" Stash watched as Anthony worked his jaw and clench his fists. Something was wrong. Anthony definitely looked scared. What was going on?

What Anthony said next was not what Stash expected to hear. Not by a long shot.

"Because he's a killer and should be in prison. That's why."

"Aren't you being a little overdramatic?" Stash bit back the nervous laughter that bubbled to the surface. At Anthony's lack of response, he felt his blood grow cold. He reached out and gripped hard onto Anthony's bicep. "You're joking, right?"

"I wish I were," Anthony said in a rueful tone.

Their gazes met, and Stash could see the agony in Anthony's eyes. And not just that, he saw dread and rage, too.

"What you're saying is that we're both in danger," Stash said.

Anthony jerked but remained quiet.

"What do you plan on doing?"

Anthony shook his head as he ran trembling fingers through his hair. "I don't know."

Stash regarded Anthony's closed fists and the beads of sweat that rolled down the side of his face. He had a feeling that Anthony didn't know what to do, and that observation didn't sit well with him.

Stash turned to Christian. The bodyguard had closed his phone and was looking at Anthony as if waiting for orders. When no such thing happened, Stash knew he had to do something. If there was one thing he knew about, it was survival and defense.

"Christian, where do you think Lawrence would be right now?"

Christian met his gaze for a moment before responding. "He landed in Paris last night, but my contact said he rented a car about an hour ago."

"Can you trust your source? How sure are they about Lawrence's plans or whereabouts?"

"I trust her implicitly."

Stash considered what to do with such minimal information. "What about a tracking system in the rental? Any chance she can find that out for us?"

"That's a negative. I already asked."

"Too bad." Stash bit on his lower lip. "It'll take him about four or five hours to reach this area, so that should give us about three hours to get out of here."

Christian dipped his head. "Yes, sir. What do you have in mind?"

"First, we need to go back to the chateau. In the meantime, call housekeeping and tell them to prepare mine and Mr. Anthony's things. We'll get there in fifteen or twenty minutes, so that should give them enough time to get everything ready. Let me call Meggie."

Stash didn't give Christian a chance to respond. He took

out his phone and speed-dialed his friend.

Meggie picked up on the first ring. "What's up?"

"Change of plans," Stash said. "Call our pilot and tell him to get the plane ready to get out of here in half an hour."

"Where are we going?"

"Not we, them. They're going back to Paris and until further notice. We are going back to Limoges."

"Mr. Eisemann's coming with us, then. All ready." She paused before continuing. "May I ask why the change?"

"It's a long story. I'll tell you all about it later. For now, keep our itinerary a secret."

"What about your father? What do I tell him?"

"Don't worry about Dad. I'll give him a call later."

"Copy that."

Stash couldn't help but smile in relief when Meggie ended the call. It was a good thing they'd all been in worse situations than this and knew how to react. Anthony, on the other hand, looked lost. It was strange seeing him so uncertain. From how pale he'd gone, Stash surmised Anthony might be thinking the same thing. He was wide-eyed and staring at Stash as though he were a stranger.

Well. They were practically strangers. Even if they'd spent the whole night talking and getting to know each other, they'd only just met.

"I'm sorry," Anthony said, letting out a stuttering breath. "I'm really sorry."

Stash frowned. "Whatever for?"

"Everything's ruined."

"What is? I don't understand." Stash looked from Anthony to Christian and back again when Christian shrugged.

When Anthony didn't respond, Stash gave him a swift smile and a reassuring caress down the side of his cheek. "I don't think anything's ruined." He looked to the front seat. "In any case, Christian, we're going to Limoges."

Christian dipped his head. "Understood. I'll let the men know."

"Thank you," Anthony said softly.

Stash took Anthony's hand in his and gave him a reassuring smile. "It's no problem."

"What's in Limoges?"

"I have property there. It's quite private, and no one knows I own it. It's actually my home base."

Anthony raised a brow. "I see."

Stash grinned before turning away to look out the window. They were nearing Paul's chateau. "Like you, I have several properties around the world. Limoges is special, and I decided to make it my home five years ago. It'll take us a five-hour drive to get there." He looked back at Anthony. "More than enough time for you to tell me everything about your brother."

Anthony stared at him for a long moment before he took Stash's hand and clasped it tightly. "As soon as we're alone, I'll tell you everything you need to know."

They sat in silence until they reached the chateau. Once there, they walked up to their suites, only separating at their respective floors. Stash was met by Flossy as soon as he entered his bedroom. He picked her up and cuddled her even as he looked over his suitcases.

He went around the room to make sure none of his things had been left out. Satisfied that the staff had packed everything, he tucked Flossy under one arm and slung the bag containing his laptop over the opposite shoulder. He was out the door in less than ten minutes and met up with Anthony at the landing.

"Need a hand?" Anthony asked, already reaching out for Flossy.

Flossy wagged her tail and began to wriggle her way out of Stash's arms. Laughing at the dog's exuberance, he deposited the squiggling dog into Anthony's waiting arms.

"I think she wants you."

"Yes, she does, don't you, little Flossy," Anthony crooned. Flossy licked at his chin, making him grin broadly. It was the first real smile since they'd learned about his brother.

"Sir? The car's ready," Gregory said from where he stepped up behind Anthony.

Stash leaned over to the side to get a real look at the man. Anthony's assistant had followed them around the whole day, but from what he'd observed, had not initiated a conversation with him or any of the other guards. He'd seen the man talk to Meggie once or twice, but most of his time was spent talking to someone on the phone. In fact, Stash couldn't recall the man talking to him at all. He turned back to Anthony and saw his guarded look. When Anthony didn't immediately respond to Gregory, Stash turned his back on him and faced Anthony.

"Shall we?"

"Yes," Anthony said, distracted with scratching Flossy's chin. After a moment, he met Stash's gaze. "Wait for me in the car. Can you give me a few minutes?"

"Of course. Do you want me to take Flossy?"

"No. We're fine," he said, clutching Flossy closer.

Anthony stepped forward and pressed his lips against Stash's cheek. Stash leaned against the kiss before running his hand down Anthony's cheek.

"Behave, little lady," Stash said before dropping a kiss on Flossy's head. Just as he straightened, he caught the flash of contempt on Gregory's face before his expression cleared. Stash didn't think to waste time or energy on the contemptuous man. Nevertheless, he gave Anthony a telling look and left him to deal with his assistant.

Stash joined Meggie and Ian, where they were waiting for him at the landing. In silence, they followed him as he walked down the stairs and exited through the front doors.

A few minutes later, Anthony joined him. Neither said a word as they pulled out of the driveway. Stash took note of the way Anthony cradled Flossy close to his chest. It was a body language Stash was quite familiar with, one of fear and uncertainty. The need to hide. If it were any other time or situation, Stash would have found the use of Flossy as a security blanket as amusing, but not today.

"Did you fire him?"

Anthony's jaw clenched. "Yes."

"Did he say why he betrayed you?" When Anthony didn't speak, Stash touched Anthony's hand. "If you don't want to talk, it's okay."

Anthony pressed his lips together and shook his head. After a moment, he relaxed, but not once did he stop petting Flossy. "No. Actually, I was just thinking about that exact question. Gregory's been my assistant for only a few months, and I didn't know he'd been in contact with Lawrence. He didn't even deny it when I asked him." Anthony looked away. "I don't understand any of this," he whispered. "Why now?"

"Several questions come to mind. How long have they known each other? Was it before or after you hired him? Was he planted by your brother or someone else?"

"I don't know. Christian had Gregory flown back to New York. My lawyer will take it from there. I hope you don't mind, but I had Christian speak with Meggie for the change of plans. They're taking him on your plane."

Stash shook his head. "I don't see any problem with that. It's a great diversion, should your brother think we're on it. I must ask, though, why you didn't use your own plane?"

"It's on its way here as we speak, so that was out of the question. The police in New York have already been contacted. They said they'd take care of him on their end."

Anthony said, shaking his head. "Lawrence has been in jail since he was twenty, about ten years now. I didn't even know he got out. They were supposed to let us know when he was up for parole."

"That's strange," Stash said. "Why do you think he's coming here? Do you know why he's looking for you?"

"Lawrence wants my position as CEO. He's always said he had a right to the position. Of course, he doesn't. And the board would never allow him to have any form of control over the companies."

Stash tipped his head back and closed his eyes. "He's a dangerous man, then."

"He is." Anthony gave a long sigh.

"Earlier, you wanted me to get out and ride in the other car."

"I didn't want you hurt."

Stash turned his head and stared. "How would that be?"

"Gregory. He would have told Lawrence we were together," Anthony said, rubbing his thumb on the back of Stash's hand.

Stash felt his heart race. "Are we together?"

"Yes."

"I have to say your confidence is astounding. We've only just met. This may all just be a one-time thing."

"Not for me. I told you last night." The answer was quick, and the tone decisive. Determined. Resolved.

Stash couldn't look away. He'd never met a man like Anthony before.

"Wow." He wanted to say more, but words failed him.

Anthony's lips quivered before he barked out a laugh. "Is that all you're going to say? Wow?"

Stash couldn't hide his irritation. "What do you want me to say? Holy fucking shit? How about, maybe I've finally found the one man who would share my life and face a future full of bigoted obstacles? Or maybe, oh my Lord, you're amazing?"

Anthony's smile didn't waver. "*Wow*'s good."

"You're full of yourself, aren't you?" Stash huffed but deep inside felt relieved Anthony's mood had improved. He folded his arms in front of him and leaned back into the car seat and glared at Anthony.

"No, I'm not. I'm just sure about things I like and know will make sense in my life. You make sense." Anthony chuckled.

The words were cheesy, but Stash couldn't stop his stomach from clenching in response.

"You're . . . you're . . . you're incorrigible."

"That I am."

Stash shook his head. "What happened to talking seriously?" Laughter died in his throat when Anthony's demeanor sobered.

"I am serious."

Anthony sounded so sad that Stash immediately regretted his words, and once more, lacked the right thing to say.

"Come here." Anthony pulled him into a tight embrace. "Let's forget about my brother for a while and enjoy the rest of the drive to your place."

Stash settled into Anthony's arms and thought about how his life had changed in less than twenty-four hours. It was all so cliché. From the way he'd fallen under Anthony's spell to the danger they were both caught in. What surprised him the most was his eagerness for his future and what it could bring him. Somehow, Anthony beside him to share the discovery gave him the courage he'd lacked before. It was all so exciting.

Chapter Eleven

A nthony couldn't help feeling in awe as he looked around the spacious bedroom Stash called *The King's Suite.*

He'd first set sight on Stash's stately chateau when they had passed through the stone gatehouse. Immediately, the history buff in him had wanted to get out and explore the surroundings on foot. The driveway alone was straight out of a fairy tale with a winding paved road leading up to a bridge crossing a moat—a moat, of all things. Stash had later told him the land the house sat on was an island fed by three rivers, and all three passed through the moat.

"No wonder you prefer staying here, it's spectacular," he said. "How old is this place?"

"According to the records, the original structure dates back to the twelfth century. It had once been a fortress that history included the Hundred Years' War. It went through several renovations through the years, but the former owners simply got tired of the maintenance and decided to sell. It had been on the market for about six years before I found it."

Anthony could only gape at the way Stash spoke about his home. There was pride in his tone, but also the nonchalance of someone who had gotten used to living in such a place. Properties were part and parcel of the Eisemann family, but none of them compared to Stash's Limoges house.

"Do you know big it is?"

Stash shrugged. "When I first bought it, the house itself was a little over sixteen thousand square feet, but we had to add a few more to keep the walls and support posts from falling, so I don't know the exact footage right now. That's with the three levels combined. Except for the kennels, I've maintained room functions as they were. It wasn't my choice, but I had to comply with a lot of requirements. As I didn't keep any dogs other than Flossy, I converted the kennels into a recreation room for everybody's use. So if you prefer swimming and weights, you can go there and work out."

The interiors were a stark contrast to the medieval structure. Every room had been decorated to reflect a more modern, minimalistic look in neutral colors. There was none of the expected antique damask curtains or embossed upholstery stretched over delicate period chairs and sofas. The simple but elegant aesthetics reflected another level of Stash Burcell's personality. But there was that other thing he'd observed.

"Tell me something," Anthony said as soon as the bedroom door closed behind the two women who'd brought in their suitcases.

"What?" Stash kicked off his shoes to one side of the room.

Before Anthony could continue, there was a sound of scratching on the door.

"Hold on." Stash opened the door again, and Flossy walked in. She ignored them, opting to jump on the bed and lie down on one of the numerous pillows.

"Coming in, I counted no less than twenty guards. I assume you have more than double the number of men lurking around," Anthony said.

"Not that many, there's only thirty assigned here at the moment. The rest are still in training with Paul's agency." Stash looked amused as he sat on a plush bench at the end of the bed.

Anthony narrowed his gaze when Stash threw his track jacket on the floor. "That's practically an army. Is there a particular reason why you need to have that many guards?" Joining Stash on the couch sounded like a good idea, and he did just that.

Stash threw him a grin before shrugging out of his shirt. It, too, flew through the air and landed on top of the jacket. "Among other things, I had to up my security once my first makeup collection was launched. Plus, my father was the one who spoke with Paul, and he suggested the upgrade."

"Why?" Anthony frowned in puzzlement. His confusion, along with a few brain cells, flew out the window when Stash started pushing his track pants down his long legs.

"You're probably thinking about my makeup, but that's where you're wrong. Nothing's just about makeup. You do realize how gnarly the beauty industry is, right? You're in it, you should know. It's a hot commodity, and counterfeit products are big business."

Stash bent over and began pulling off his socks. The position tightened the skin on his back. Anthony reached out and touched the smooth skin there, stretching his fingers until his palm lay flat. "Still, it's a bit overkill, don't you think? I never had to up my personal security for it, and we've launched hundreds of lines."

Stash sat up, letting out a groan of satisfaction after pulling his hair free of the elastic band holding it up. "True, but each one of your companies has its own CEO. No one really has any idea who is behind the development of each product. I don't have that privilege. And then there's the way I look. I'm kind of a prime magnet for hate crime." Through the length of his loosened hair, he peeked at Anthony over his shoulder and gave him a slow wink. "Also, I'm sorry to say this, but you're not that famous, Ace."

Anthony raised a brow at Stash's mischievousness. "Really?"

"Well, let me correct that." Stash stretched his arms over his head and pressed against Anthony's hand.

The new position made it possible for Anthony to close his

arms around Stash's naked torso. Stash leaned into the embrace and reached over his head to wrap his hands around Anthony's neck, bringing them closer. It made it easier for Anthony to gently bite Stash's exposed shoulder. Not hard enough to make a mark. He would not dare injure that beautiful skin.

"Oh, I like that." Stash hummed his appreciation before continuing. "Your name is famous, sweetie, but no one really knows what you look like. If you walk down the street, they won't know who you are, and that's because you're not the face of your makeup line. In my case, specific body parts *are* the face of the line. My anonymity intrigues my audience, and once they get a hint that I'm releasing something, people will try to get to it before it launches. People can go crazy, do shitty things, just to get a hold of whatever it is I'm putting out there. Get it to the highest bidder and make the most at my expense."

Anthony kissed the spot he'd bitten, dropping his hands down to Stash's abdomen, spreading his hands so he could feel every inch of the soft skin there.

"How badly has it gone that you needed an army of guards?"

Stash twisted, stretching a leg up and to the side until he sat astride Anthony. The new position made it possible for Anthony to grab Stash by his buttocks and pull him closer. With their groins pressed together, there was no doubt in Anthony's mind that Stash could feel his hard erection hidden beneath the fabric of his pants.

"Oof . . . I've had people walk into parties and pretend to be long lost friends or relatives," Stash said in a flippant manner. "It's late. I'm tired, you're tired, and I want you in my bed."

"Thank you." Anthony didn't mind the sudden change of topic, especially when his stomach growled. "How about we take a shower first and then go have dinner?"

"Great idea. Priorities first," Stash said, and dropped a kiss on Anthony's lips.

Anthony leaned in to deepen their connection, but Stash was already up and on his feet. He looked at the hand Stash extended to him. When his stomach growled louder, he took Stash's hand since he could no longer deny his body had other ideas than sex.

"Okay, okay, let's go take that shower. Where is it?"

"Over thataway," Stash said, pointing a finger to somewhere behind Anthony.

"Let's go, then." Anthony turned and pulled Stash along with him.

Once inside the bathroom, Anthony let go of Stash's hand and quickly began taking off his clothes. The combined need for food and sex enhanced his arousal, and seeing Stash lick his lips gave him a deep feeling of satisfaction.

Stash got inside the shower cubicle and began turning on the controls.

Anthony noticed the fixtures were the same as he had in his own private homes and silently approved. It seemed they had a lot in common.

Divested of his clothes, he kicked them into a pile before picking them up and throwing them into a basket set by the corner. Stash had already begun shampooing his hair and had his eyes closed by the time Anthony stepped in to join him in the small space.

"I'm coming in, don't get startled," Anthony said, not wanting to risk an accident.

"Come on in," Stash said as he turned under the spray to rinse his hair.

Anthony stepped up until his chest pressed against Stash's and closed his eyes under the spray. He moaned in pleasure when the water washed over him. The temperature was just right.

"You do your hair, I'll soap us down." Stash's voice broke through Anthony's reverie.

"Thanks." Anthony nodded. "Sorry, but no sex in the shower."

Stash chuckled as he ran his soapy hands down Anthony's body. "I hope not. Have you ever had soap get inside your butthole? Stings like hell. Also, accidents can happen, and there's glass everywhere."

Anthony approved. "No, I've never had it up there, but I can only imagine. Sex in a shower sounds all erotic and stuff, but it's not for me. My imagination runs wild on what could go wrong."

"Broken bones, among other things," Stash said, his voice muffled under the spray of water.

"I'm really beginning to like you, baby," Anthony said.

"Oh, how sweet. But only just now?"

Anthony groaned when Stash went down on his haunches and began to soap his erection. "What are you doing? Stop that."

"But sweetie, we need to make sure we're both squeaky clean," Stash said, adding an innocent smile.

Anthony was forced to close his eyes and count to a hundred. His knees began to shake, and knew he couldn't keep his balance. "If I fall in here, how are you going to get me off the floor?"

Stash glared up at him. "All right, all right, wow, you're paranoid."

"Yes, I am." Anthony nodded emphatically. "Come on, let's finish in here and get some dinner. I'm really hungry."

Stash stood and dropped a kiss on Anthony's lips. "I'm done. Let's get some food."

Fifteen minutes later, they sat in the kitchen, devouring ham omelet sandwiches laid out on the island. They sat side by side as they ate, not speaking much. After one bite, Anthony found he was even hungrier than he'd originally thought. One look at Stash, taking a huge bite out of his sandwich, and Anthony knew he'd been just as hungry.

"What time is it?" Stash asked around a mouthful of sandwich. "I forgot all about our meeting. It was supposed to be tonight."

Anthony checked his phone. "It's after eleven. What about your father?"

Stash shrugged. "Well, he didn't call, so there's that. Are you done? I want to go to bed."

"I'm done." Anthony couldn't help but laugh when Stash jumped off the stool and pulled on his arm. "No need to rush."

"I want to go to bed," Stash said with a mock growl. "Now."

"You're such a brat," Anthony chastised. "Let's put the dishes in the sink first."

"Ugh, why are you such a good boy?" Stash complained, let go of Anthony's arm, and started picking up the dishes while Anthony picked up their glasses.

"Because my parents raised me well. Mom was very strict when it came to doing chores. Even my dad told me off whenever I acted entitled in front of the help. My nanny, on the other hand . . . Mrs. Louis didn't spare the rod and spanked my butt if I acted like a spoiled kid in her eyes. I learned to behave at a very young age." Anthony put the glasses in the sink, took the dishes from Stash, and set them inside as well.

"How many times did she spank you?"

"Two times." Anthony chuckled under his breath. He turned on the faucet and began to wash the glasses and dishes, in that order. "I was so scared of her—the way she would widen her eyes. Just a fraction of a second, mind you, but she made sure I never missed it. For me, it was enough warning. She was scary."

"So she wasn't abusive?"

"No. She was the most loving nanny, and I loved her."

"What happened to her? Is she still alive?"

"Oh yes. She's still with us, but she's busy running the household at the Eisemann estate. That's the family property in New York. In Saratoga." Anthony stopped there. He took a deep breath and mentally shook off the dark thoughts that tried to overcome him.

Finished with his chore, he turned off the water and wiped down the surfaces with a paper towel. Done, he threw the soiled paper into the garbage can. "She was also the only one who was brave enough to talk to my parents about Lawrence. If not for her, I don't know what else Lawrence would have done."

"I'm glad you had her."

"So am I," Anthony said in a tight voice.

He hadn't been lying about Lawrence earlier, but he couldn't find the courage to tell Stash everything. Shaking off his gloom, he gave Stash a smile and took his hand. "Come on, let's go upstairs."

They walked back to Stash's bedroom in silence. A movement outside made Anthony stop and look out the window. He saw the figure of a man with his back toward them.

"That would be Andrew," Stash said. "Jonathan and Curtis should be with him on that side of the house. There are nine guards on night shift, along with the two who man the cameras and sensors."

Anthony nodded and filed the information to the back of his mind. He couldn't help but admire how Stash handled the presence of so many guards securing his home and person. Security was a common thing in their circle, but even he had to admit that Stash was a whole other level.

They reached the bedroom and entered to Flossy's

questioning bark. She was standing on one of the pillows and wagging her tail in greeting.

"It's just us, baby girl," Stash said, picking up Flossy in his arms. He turned to Anthony and handed the dog to him. "Hold her for me. I need to go to the bathroom."

Anthony sat on the bench that Stash had used to tease him earlier and waited until he heard the bathroom door open and Stash walked out smelling of toothpaste.

"Your turn," Stash said, taking Flossy from Anthony.

"Okay," Anthony said, stifling a yawn and took his turn to brush his teeth.

He stared at his reflection in the mirror, seeing the dark circles under his eyes and the exhaustion clearly etched on his face. He had to admit that his stress and worry over Lawrence had made him feel tired and worn out.

When he walked out of the bathroom, he entered the darkened bedroom. There was a nightlight in one corner, but it barely illuminated a couple of feet. He suspected Stash was as tired as he was, so he briefly studied the path toward the bed before closing the bathroom door. Not entirely. He left it open a crack and did not bother to turn off the light in there.

Anthony did not know how Stash preferred to sleep, but he personally liked to have some light on. The darkness was something he had learned to fear.

With quiet steps, he slowly maneuvered his way deeper into the room until he reached his side of the bed. He carefully lay down on his back, pulling the covers halfway up his chest. Beside him, Stash moved toward him, so Anthony extended his arm and pulled him closer. Only when he was satisfied his arm wouldn't get numb under Stash's weight did he close his eyes and allow himself to relax. He smiled and didn't complain when Flossy moved over his head and lay down at the top edge of his pillow. Somehow, her presence there added a reassuring comfort he didn't know he needed.

Chapter Twelve

Stash woke to the sound of gentle panting next to his ear. He opened his eyes to Flossy lying above his head, on the pillow that should have been his. As usual, the tiny dog had managed to take over his pillows, leaving him sleeping without. It was a morning ritual that always made him smile. He reached up a hand to pick her up and cuddle.

"Good morning, little lady. How are we today?" His greeting was met with licks to his earlobe.

A quick check of the space next to him and a glance around the bedroom, revealed that Anthony was nowhere in sight. He wondered where he could have gone at such an early hour as he reached for his phone to check the time. It was barely seven o'clock.

Flossy whined and began to pant in earnest.

"Hold on, sweetie. Let me go to the bathroom and then I'll take you outside."

Ten minutes later, he hurried after Flossy, who sprinted ahead of him. Marie, his housekeeper, beamed up at them.

"Good morning, Stash. Mr. Eisemann woke up at five this morning and took a walk around the gardens," Marie said, handing over Flossy's leash.

"Thank you, Marie," he said. Flossy stood still and allowed him to clip the lead onto her collar. "Has he had breakfast yet?"

"Not yet. He's having coffee by the back garden."

"All right. Let me take care of Flossy here first and then I'll join him there. Serve breakfast in twenty minutes, please."

"Of course, sir," Marie said.

It took Flossy more than twenty minutes to finally be done with her walk. Stash didn't want to keep Anthony waiting, so he hurried Flossy, taking the path through the forest he knew would take him to the garden faster.

He returned the greetings from the gardeners and maintenance crew but didn't stop to talk to them as he normally did. However, one of his security men stepped out from the shadows and blocked his path, stopping him in his tracks. Flossy barked a greeting and didn't stop until the man stooped down to pet her head.

"What is it, Coleman?" Stash said. His gaze went to Christian, standing a few feet behind Coleman.

"Sir, Mr. Eisemann's guard, Christian, is wondering if he could speak privately with you." Coleman gave Flossy a final pat before standing up.

Stash wondered what Christian had to say and nodded his assent. "Thank you, Coleman, I'll speak with him." He walked over to where Christian stood. "What can I do for you, Christian?"

Christian met him halfway. "Mr. Burcell—"

Stash cut him short with a raised hand. "Call me Stash or Mr. Stash, or even sir. Mr. Burcell is reserved for my father."

"Mr. Stash, I wanted to talk to you about Mr. Eisemann if you don't mind," Christian said.

"Go ahead?" Stash tilted his head in the direction of the back gardens and flicked on Flossy's leash to signal to her to lead the way.

"Mr. Eisemann slept with you last night."

Stash paused and looked at Christian. The words were a statement, and he wondered if the man was against his developing relationship with Anthony.

"You have a problem with that?"

"No, sir. Please, don't get me wrong. I just wanted to ask

you if Mr. Eisemann had any nightmares last night. You see, he gets anxious whenever the subject of his brother comes up," Christian's whispered. "We were worried, since he woke up really early this morning."

Stash frowned and shook his head. "Not that I'm aware of, no."

Christian looked relieved. "Thank you, sir. Can I ask you a favor to let me know when or if he does?"

"Does it affect his work that much?"

"I'm not going to lie, it does affect him, even if he looks unaffected. Through the years I've served him, his nightmares can be quite severe at times. With both his parents dead, it's important to tell his psychiatrist."

"Lawrence did a number on him, didn't he?" Stash's heart pounded in his chest. There was more to Anthony's history than he'd initially thought.

"It's not my story to tell, sir," Christian said quietly.

Stash considered the favor and found it reasonable. "Talk to Meggie and Ian. Tell them as much as you're allowed, so they can coordinate your men with mine." Stash began to walk once more, and Christian followed him in silence. He appeared to be thinking over the suggested teamwork.

"Can I trust Meggie and Ian, sir?" Christian said when they neared the edge of the forest.

Stash understood Christian's hesitance. Meggie would have done the same thing. "Implicitly."

"Thank you, sir," Christian said, bowing his head.

"Oh, and Christian?" Stash said when Christian stopped walking.

"Yes, sir?" Christian's shining gaze locked with his.

"Thank you for letting me know, and for trusting me. Let me assure you that no harm will fall on Anthony's head. Not while we're together."

"Are you? Together, I mean?"

The concern behind the question made Stash smile. Now there was a loyal man.

"Yes, we are."

Christian rocked on his heels and bowed his head once more. "Thank you, sir. I'll advise the men."

"Do that," Stash said. He waved goodbye and continued on his way.

Stash mulled over his conversation with Christian, finding it hard to imagine the kind of horror Anthony had gone through to cause nightmares. Christian implied a psychiatrist was also involved, so it must have been bad. He let out a long sigh. He'd learned long ago to go with the flow of being someone who was unacceptable. He was more than familiar with society's darker side. Abuse came in many guises and didn't recognize social status, financial stability, gender, race, or color. So why did he think Anthony would have been spared?

By some twist of fate, he and Anthony had connected on a level he'd never thought possible. And in a short period of time. Christian appeared to trust him as well, which was altogether more of a surprise than his developing relationship with Anthony.

The forest gave way to the bright and open manicured lawns of the back gardens. Across the wide expanse, he spotted Anthony sitting in the shade of a white umbrella, a cup of coffee in his hand. He was staring into the empty space in front of him and didn't appear to have noticed Stash's presence.

Stash considered him for a moment, and there was no question in his mind that he would help. Pasting on a bright smile, he crossed the distance, lengthening his steps so he could be near Anthony quicker.

"Good morning. I hope I didn't keep you waiting. You're not too hungry, are you?" he called out as he walked across the lawn.

Anthony visibly jerked in his seat, turning a startled gaze in Stash's direction before it changed to one of pleasure.

"Good morning to you, too. Hurry up, the food looks amazing, and I'm starving." Anthony flashed a huge smile. He set his cup on the table and stood up.

"No need to get up." Stash returned the smile.

Flossy began to bark and bounce on her hind legs. When she started pawing the air, Stash interpreted her excitement to reach Anthony. Once freed from her restrictions, she bounded across the lawn and jumped into Anthony's arms.

"Oh, ho, I think she likes you," Stash said.

"Yes, I think she does," Anthony said.

The smile transformed his face, but Stash saw the dark circles under his eyes. Christian's caution came back.

"How did you sleep? I hope I didn't cause nightmares with my snoring?"

Anthony shook his head and extended his arm so Stash can walk into his embrace.

"Good morning," Anthony said in a low voice before dropping a kiss on Stash's lips. "You and Flossy are great bed partners, and no, you didn't snore."

"Nice to know." Stash purred and kissed him back. He decided not to mention what Christian had told him. There was more than enough time for that. For now, he was hungry. He looked at the food laid out on the table next to the one where their plates were set. "Shall we eat?"

"Yes, please." Anthony set Flossy down on the ground before quickly picking her up again. "She's going to be all right? Or should we put her back inside?"

Stash shook his head. "Nah, she'll be fine, you can let her down. She's got the run of the property. Just don't allow her to guilt-trip you into giving her food off the table."

"Understood." Anthony nodded, put Flossy back on the ground, and followed Stash to get some food.

They ate in silence. Stash was still hungry after he finished his first plate. He hesitated but finally decided to get himself a second serving. Except for the silence and the flitting frown that creased Anthony's forehead every so often, he appeared to enjoy his food and asked questions about the estate.

"So it took you two years to finish this place?"

"Yes. Two excruciatingly expensive years, but it was worth it," Stash said. "The historical society had a lot of requirements that we had to fulfill before they gave the go signal for the next phases."

"It's a fantastic place, I'll grant you that. I don't know if I could have had the patience to take on a project like this." Anthony looked around the gardens and up at the steeples.

"I know what you mean. It's different when it comes to constructing a modern building. We still have to abide by the restrictions, but the historical society is on a whole other level. It's a huge decision to make, with a whole lot of money involved. Granted, I bought this place cheap, but the rest of it was a bit much. There was a point in time when I wanted to give up."

"Why this place, though?"

"I guess you can blame it on my love of fairy tales. And nothing beats French architecture. I took one look and decided I could save the building. It all turned out for the good, because it's now a place where I feel safe and I don't have to deal with society's censure. The estate is large enough to detract visitors."

Anthony turned to face him again. "I guess that's what counts the most, doesn't it?"

Stash nodded. He reached for the carafe and topped his cup for the second time that morning. "Paul sent in his team to set up the internet connections, backup servers, and his security company took care of the security cameras while construction was going on."

"Paul has established CyNapse as a leading brand in security and technology. He and his husband are quite the team with their research and development," Anthony said.

"You want to see what he did to my office?" Stash said, setting his cup down.

"Are you wanting to show off?" Anthony grinned. After the food and two more cups of coffee, he looked more relaxed than he'd had previously.

Stash's smile widened. "I must admit, I am quite proud of what I've got in there. Also, we need to talk about a few things in private, and that's the best place to do it."

The abrupt turn of subject erased Anthony's smile, and Stash wanted to kick himself for his lack of sensitivity. But business was business, which was why they had arranged the meeting in the first place.

When Anthony didn't immediately respond, Stash offered another option. "If you want, we can postpone the meeting until Dad decides to get here, but I have no idea when that will be."

"No, let's get this over with. Do away with all the formalities." Anthony shook his head. "I don't mind doing this now. Unless you're asking me to commit a crime."

Stash stood up and held out his hand, glad when Anthony took it in his.

"Lead the way," Anthony said as he stood.

Stash held back his laughter when Anthony began leading the way instead of the other way around.

"Do you even know where we're going?" Stash asked when they reached the staircase.

Anthony stopped and turned to look at him. "Nope."

"Second-floor study, next to our bedroom."

"Our bedroom," Anthony repeated in a soft voice.

"Well, we're both sleeping in it," Stash said, feeling suddenly embarrassed. "There are ten other rooms to choose from should you want one."

"Don't even think to go back on your word," Anthony warned.

Stash beamed, relieved, but at the same time anxious over the implications of their conversation.

"I don't know about you," Anthony said when they reached the second-floor landing and turned toward their bedroom. "But I feel as though I've known you for a long time."

"It's kind of scary, isn't it?" Stash tightened his grip on Anthony's hand. "I mean, it's only been two days."

"Let's take our time getting to know each other more, okay?" Anthony suggested.

Stash looked at Anthony and wondered who he was trying to reassure. "Okay, we can do that. Well, first thing on the agenda is, I need your help."

"Okay," Anthony said.

Stash rolled his eyes. "You're easy, you know that?"

When they were two doors down from the study, Stash pointed at the door just past their bedroom "Through there."

Anthony stopped and examined the hallway. "Is it my imagination, or is your study even bigger than the bedroom?"

"There are only two rooms in this wing, if that's what you're asking."

"Incredible. Okay, let's get this over with. I want to enjoy the rest of the day with you, if you don't mind."

Stash smirked. He stepped ahead of Anthony and stopped in front of the doors that looked like the ones to the bedroom. He placed his palm on a scanner off to one side, and the doors slid open. "Come on in."

Anthony gave Stash a wink. "I find it easy to say yes to you."

"Oh, you're sweet." Stash crooned, leaning over to kiss Anthony on the cheek before going over to his desk at the far end of the room. On a wall behind the desk hung an elaborately framed painting of an old man. The surface of his desk was one big touchpad, and he woke it with a simple swipe on its surface.

"I don't have a desk like that. Where did you get it?" Anthony walked over and examined it closely. He touched the surface in awe. "This is amazing."

"It was a gift from Paul, after the construction was done. He said if I wanted to stay here the rest of my life, I might as well get the best technology he can offer. I didn't say no. It's beautiful, isn't it?"

Anthony narrowed his gaze on Stash when the desk lit up. When the apps and other icons showed up, he closed his eyes and moaned. "I'm going to have to talk to Paul. This is unfair. Just because you're sort of cousins doesn't mean you should get all the good stuff. What's it called?"

"Paul said it's simply called *The Desk Top*."

"Quite the understatement," Anthony murmured.

"I'm sure he wouldn't mind giving you one. For a price," Stash added. He beamed when Anthony glared at him. "Take a seat, let's begin."

"Can I play with it after we're done?" Anthony asked, his gaze still locked on the desk.

"Yes, I promise you can." Stash sat down and started pulling up files.

Anthony took his seat opposite Stash. "What are those?" His words were clipped and straight to the point.

At the change of tone, Stash looked up and almost did a double take. Unlike earlier, when Anthony had been deep in thought and then playful, this Anthony was sober and focused.

"I need you to listen first before you agree to anything," Stash said, slipping into business mode as well.

"I'm listening."

"I need your approval so your company can help fast track the development of a lip gloss formula that I've been trying to get on the market."

Anthony immediately nodded. "Give me the proposal so I can approve it."

"Are you not even going to ask what flavor I want you to develop for me?" Stash stared in amazement. This was no way to conduct a business.

Anthony narrowed his eyes. "Okay, I'll bite. What is it?"

Stash couldn't help rolling his eyes. "First, I need help eliminating the flavors of the ingredients I'm using for the gloss. Despite all claims to the contrary, there's a lingering chemical aftertaste that I personally cannot stand. Sometimes, when I eat or drink anything, the taste gets stronger and . . . weirder, for lack of a better term."

Anthony shrugged and leaned back into his chair. "That's doable. When do you need it?"

They proceeded to talk through the details of Stash's vision before agreeing to go to the factory the following month.

"All right, now that we're done with what you need, what's the other thing you wanted to discuss with me? Asking to make use of the lab shouldn't require all this secrecy."

Stash had discussed his proposal with his father for several weeks and knew what he wanted to say. Now that Anthony was sitting opposite him, he hesitated. Finally, he decided to go for it.

"Well, here's the thing. What I need to talk to you about is actually connected to that lab—in particular, Eisemann Foods. I know you have two others, but EF is the one I really want to work with because that's where they specialize in flavor chemistry."

"Yes, I know. What about it?" Anthony tilted his head to the side, his gaze direct, and all business.

"I wanted to talk to you about using EF after the general

manager made excuses that didn't make sense. Instead, I reached out to the president of EF next, but he wouldn't even take my calls. I talked to my father about it, and he suggested that if I really wanted to work with EF, I should reach out to you."

Anthony's demeanor changed. A frown appeared between his brows, and his eyes narrowed. "They wouldn't see you?"

"Not the president, not the general manager, no one." Stash shook his head. "At first, I got irritated, but then I wondered about why they would refuse my money. I asked Meggie to dig around, and she discovered that EF was not taking on new clients. Another source said it was a usual precaution when a company was going to be put up for sale."

Anthony's expression tightened. "EF is not for sale. Where the hell did you get that idea?"

"Hold on, don't go getting angry on me. To test the information, I made a bid on EF and only told Dad about it after the fact. He reacted the same way you just did, all huffy and puffy. By the way, Dad also denied that EF's for sale."

"Were you able to buy any shares?"

Stash made a face. "Unfortunately, yes. Quite a few, actually. Cost me ten million dollars for a couple thousand shares."

He tapped on one of the folders, and it opened to reveal digital images of the sale. Anthony leaned over the table and began to read. The more he did, the more his lips tightened in anger.

"After I got the confirmation they received my money and got the documents to back it up, I showed them to my father, and he was just as alarmed as you are. In any case, he immediately decided to call you. Hence this meeting. He wanted to tell you personally about my discovery. Dad was furious that someone is pawning off company shares without permission from the board. I also found out that someone's buying shares from many of the individual shareholders." Stash opened another document and slid the image to Anthony. "This is a list of shareholders who sold their shares. I'm not one hundred percent sure it's complete, but I'm certain you can take care of that from your end. Also, can I just say that I don't think they knew this goes against company bylaws. They only saw dollar signs."

"When did you find out all this?" Anthony didn't look up from the documents.

Although Anthony appeared calm and composed, Stash noticed his right eye began to tick.

"Five days ago. We reached out to you as soon as we could, but as I said, not until I was able to gather all the evidence. I bought-in two weeks ago, received confirmation within the hour, and got the share documents five days ago. The dates of each transaction are in the documents. Dad insisted on telling you immediately, and I agreed. He and your dad had been friends for a long time, and he thought it only right to tell you about it."

"Do you know how much is involved?"

"Dad took over that part," Stash said, already opening another file. "Here are all the figures he sent me. I looked over the numbers. They're quite minimal, but I suspect they either just started this or are doing it on purpose, so no one notices the movements until they drop the ball and try to pull a stunt. I think there's an upcoming general meeting, so they'll probably do it then. At least, if I were them, I'd wait until that time to create more drama."

Anthony looked up from the images, his gaze filled with determination. "I can't thank you enough for this. This isn't what I expected at all. Tell Adrien not to worry. I'll take care of it."

"Do you think this could be related to Lawrence? Maybe this is a move so he could take control over the board?"

Anthony straightened and placed his hands on his hips. "I don't know, but anything's possible, so I'm not letting down my guard. Don't worry, I'll find out and deal with this. As for Lawrence, if he's the one behind this, it's a stupid move. The board made a resolution to ban him from being connected in any form with any of the companies. Even if he chose to apply for a janitorial job, he wouldn't get it."

"Hey, you don't have to face this alone, you know," Stash said, running his hand up and down Anthony's hips.

"Thank you. You have no idea what that means to me." Anthony took Stash's hands into his, pressing his palms around them in a tight grip. He didn't meet Stash's gaze, focusing instead on their clasped hands.

"Dad also said that you have his vote."

Anthony nodded, but he still didn't look up. Stash leaned forward so he could peer into Anthony's face.

"Hey, what's going on in that head of yours?" Stash whispered. "Why so gloomy?"

"I'm not." Anthony insisted.

"Tell me what you're thinking."

Anthony took a deep breath and opened his mouth, then closed it, and continued to stare at their hands.

"Ace?"

"I just realized something," Anthony said, his voice so low that Stash had to strain to hear him. "I . . . I've never been in a relationship before. Dated, yes. And a lot of sex."

Shaken, Stash didn't know how to respond to the complete shift in topics, topped with an unexpected confession.

"There has only been one person I cared enough about to tempt me to take that step. That person's you." Anthony stopped and shook his head.

Stash nodded but still didn't know what to say. What did someone say to a confession like that? He wanted to respond more than anything but was almost afraid to hear what

Anthony would say next. Anthony's lips tightened, and it took him a few more seconds before he finally looked up.

"You scare me."

Chapter Thirteen

"You really scare me," Anthony repeated.

The words were basically an admission of his weaker stance regarding his involvement with Stash. It was a risky move, one he would never have taken had it involved money. His growing feelings for Stash, and his dreams of taking their relationship a step further, emboldened him. He only hoped he wasn't making a mistake. That he'd read Stash correctly. That he was not the only one feeling like this.

Anthony, again, studied Stash's hand pressed between his larger ones. The differences between their skin tones were clearer close up. His, a pale, blotchy pink compared to Stash's alabaster smoothness. Easing the pressure, he cradled the slim, elegant hand and continued to study it. He couldn't be more different than the man who was becoming important to him in ways he was even afraid to admit to himself.

"Why do you say you're afraid of me?" Stash attempted to pull his hands free.

Anthony tightened his grip once more. He wasn't ready to let go yet. At that point, he didn't know if he could ever let go.

"I'm really messing this up," Anthony muttered under his breath. How was he going to do this?

Stash shook his head. "Yes, you are. Ace, just spit it out. What have I done to make you afraid of me? I mean, do I look scary?" Stash twisted to pick up his phone. "Is my mascara running? I thought this was waterproof. Can you let go of my hand? I need to see what my face looks like."

Anthony chuckled. "You're makeup's fine, Stash. Relax."

"Then what the hell are you talking about? If it's not my makeup, what is it?"

"It's not your makeup." Anthony shook his head. "What I'm trying to say, if you can just sit still for a minute so I can finish, is that others may look at you and think you're weak. They probably think they can flick their fingers at you, and you'd fall over your backside."

"I'm not weak. Excuse me," Stash huffed.

"Exactly." Anthony raised Stash's hand and kissed the knuckles. "You're the strongest person I know and also one of the most intelligent."

"Why, thank you." Stash beamed, practically preening. "That's a really nice thing to say."

Anthony laughed so hard his body started to shake. "Sorry to break it to you, baby, but you really are scary. I thought Meggie was because she can be so loud, but I changed my mind. You're the expert in terrorizing the enemy. You trained her, didn't you? Not the other way around?"

"I don't know what you're talking about," Stash said with exaggerated innocence. "Can I have my hand back now?"

"Come here." Anthony pulled Stash up to his feet and into his arms. "Have I thanked you yet?"

"You have, but I wouldn't mind hearing it again." Stash smiled mischievously. "Now, let me go. I need to go to the washroom."

"I'll be here." Anthony gave Stash a kiss on the cheek before letting him go.

As he watched Stash leave the room and close the door behind him, Anthony realized how deeply he was falling for the man. It wasn't going to be an easy drop, either. It was as though he'd spent most of his adult life like a bird on a wire who had suddenly lost its balance, and no one was there to catch him. Besides, now that the fall had started, there was absolutely nothing he would change.

He went back to the chair he'd vacated and stared at the stack of documents Stash has pulled up for him. Right there was just part of the proof of an insidious betrayal that could have ruined his company had it not been for Stash.

Anthony had always taken pride in his self-control, but when Stash had started showing him the detailed data, he'd almost lost it. That it had taken a third party to show him what was going on within his own company had been like a punch to his gut and ego. If he were physically capable of kicking himself for his lack of insight, he would have done it. He clenched hands into fists.

How stupidly naïve he'd been, thinking he was untouchable as chairman of one of the world's largest conglomerates. That someone would dare make a move to ruin his company at this level made him feel like an inexperienced noob. Rage made his heart pound, and the resulting adrenaline rushed through him, but it was a high he was more than familiar with. In fact, he welcomed it. Dealing with challenges had always been like a game to him, and this time, he had the upper hand. Thanks to Stash, he had the evidence he needed. First, he needed to deal with the Eisemann Foods executives.

With grim determination, he picked up his phone and contacted his lawyer, Maxwell Kauffman.

"Anthony, what can I do for you?" Max yawned.

Anthony berated himself for not considering the time difference. "Max, I apologize for calling so early. But there's something I need you to do for me and, I need it done yesterday."

"That's all right, you wouldn't be calling me from your personal number if this were not important. What do you need?"

Anthony gave Max a brief overview of what had happened and what he wanted done.

Max listened and didn't interrupt until after Anthony was

done talking.

"Here's my advice. First, you suspend the administrative officers and staff of EF from the general manager down to the secretarial pool. Assign someone from the main office to fly in and supervise the operations there. Also, issue an order for internal followed by external audit for comparison."

"Do it," Anthony said.

"Done. Next, Frank Schoffield. He's been the president in charge of EF for over twenty years. We don't know how deeply he's involved, but his actions and probable involvement is a sensitive matter. We should take our time before we do anything drastic that would rile him and cause problems. The suspensions alone will already make him suspicious, but you can ask your team to think up something, like an emergency cleanup or something radical, but not so extreme it's unbelievable."

Anthony nodded. "We can do that. Cause some drama. Now, can I indefinitely suspend Schoffield's privileges and involvement in EF and other companies under the Eisemann Industries umbrella?"

"Yes, you can, but be prepared to defend your actions when the board starts asking questions," Max said.

"Easily done. I have enough evidence of probable involvement."

"Well, see, Anthony, probable is not conclusive. Why don't you wait until such time you have indisputable proof before you take action? I know you're pissed and want to take immediate action, but as your lawyer, I'd advise you to wait. Once we get everything documented, then we can throw the book at him. We want to avoid an expensive lawsuit. We need to get back Schoffield's shares and take control of them."

Anthony looked up when the door opened, and Stash came back inside the office.

"All right, Max. I'll leave everything up to you, I've got to go," Anthony said.

"Can I call you anytime? Or do you want me to go through Gregory?" Max asked.

"I just fired Gregory," Anthony said, smiling at Stash when he glanced in his direction. Stash smiled back but didn't say anything as he sat down.

"Is he involved in the illegal sale? What do you want me to do with him? Is Cochran aware of the situation?""

"Send someone to listen in on the debriefing. We think he may be involved with Lawrence but not sure to what extent. Also, as my assistant, he was privy to a lot of information I cannot afford to get leaked."

"Lawrence? He's in jail, isn't he?"

"We just found out he got out on parole." Although Max was a corporate lawyer, Anthony proceeded to brief him about the situation. "Cochran was advised about the situation as soon as we found out. He hadn't been informed either, and he's finalizing formal complaints to that effect."

Max whistled. "And Gregory kept that little fact from you, didn't he? Okay, I'm going to send Sam over to Cochran to find out everything we can. The two cases may not be connected, but it's best to be in the loop of things."

"Thank you, Max," Anthony said.

"I'll talk to you soon. Bye," Max said before quickly ending the call.

Anthony pushed his anger to the back of his mind, confident that Max would take care of things from his end with his usual efficiency. He walked around the to-die-for-desk-sized-tablet and pulled Stash to his feet. Stash looked momentarily confused until Anthony wrapped his arms around him.

"I'll take your offer of help if you don't mind?" Anthony whispered into Stash's neck.

It had been an easy decision to accept Stash's offer of help. It revealed a loyalty from a corner he'd hoped for but never knew he'd already had. He'd known the elder Burcell had been a friend of his father's for years but had no idea they had been that close. He wondered why that was and vowed to discover the reasons.

"I don't mind at all, you didn't even need to ask," Stash said, hugging him back.

Time stood still. For Anthony, it was a time to be grateful, and all he wanted was to enjoy the moment. After a while, Stash stood back and gazed up at him.

"Let me go and print out the documents. I'll also send all the electronic files to you. What email do you want me to send them to?"

Anthony caressed Stash's cheek as he considered his choices. As chairman, he had a company email where all official documents were usually uploaded. However, this was a different situation and would need a private account. One that no former or presently employed personal assistant could access. He pointed to the table.

"Do you mind if I use that incredible table of yours? I think I need to create a different account."

Stash patted Anthony's chest and grinned broadly. "Go for it."

Anthony suspected Stash knew his true intentions—he wanted to play with the new toy. He rubbed his palms together and took the chair Stash had vacated. After a moment's hesitation, he tapped to open a browser. It took him some time to get used to the giant-sized gadget, for it had an unexpected learning curve. Or curves. First, although it was one giant tablet, there was some trick to the amount of pressure to apply for it to respond. Second, the screen was highly sensitive, and a mere caress would open different windows so quickly it almost scared him. Third, he'd never actually created an email account—his assistants and other secretaries had always done it for him, so he got a little aggressive when he couldn't get past having to choose a password that didn't involve his birth date. Stash came to his rescue by sitting beside him and stepping him through the process.

"Send it to that account," Anthony said when the new email account was finalized.

While Stash started uploading the numerous files, Anthony linked his phone to his new email account. The connection took seconds to connect, quickly followed by another beep that announced the email had been delivered. He clicked his tongue.

"I really need to talk to Howell," he muttered as he checked his email to see if all the files came through successfully. He nodded in approval when he saw they all had.

"How many copies do you want me to print out?" Stash asked, his hands hovering over the virtual keyboard.

"Just two for now." Anthony couldn't resist dropping a grateful kiss on Stash's head. "I can't say thank you enough, baby."

"You keep saying that," Stash said, beaming up at him.

"And I will never stop saying it." Anthony sighed as he admired The Desk Top. He was really going to have to upgrade his systems.

While waiting for the printer to finish its task, Anthony took the time to go over what had already been completed. Stash kept watch over the machine, sorted and stapled according to their order of printing. There was a lot of information to absorb, and soon Anthony lost himself in analyzing the names and numbers involved in the illegal sale of his company's shares. The more he read, the calmer he became. There was no room for anger, not in this kind of game. A phone rang, and Anthony checked to see if it was his phone.

"It's mine," Stash said, holding up his phone. He frowned at it. "It's my dad."

Anthony nodded and went back to reading, but soon

couldn't help listening to the one-sided conversation.

"Yes, I just finished explaining the situation to him. I'm finishing up printing the documents . . . uh-huh . . . he took it pretty well, considering." Stash looked up to the ceiling and rolled his eyes.

Anthony had to bite down on his lip to keep from laughing out loud.

"No, he didn't ask a lot of questions, just took in the information. He's been studying the ones I'd finished printing so far. Ah, as for the use of the lab, he agreed to it, but I'll need to fly over and visit in person. Okay, I'll see you next week."

"Everything all right?" Anthony looked up and watched as Stash continued to gather the finished printouts as they were spat out.

"You heard. Dad just wanted to confirm I gave you everything you needed." Stash chuckled. "Dad's a worrywart. He can never be satisfied unless he's right in the middle of everything."

Stash chattered on, but Anthony's thoughts had gone back to the situation. He bit on his lower lip as he thought about what his next move would be. There was no doubt in his mind this was a problem that would need his full attention. It was unfortunate that it should come at an inconvenient time. He truly wanted to spend more time with Stash and learn everything he could about the man. However, circumstances like these needed to be nipped in the bud, and he couldn't trust anyone else to do it for him. With a start, he realized that for all his wealth and accrued financial — and maybe political — powers, he had absolutely no one to trust.

The thought gave him pause. Anthony stared at a wall for a long time. He could only think of one word. Pathetic.

And yet, here was Stash Burcell, someone he'd not even known existed when he should have, giving him all the ammunition to save his company from being sold out from under him. He grimaced at the thought of having to inform the board of directors and major stockholders about the situation. First step was the need to call for an emergency board meeting, and the bylaws required him to give the directors at least seventy-two-hours advanced notice.

"Finally," Stash exclaimed.

"I take it the printing's all done?" Anthony looked up to see Stash wave a sheaf of papers.

"Yes. Let me finish stapling these together, then let's have some lunch, please. I'm starving."

At the mention of food, Anthony's stomach growled loudly. He set the papers he was studying on the table beside him and pushed himself off the chair.

"How long have we been in here?" Anthony stretched his arms above his head and felt his spine crack in places. He winced at the sudden relief that crept up his back.

Stash picked up his phone. "Uhm, we came in here around nine, it's almost one now. That's over four hours. No wonder we're hungry," he said, looking down at the stack of documents. His hair fell over his eyes, which he flicked back with a hand.

"Let's get out of here." Anthony slung an arm around Stash's shoulders, and they left the office.

Neither of them lingered over lunch. As soon as they were done, Stash requested their coffee to be delivered to the office. The rest of the afternoon passed by in a blur, and it wasn't until Anthony had read every inch of documentation that he decided he needed a break. He closed his eyes and pinched the bridge of his nose. Although he was used to working all hours, he was emotionally drained, and all he wanted to do was spend what was left of the day with Stash.

Anthony looked around and found Stash sleeping across from him on one of the sofas. He didn't know how long he sat there, studying Stash's form and listening to him snore softly under his breath. It was a moment he would forever remember as a turning point in his life. There was no turning back for him. Why it happened to be Stash over anyone else was beyond him, but he didn't mind.

He rushed over when Stash shifted and began to slide off the sofa. He barely caught him before he fell to the floor.

"Hey, it's okay," Anthony said when Stash floundered to regain balance.

"I nearly fell, didn't I?" Stash muttered as he sat up.

"I take it this wasn't the first time?"

Stash shook his head and ran his fingers over his hair. He grimaced when his fingernails snagged on some tangles. "I specifically chose that sofa because it is comfortable. It's just a little bit too narrow."

"Okay." Anthony chuckled, shaking his head. "Come on, it's time for dinner." He held out a hand, and when Stash took it, he pulled him up to his feet.

Outside the office, two men stood to attention. Anthony recognized one of his own guards, the other he didn't know. Most likely one of Stash's. The men followed them down the hall and staircase only to fall back and stand guard outside a room where food was laid out on a long table.

"You know what?" Stash said, linking his arms through Anthony's.

"What?"

"We need more than just you and me to work over this situation. We need recruits. Do you mind if Meggie joins us?" Stash asked as he took a seat.

"I don't mind." Anthony shrugged. "In fact, I'll ask Christian to join us as well. What do you think?"

"Good idea," Stash said. He turned and motioned to one of the servers, who stood by the buffet table. After a few whispered words, the server turned to do as asked. A few minutes later, Meggie and Christian came in. While Meggie sent Stash a questioning look, Christian looked self-conscious and uncomfortable as he was being served soup.

"Relax, Christian," Meggie said, unfolding a napkin and laying it over her lap. "We're usually not so formal, but here in Limoges, we kind of have to go with the flow, if you get what I mean."

"Stash inherited the staff, didn't he?" Anthony had observed that for all of Stash's informal ways, the staff went about their duties confidently and with an air of pride.

"Yes, it was one of the things I insisted on retaining when I first bought this place. People value their tradition around here, and as the property came with the farmlands and tenants, it was an easy decision to make." Stash shrugged his shoulders nonchalantly.

A rush of pride coursed through Anthony. Every time he was beginning to think he had gotten to know Stash, something new would come up.

"I heard your father called," Meggie said.

The change of topic was delivered so smoothly it took a moment before Meggie's words registered. Anthony looked at Meggie in surprise. Did her close monitoring on Stash include tapping into his phone? Her familiarity with Stash was not what one would see in a typical employee and employer relationship. But he had no doubt theirs was a relationship based on love, friendship, and deep trust in one another.

"He wanted to know if I had spoken to Anthony about that issue," Stash said in a calm voice.

Christian lowered his spoon and looked from Anthony to Stash.

"I take it everything's taken cared of?" Meggie asked as she continued to eat.

Stash nodded but didn't say anything. Christian looked lost and glared at the three of them. Anthony didn't want to say anything while there were others about, so he kept on eating, all the time keeping a close eye on the interaction between Meggie and Stash.

Christian's face turned grim, and Anthony leaned in to reassure him.

"I'll brief you after dinner," Anthony whispered.

Christian visibly relaxed and continued to eat. By the end of the meal, the tension between Christian and Meggie had eased, with Christian initiating a conversation with Meggie. When their plates were getting cleared off the table, Stash suggested dessert on the patio. Anthony held back his amusement when Christian excused himself only to be stopped by Stash.

"Christian, why don't you and Meggie go ahead to the patio. Anthony and I will follow in a minute."

Both Meggie and Christian looked confused, but Stash insisted, waving them out the door.

When they were left alone in the dining room, Anthony turned to Stash. "Is there something you wanted to talk to me about?"

"No. I just want the two of them to get to know each other better." Stash exaggerated a slow wink.

Momentarily bewildered, Anthony looked back to where Meggie and Christian had exited. "Did I miss something?"

Stash grimaced. "Meggie doesn't usually make these types of requests, but she messaged me earlier and asked if Christian could join us for dinner."

"You mean, she's interested in Christian?" Anthony couldn't believe what he was hearing. "But she's so . . .so . . . domineering."

Stash's mouth fell open. "And Christian's a what? A wimp? Is that what you're saying?"

"Well, no, but—"

"What are you saying then?"

"I'm kind of intimidated by her," Anthony whispered.

Stash gawked at him before he tilted his head back and began to laugh. When tears started to fall down Stash's face, Anthony's cheeks heated, and he closed his eyes.

"Stop it," he hissed.

"I'm sorry." Stash covered his mouth with a hand in an obvious attempt to control his mirth. He failed. His laughter only got louder.

Anthony threw his napkin on the table and stood up. "I can't believe you're pitting them together."

"Why not? I mean, Meggie's never expressed any interest in anyone before Christian. I mean, he is gorgeous, in a straight-laced, conservative sort of way."

"You're hopeless. If Christian runs back in here screaming for help, I'm blaming you for it." Anthony muttered, then he paused and glared at Stash. "What do you mean, Christian's gorgeous? Explain yourself."

"Don't underestimate your man, Ace. Christian's as pretty as can be, all buff and macho. And that's just his body. His face, oh my. And what about those pouty lips." Stash fanned himself dramatically. "He knows he's pretty, too, but what I can't quite figure out is what he thinks about Meggie. I bet he's never met his match before and doesn't know how to deal with a strong-willed woman. Did you notice how he was looking at Meggie earlier? Oh yes, he wants her."

Anthony couldn't stop his own grin. He had noticed the covert glances Christian kept throwing at Meggie. "How did he look? Come on, spit it out."

"You know what I mean." Stash sniggered. "Like he was hungry."

"I didn't know you were a matchmaker, among other things." Anthony shook his head. "Their budding romance will have to wait, though."

Stash tilted his head to one side. "You're thinking of going back to the States."

"I don't think I can handle this investigation properly from here. Also, I have to arrange for an emergency board meeting so we can nip this in the bud. Before that, I'd need to talk to the directors privately. Assess where they individually stand in this situation."

"Do you think any of the other directors are involved?"

"I don't know, but one can never tell," Anthony said, wrinkling his nose.

"When do you want to leave?" Stash said, looking thoughtful.

"The bylaws state the board members need a minimum of three days notification before I can call the emergency meeting."

"I guess you'll leave as soon as possible, then."

Anthony nodded. "Yes. I should be able to leave tomorrow morning and still have enough time to investigate who's behind this. Come up with different solutions on how to deal with the perpetrators that would be agreeable to the majority of the members. I have the majority shares, but it would still be nice to have everyone, or at least most of them, support me."

"I agree. You can count on Dad's support."

"Yes, I know that now." Anthony smiled, his heart warming at the thought that he had at least one director he could trust implicitly.

"Did you have any doubts?"

"I knew Adrien supported me. I just didn't know to what extent. After what you've told me today, I no longer have any doubts that he's a loyal friend and colleague."

Stash's brows drew together. "I knew your father and mine were close, but even I had no idea how close they really were."

"Yes. I was thinking about that earlier," Anthony said.

Most of the elder directors had inherited their shares from the founding directors, who'd helped Anthony's grandfather when he'd set up the first company. Adrien Burcell had joined later, after buying into the directorship. The only way that could happen was getting full approval from the CEO of the time, Anthony's father, Murdoch.

"We need to find out why they never told us anything," Anthony suggested. "Or why they had a falling out."

Stash's frown deepened. "Why would you assume that?"

"Well, I never heard my father talking about Adrien unless it had something to do with the company." Anthony shrugged.

"No. You're right." Stash leaned forward. "But that doesn't really mean anything. Maybe they just got too busy running their companies. But enough about that. I was looking forward to spending some time with you. I guess that's out of the question now."

The despondent look on Stash's face made the decision easy for Anthony. He reached out and took hold of Stash's hands.

"Not really. Think of this as nothing more than a minor hiccup over something that we never planned in the first place." He shrugged. "Hey, I know it's early days yet, but I don't want to go and leave things as they are between us. What's your schedule like the coming week or two?"

"Nothing I can't reschedule. But there's that visit to your lab that you suggested this morning."

"Come with me, then. Fly back to New York with me. I can't promise I'll be with you all the time, but I've made it a habit to go home every night."

"Oh, you have, have you."

"What do you say? Join me, or stay here? Alone. With Fluffy." Anthony squeezed Stash's hand between his palms. "Please?"

"What if I say no?"

"I guess I'll survive," Anthony said, letting go of Stash's hands.

"God, you're so sweet." Stash reached out and pinched his cheeks.

If it had been someone other than Stash, they would not have liked how Anthony would have reacted. Being around Stash the past few days was changing him in so many ways. He smiled. "I aim to please, baby."

"Okay, let's tell Meggie and Christian about the change of plans."

"Good. I saw the mousse earlier, and I'm really craving some chocolate."

Christian stood to attention when Anthony and Stash joined him and Meggie on the patio. Anthony waved him back to his seat and waited for Stash to sit before taking the seat next to him. The mousse tasted just as good as it looked, and he couldn't refuse when Stash offered him his leftovers.

Anthony closed his eyes as the sweet taste hit his palate and then groaned when he suddenly remembered something.

He turned to Christian and leaned forward so he could speak in low tones. "Do you happen to know what happened to Genevieve and Jade?"

"Yes, sir. They stayed back in Saint Pierre."

"Damn it. Well, cancel their appointments but make sure to double compensate them for wasting their time. Make arrangements to fly them back to Paris."

"Yes, sir."

"Oh, and about Renault? Change the time of appointment in New York. Make it the day after we get there. We'll be staying at the Upper East Side house. Contact Banks and let him know we're coming."

"Yes, sir." Christian's always-calm demeanor didn't falter.

"When are you thinking of going back?"

"Tomorrow morning."

Christian's only response was to nod. Meggie continued to eat, but there was no mistaking that she was listening to their conversation.

"I'm going to miss this food when we leave." Anthony groaned and patted his stomach.

Meggie's mouth dropped open. "We?"

"We're going back to the States with Anthony," Stash said, not looking up from his dessert.

"Which state exactly?" Meggie raised an eyebrow and folded her arms in front of her.

Stash looked up. "New York, right?"

"Yes, that's where the main headquarters are." Anthony smiled at Stash before glancing at Meggie. "And here I thought you were listening to my conversation earlier." Anthony leaned his arms on his thighs. "Of course, you'll be staying at my place. Christian will take care of the details."

"Of course." Meggie rolled her eyes.

Anthony recognized the caution behind Meggie's negative attitude. He still did not know how deep her relationship was with Stash, but he suspected a lot of worry beneath her brash behavior.

"I just thought of something," Stash said, tapping a finger on his chin. "You mentioned the emergency board meeting." At Anthony's nod, he continued. "I know you fired Gregory, and that Christian has been acting as your de facto assistant. My question is, do you have anyone who can take Gregory's place?"

"I can do without an assistant, although having one would make my job easier. Why, what are you suggesting?"

"I was thinking that Meggie could take over that job. Temporarily. Until you find someone you can trust to work with."

"Who? Me?" Meggie quickly sat up in her chair, her voice

rising in volume.

"It's just a suggestion, Meggie. If you're not willing to help, I perfectly understand."

"I am your assistant, and I take care of your security detail as well. Who do you think I am? Wonder Woman?"

"Well, as I said, it was just a suggestion. Also, my schedule is clear the next couple of weeks, and the rest we can reschedule."

Meggie's expression hardened. "Bitch."

Anthony opened his mouth to call out Meggie's impoliteness, but to his surprise, Christian beat him to it.

"There's no need for rudeness, Meggie. If you don't want to help out, we'll understand. However," Christian added quickly when Meggie turned a hard gaze in his direction, "I wouldn't mind your help training me to be a better assistant for Mr. Eisemann. I've been guarding his back for ten years, so I know what his assistants do."

Meggie's hardened expression turned thoughtful as she appeared to consider Christian's suggestion.

"I was just observing the way you help out Mr. Stash, and I can see the logic of you being both the head of security and personal assistant. I get the security stuff, and I can schedule things, but I don't know the rest of it."

"Do you know how to write out reports?" Meggie asked.

Christian glared and leaned forward. "It's a must to know how to write reports as head of security. I do it on a daily basis. Twice. Daily."

"Granted, but what I meant was analytical reports. Global analytical reports. It's a must for personal assistants to guarantee their boss won't have to stress out over mundane matters. It's not all about serving them coffee, you know."

"If you teach me, I can learn," Christian said without missing a beat.

The air turned electric, and Anthony thought it wise to

leave the area just to avoid having his hair stand on end. He could no longer deny what Stash had implied earlier. Their two heads of security had an intense reaction to one another. It was disconcerting to be stuck in the middle of two volatile personalities.

He leaned toward Stash and whispered. "Let's leave these two alone to hash out the details."

Stash sucked in his lips and bobbed his head several times. It appeared he was having a hard time holding onto his composure. Anthony was caught in the same predicament. He desperately tried to keep a straight face as Meggie and Christian continued with their discussion. Although it sounded more like they were in the middle of a hostile negotiation than a friendly chat, he guessed they were, in a manner of speaking.

Quietly, he hurriedly and gracefully excused himself. He pulled Stash along until they were once more back inside the house, where he finally lost control. They were still laughing when they slammed the bedroom door behind them.

CHAPTER FOURTEEN

"Oh, my God, that was intense." Stash breathed hard as he leaned against the door and closed his eyes. "And so sexy. I never thought Christian would be Meggie's match, but he certainly proved me wrong."

His eyes snapped open, and his breath caught in his throat when Anthony pressed into him with the full length of his body. He met Anthony's intense gaze, and it was impossible to look away.

"*You're* sexy," Anthony said in a low growl.

Anthony lowered his head, and Stash closed his eyes, breathing rapidly in anticipation. He was hungry for the kiss he knew was coming. When Anthony's mouth touched his, he let out a moan and opened his mouth. There was no tenderness or wariness to it.

Stash had never thought a kiss could bring him so much happiness. All thoughts flew from his mind when Anthony cupped his jaw. He leaned in, pressing against Anthony's warmth as he deepened the kiss, sliding his tongue inside. He groaned again and took in everything that Anthony gave. The hardness of his body, his soft lips, the scent of his cologne that smelled freshly erotic and masculine. Anthony made his head spin, and with him pressed so close, it only made Stash want him more.

Anthony threaded his fingers into Stash's hair, turning his head to the side, exposing his neck. Then Anthony broke the kiss and made his way down the side of his neck, kissing and nipping the sensitive skin there. Each soft touch sent ripples of desire down Stash's cock. If Anthony continued to wreak havoc on his senses, he was going to lose it in his pants.

"I love whatever scent you're wearing. All fresh, delicious, and sweet," Anthony said against Stash's neck. "God, I can't get enough of touching you. You have no idea how your skin feels on my hand. It's like warm silk."

The words made Stash shudder. His knees weakened, and he had to grasp onto Anthony's arms to regain his balance.

"It's just soap," he managed to gasp out.

Where their bodies touched, the heat between them brought him to the brink of pain. Stash could swear he was going to burn up. Yet he wanted to get closer, to fuse himself with Anthony. In desperation, he dragged his fingers through Anthony's soft hair, feeling the fine texture, pulling at them until Anthony groaned deep in his throat and pulled away. Stash grudgingly let him go. When Anthony discretely adjusted himself, Stash felt a deep satisfaction. He had caused that.

Stash locked his gaze with Anthony's and began to take off his belt and toed off his shoes. Within seconds, he had stepped out of his pants and let them drop to the floor. He was unbuttoning his shirt when Anthony started undressing, not once looking away from Stash.

Neither of them stopped to examine the other's nakedness as they reached out for each other. Their bodies slammed together, and their lips met in a hard kiss that took a moment of adjustment. Teeth and tongues got in the way until they finally figured it out.

Stash lost himself to the overwhelming feelings flooding his body. One kiss was followed by another. Teeth nipped at lips. Heat flared between them as they ground their bodies together. He felt as if he were drowning in an explosion of sensations and wondered whether he would survive the encounter.

A momentary thought crossed Stash's mind but was quickly swept away when he was lifted off his feet. He automatically wound his arms around Anthony's shoulders and wrapped his legs around Anthony's waist to anchor himself as he was carried across the room and gently lowered onto the bed. When Anthony straddled his waist, he reached up to touch him, appreciating the smooth, hard muscle of his chest, his slim waist, and his strong, thick thighs.

Anthony kissed Stash, then slowly worked his way down to his navel. He glanced up briefly before bending down and swallowing his cock. Stash gasped, arching his body to get closer to the mouth that was causing havoc on his sanity. His desperate fingers reached and grasped the headboard, gripping the wood and holding on. Anthony's tongue played with Stash's slit, sending sharp thrills of pleasure through his shaft. His amazing mouth was doing crazy things to his cock. Just when he thought he couldn't stand anymore, Anthony pushed slick, thick fingers deep past his ring of guardian muscles.

"Ah, please. Please!" Stash begged as Anthony's fingers started to move in and out. He thought he could breathe through the riot of sensations until Anthony curled his finger and massaged the little bundle of nerves inside him. He screamed and came hard, emptying himself into Anthony's mouth.

Lights sparkled behind his eyelids, and he thought he would lose consciousness. Only Anthony didn't allow him respite. He kept sucking on Stash's cock. The steady suction and constriction of his throat had Stash whimpering and trembling uncontrollably with the pleasure-pain of his orgasm.

As the tremors subsided, Stash became aware of Anthony moving. He opened his eyes in time to see Anthony retrieve essential items from his pants. Anthony crawled back on top of him and placed lube and condoms beside them on the bed. Anthony settled between Stash's legs, gently arranging him so his legs encircled Anthony's hips.

Stash reached up and wrapped his arms around Anthony's neck, pulling him into a wet, open-mouthed kiss. He tasted himself on Anthony's tongue. Had he not just come so spectacularly, he would have shot his load right then and there.

"I want to know how you feel around me," Anthony murmured.

Stash nodded, inhaling sharply when Anthony's fingers slid inside him once more. He couldn't wait to feel the burn and gratification of penetration — needing to feel Anthony impaling him. Anthony reached for a condom, but Stash beat him to it.

"Let me," Stash said. He used his teeth to open the wrapper and quickly slid the condom down Anthony's hard shaft.

Anthony groaned while Stash took his time, spreading a messy amount of lube over his length.

"Stop teasing me," Antony said in a harsh voice. "Show me how you want me. Guide me inside you."

It was clear to Stash what Anthony was thinking. He reached down and grasped Anthony's cock, sliding his hand up and down to spread the lubricant evenly over his thick, engorged shaft. He licked his lips in anticipation, since his hand could not fully encircle the shaft he held. For a moment, he studied its size and wondered at the possibilities.

"What's wrong?" Anthony asked with a look of concern.

"Nothing." Stash flashed him a smile and quickly positioned the bulbous head at his entrance. With his heart rate skyrocketing, he pulled on Anthony until he slowly pushed forward.

At first Stash felt his body's resistance, but he wanted this more than anything, so he took a deep breath. When Anthony began to penetrate him, he willed himself to relax some more, unable to hold back his pained gasp at the slow stretch and burn. Stash placed his hand against Anthony's hip and pushed against him to give himself a moment to adjust. Anthony shifted, lifting Stash's thighs and ass higher.

"Am I hurting you?" Anthony breathed, sweat beads decorating his temple. The worry was evident in his eyes. He was holding his control by a thread.

Stash nodded and closed his eyes. "A bit. It's been a while."

In reality, it felt like Anthony was splitting him in two, but he didn't want to scare Anthony away. He really wanted this to work and let out a strangled sigh of relief when the cockhead eased through and Anthony was inside him. Not fully, but at least halfway.

"Hold on, let me get some more lube." Anthony slathered Stash's entrance to aid his penetration. "You're so tight." He leaned down and kissed Stash as he successfully slid in. He slowly flexed his hips, going deeper with every move. "Tell me to stop if it's too much."

Stash shook his head. He had never felt so full, yet he knew there was more to come. "No. I want all of you in me. Don't you dare stop."

"Thank God." Anthony stared at where they joined and rotated his hips.

Stash's passage eased under the momentum of Anthony's deep motions, his passion growing with each thrust.

"Ahh . . . Ugh . . ." Stash groaned, caught in the sensual ride of pleasure. He simply couldn't get enough.

Perhaps Anthony took the sounds Stash was making as encouragement, for he powered into him, each strong thrust slapping against flesh. Anthony went up on his knees, dragging Stash by his hips and lifting his legs over his shoulders. He never once ceased his movements, pounding deep and hard into him. That was the moment Stash lost all sense of control over his body. He whimpered at the intensity of the pressure over his prostate and tried desperately to grasp onto Anthony's shoulders. His hands slid from the slick of sweat.

Stash opened his eyes, straining urgently to meet the hard pounding strokes with some of his own. He didn't have much time left. His vision blurred as he soared to heights he had never experienced. He gripped onto Anthony's hips, his fingers sinking into the flesh there, but there was no withholding his body's response. He erupted, and time stopped. When he came to, he realized Anthony was no longer moving, but incredibly, he was still deep inside of him, hard, pulsing, and ready to go.

"You have got to be kidding me," Stash gasped out.

Anthony leaned down, dropping a kiss on his lips. "You want me to stop?"

Stash thought about the question seriously . . . for about a second. "Nope."

"I thought not." Antony chuckled under his breath as he pulled out.

Stash wanted to shout his dismay, but the words flew out of his head when he was flipped onto his stomach. Before he could say anything, Anthony had him repositioned on his knees. He was still trying to get his face out of the mattress when Anthony plunged into him once more, making him cry out in surprise.

The new position meant Anthony's cock plunged even deeper, and Stash felt every inch of the glorious hardness. He had to bite down on the sheets to muffle his screams of pleasure. Anthony gripped his hips hard, and Stash knew he was going to develop bruises there. Stash contracted his muscles, ensuring Anthony would feel the pressure. He sneaked a peek over his shoulder, pleased to see the rapture on Anthony's face. Incredibly, it only made Anthony pummel into him harder and faster.

All Stash could do was close his eyes and enjoy the ride. He dug his fingers into the wood of the headboard and relaxed into the rhythm. After coming twice, he was beyond exhausted, but he didn't want to deny Anthony his pleasure. After a few more strokes, he finally felt Anthony stiffen, and his large cock pulsed inside him. The warmth spread, and to his amazement, Stash came for the third time. It wasn't as mind-boggling as the first or the second, but it was enough. That was the last thing he remembered before darkness took over.

Chapter Fifteen

Despite every attempt to get to New York as fast as they could, things didn't quite go as Anthony planned. When the plane reached the airspace over New York, he thought Stash would go ballistic for every hour they spent circling JFK. Stash looked so nervous that it took him and Meggie to reassure him that everything was going to be all right. For a moment, Anthony thought Stash would need a sedative. Discovering Stash was afraid of landings was a surprise, but now that he knew about it, he would know what to do in the future.

By the time they finally received permission to land, they were flying on fumes. They touched down at half-past midnight, so it was half-past two in the morning before they reached Anthony's home on the Upper East Side. They were all tired, so Anthony waved away the sleepy butler who'd opened the door for them and quietly led Stash to his bedroom on the second floor, where they promptly fell asleep. They didn't even bother to shower.

The next thing Anthony knew, the alarm on his phone went off, and he opened his eyes to the morning light. He stretched out his hand for Stash when he heard the man in question singing in the bathroom. After a few lines, he bit on the inside of his cheek to keep himself from laughing out loud. As voices went, Stash didn't have the best, but at least he wasn't off-key. He even sounded better than others. That was what counted most.

The exhaustion from the previous day lingered in his bones. He was tempted to stay in bed for the rest of the morning until a knock on the door made the decision for him.

"Hold on," Anthony said, getting to his feet. He looked down and belatedly realized he was naked. He grabbed his silk robe, hanging on the floor stand, and was still shrugging into it when Stash walked out of the bathroom.

"Hey, you." He walked over to Stash and dropped a kiss on his forehead.

"Good morning," Stash said with a bright smile.

He must have investigated in the bathroom, for he was wearing another of Anthony's robes.

Anthony smiled in return. "Did you sleep well?"

Stash nodded. "Yes. Surprisingly so. Despite the lack of hours."

"Good." Anthony cupped his hands around Stash's shoulders and dropped a kiss on his neck. "I'll go wash up. Can you see who's at the door?"

"Okay, you go ahead," Stash said.

Anthony didn't wait to see how Stash would deal with the early visitor. He stepped into the bathroom and almost did a double take. The steam was so thick he could hardly see where he was going. Shaking his head, he flipped a switch on the wall, and the whirring sound of the fan started. Soon the room cleared as the steam got sucked into the exhaust pipes.

He could hear Stash talking to someone outside and paused to listen. When he heard Christian's voice, he went ahead and took his shower. Once he was done, he went through to his walk-in closet and saw his bags, alongside another set. Stash was kneeling beside them, taking out his clothes and other things from one of his bags.

"Why are you the one doing that?"

"Someone called Banks, I think he introduced himself as your butler, came with Christian," Stash replied. "He and a couple of ladies brought in our bags."

There was something about the way Stash spoke as he pulled out his things that gave Anthony pause. Gone was the bright smile and sing-song inflection. Replacing it was a flat monotone. Stash's movements were too brusque, almost robotic.

"What happened? Did someone say or do something?" Anthony felt a sudden surge of anger rush through him. What could his butler have done to wipe out all the joy from the room? From Stash?

"Nothing, actually. No one needed to say anything." Stash looked up and smiled, but he couldn't hide the hurt reflected in his eyes. "Don't worry, I'm used to it. It's okay. They don't know who I am. I don't care." He shrugged and turned to deal with the rest of his things.

Anthony immediately knew that someone on his staff had done something, and Banks had done nothing to correct them. He stared at Stash's awkwardly held shoulders and raised chin. There was nothing he could say right then that wouldn't come out as crass or impolite. Plus, he didn't want Stash to witness that side of him. When Stash got busy with drying and styling his hair, Anthony snuck out of the dressing room and took out his phone. Fifteen minutes later, Stash came out dressed and prettied up, and Anthony led the way to the breakfast room. Neither of them said much as they ate their food.

Halfway through their second cup of coffee, Meggie entered the room, followed by a stern-faced Christian. There was no mistaking Meggie's anger from how her nostrils alternated between an all-out flare and pinched, but she didn't say a word.

Anthony didn't blame her. He was just as angry, if not angrier, than Meggie. He wondered how she would deal with the situation had it happened in Stash's home.

Anthony didn't miss the wide-eyed looks the household staff exchanged with each other when they looked at Stash. Their confusion became more evident after Anthony gave them implicit instructions to make room for Stash's things in his walk-in closet.

After breakfast, Stash announced he would be up in their room the rest of the morning, claiming he had an online conference with one of his designers. Meggie prepared to follow him.

Stash shook his head. "No, you stay down here. Help Anthony with whatever needs to be done before the meeting on Thursday. Also, it's just a conference call. It's not as if I haven't done it before. I'll be okay. Just don't let anyone disturb me." He immediately turned his back on them and left the room.

Not giving Meggie a chance to respond bothered Anthony a lot. When Meggie turned her glare on Anthony, he could only shrug it off. There were things he could do to salvage things between him and Stash, and anger was not among them. Although he did fantasize about doing something more physical, as usual, his logical side intervened. Plus, if he gave in to anger, he knew it would disappoint Stash, and that was the last thing he wanted.

In a matter of hours, the actions of a few had managed to ruin his mood. That they were done by an irrelevant few was what truly got under his self-control. His relationship with Stash was in its early stages, but he had hoped to avoid complications like what had happened. Embarrassment sliced through his already bruised ego, and he never wanted to see that kind of hurt reflected on Stash's face ever again.

Things hadn't improved by lunchtime, and Anthony could see Stash getting tenser by the minute. When he caught one of the servers twisting her lips in obvious distaste behind Stash's back, Anthony knew he would be reducing his staff.

There was nothing he could do about what he knew was just the first taste of society's reaction once his relationship with Stash became public. However, there was something he could do about who worked for him. This was his home, after all.

After the meal ended, Stash quickly excused himself. There was nothing he could say that would ease Stash's tension.

He turned to Meggie. "Why don't you go upstairs and stay with Stash while I finish down here." The least he could do was make sure Stash had his friend with him. While he . . . Well, he was going to have to deal with something distasteful.

Meggie threw her table napkin on the table and stormed out of the room with quick, angry steps. Anthony waited until Stash and Meggie's footsteps faded. Then he turned to Christian.

"Bring Banks to the office in twenty minutes, please." Anthony threw his own napkin down on the table and stood. His chair scraped and crashed on the floor behind him, but he was beyond the point of caring.

Anthony entered his office and made a quick call to Max's office. By the time he put down the phone, his mood had improved. Whistling under his breath, he took out a piece of stationery from a drawer on his desk and began making a list of instructions. He was still writing when three successive knocks sounded on the door.

"Enter."

Anthony glanced up when Christian came in with the butler following right behind him.

"Good afternoon, sir." Banks' tone was formal, and he bowed his head in greeting.

Anthony didn't respond. He glared at Banks for a second before pulling out a file Christian had handed him that morning. He glanced at the contents, knowing he'd already read it, but he kept reading just so he could ignore Banks.

Today was going to be the beginning of a new life. It was

time to make changes in his personal lifestyle, as well as the people he surrounded himself with. Whoever they were would depend on how they accepted, reacted, and interacted with Stash as a constant in his life.

While he had been writing out his list earlier, one question kept repeating over and over in his mind. How ready was he to identify and filter out who his real friends and family were? Admittedly, he didn't know the exact answer to his own question, but there was one thing he was certain of — he was going to have to deal with a lot of complications. A beeping coming from Christian's receiver broke through the silence. Anthony watched as Christian checked on whatever message was relayed to him.

"Sir, Mr. Kauffman and his colleague, Mr. Sanders, of Kauffman and Kauffman have arrived," Christian said.

"Tell them to come in here," Anthony said, closing the file with a snap.

"Shall I leave, sir?" Banks asked.

"No. Stay where you are." Anthony stood when the two lawyers came in, and he grabbed his list from his desk.

"Thank you for coming so soon, Sam. How's your father?" Anthony approached and shook the hand of Max Kauffman's son.

"He told me to come over as soon as I could," Sam Kauffman said, grinning at Anthony. "You could have just called me, you know."

"Well, I wanted this to be as official as legally allowed. Did you bring the documents?"

"Yes. I can take it from here."

"Thank you again, Sam. Here's the list you requested." Anthony held out the document, and Sanders took it from him and started reading. "I'll leave you to deal with this, gentlemen," Anthony said and left the room without once glancing at Banks. Christian made as if to follow him out, but Anthony stopped him.

"Stay and assist Mr. Kauffman and Mr. Sanders, will you? Give me a report after they've dealt with the situation."

"Of course, sir," Christian said with a curt nod. The grim set of his jaw indicated his willingness to take on the task.

Christian's expression reflected Anthony's mood. He found he had little patience when it came to situations that hurt Stash. It was something new he'd learned about himself shortly after meeting Stash. Suddenly encouraged about how he'd dealt with the small complication, he decided to take Stash out and about. He didn't even care if all Stash did was shop for makeup at Saks.

Anthony walked into the bedroom only to stop and stare at Stash, who had put on a long, light brown wig with two chunky strips of hair on either side of his face dyed a lighter, yellow blond. The flawlessly applied nude makeup emphasized Stash's androgynous looks, and Anthony was once more struck speechless. After about a minute of Stash waiting for him to speak, he finally cleared his throat and found his voice.

"You look stunning," Anthony said.

His words may have been what Stash needed to hear for his face broke out into a broad smile, and a blush reddened his cheeks.

"It took you long enough, but thank you," Stash said, meeting Anthony's gaze.

"Meggie, why don't you go downstairs and join Christian? I need you to help him deal with something," Anthony said, tearing his gaze away from Stash.

"What is it?" Meggie said but didn't move from where she sat on a plush chair by the window.

Anthony took out the file and a copy of the list he'd written. "Here, why don't you deal with the changes I've planned, while I take Stash out shopping."

"And that's my cue." Stash jumped up from the stool he was sitting on and picked up an expensive crocodile skin handbag. "I'll wait for you downstairs," he said and flounced away.

Anthony cringed when the door nearly closed on the ends of the waist-long wig.

"You're not going out alone. I'm assigning you two guards," Meggie yelled after Stash. "And Ian. You're taking Ian with you." She shook her head and continued to glare at the closed door a moment longer before turning back to Anthony.

Without a word, she took the file and list from him. After a cursory glance over the contents, she looked up. "You're trusting me to deal with this mess?"

"Yes. I want Stash happy, and you're the one who knows him best regarding these things. Christian's downstairs with the lawyers and doesn't know you're getting involved. He'll understand once you give him the instructions."

Meggie pursed her lips as her eyes went back to the file in her hand. "How long do I have?"

"Well, let's see. It's almost two, and it'll take you about two to three hours to get the job done. Right?"

"No." Meggie shook her head. "How about you take Stash shopping and then dinner somewhere right after. I should be done by eight or nine tonight, so go and enjoy yourselves."

"Thank you, Meggie," Anthony said. "I don't like complications, and I trust you don't like them either."

"You read me correctly," Meggie said. "Can I be honest?"

"Of course. Say what you need."

"Why are you firing your staff?"

Anthony had expected the question. "I'm not. I'm merely changing agencies. Anything else?"

Meggie pursed her lips and nodded, though Anthony could see she knew he was not telling her the whole truth.

"Okay, I'll give you that." She paused and took a deep breath. "I've known Stash since we were both babies. I was with him when he first thought he was in love and stood by his side through all the teenage angst you can ever imagine. And then you came into the picture. I've never seen him act like this with anyone. Ever. You don't look like you know what you're doing, and yet you seem to be enjoying yourself. In fact, I can see that you care for him a lot. Like, a lot, a lot."

Meggie had stopped talking, but Anthony could tell she still had plenty to say.

"I know you want to get everything off your chest, so please, continue. I'm listening," Anthony said.

Meggie's brows lifted briefly, but then she placed her hands on her hips and faced him square on. "All right. I'm going to be blunt with you. I've seen Stash hurt countless times, but he's the type who'd never say anything bad about anyone. He keeps everything hidden. Keeps it close. Don't be fooled by that charming smile or the happy façade, his feelings run deep. Now, see, I consider Stash as my brother, and in my heart, he is. He and Ian both. Note the order of preference. The last time somebody made Stash cry, the guy ended up in the hospital. It could've been worse, but then Ian stopped me. Not that I needed to tell you that, but yeah, I can get very protective. How do you think I'll act should this all end badly?"

Anthony continued to stare at Meggie as he thought over how to respond. No one had ever spoken to him the way she just had. Not even his parents or relatives. He was entitled that way. However, what Meggie said was heartfelt, and he understood where she was coming from and respected her for it.

"If you were to attempt to harm me, rest assured, you'd never succeed." He smirked. "One, you'd have to get through Christian, and the least I would expect is that you're his match and would have a hard time beating him. Second—and I'll only say this to you once—I will never willingly or consciously do or say anything that will hurt Stash. That is my promise to you. Does my answer satisfy you?"

Meggie's brows lifted briefly, then she nodded. "It'll do. For now. As for Christian, I beg to differ. I'm better than he is. Faster, too."

Anthony couldn't help chuckling. "I almost believe you." Anthony held out his hand, and when Meggie took it, he gripped it for a second before shaking it. "We're in agreement then. Now, let me go find Stash before any more complications come up. I'll take care of his security, don't be troubled about it."

"Excuse me, but I'll never stop worrying over Stash." Meggie sighed and clutched the files closer to her chest. "You're a complication I didn't need, Mr. Eisemann. Now go and take Stash shopping. He's been dying to buy some blinged-out watches, among other things."

Anthony laughed quietly to himself as he went to find out where Stash had gone to. He didn't have to search far, for he found him waiting at the bottom of the stairs. Standing beside him were Christian and Ian, as well as two other guards. Anthony should have known that Christian would not want Meggie to one-up him in the security game.

Two hours later, Anthony found himself silently observing Stash as he looked around the private viewing room. Bertrand had not failed him, and as promised, had arranged for the latest collection of his different luxury lines to be on display. At that moment, Stash was checking out a diamond-encrusted watch. The watch itself was so thin it astounded Anthony how the craftsman had managed to buff as well as mount the stones on it, there was so little metal. The one Stash had picked out was not particularly to his taste, but when Stash put it on, Anthony couldn't help thinking it looked exquisite and gave his nod of approval. Stash took out his wallet, but Anthony was quicker.

"Oh no, this is all on me, sweets," Anthony said and smiled when Stash didn't respond.

Stash put away his wallet, the blush on his cheeks betraying his pleasure. Anthony ignored the warmth he felt spreading in his chest, but there was nothing he could do to wipe the broad smile off his face. Much to his surprise, Anthony found shopping with Stash to be enjoyable. Memories of their turn around the village in Saint Pierre sent tingles through his body.

Two hours later, Stash was done with his shopping. Anthony hadn't even bothered to find out the amount when he handed over his platinum credit card for each purchase. A surge of satisfaction thrummed through his veins as he watched Stash take possession of every delicately wrapped item.

Anthony wondered if he should tell Stash that he was the first person he'd personally bought and gifted an item to. Before Stash, all gifts had been bought by his personal assistants, or by his mother when she'd been alive.

After arranging for their packages to be delivered within the hour to his home, Anthony asked Stash what else he wanted to do. To his amusement, Stash pulled him into a candy store, of all places. Anthony thought his face was going to split from smiling. Being with Stash kept him entertained, from the way he interacted with the salesclerks to how he conversed with children. It turned out Stash was a child magnet. Anthony didn't know what it was, but one mother mentioned her child thought Stash as pretty. Anthony couldn't agree more.

Christian helped break the monotony of malling by calling in several times to give updates on what was going down at his house. It appeared that Meggie had been in her element interviewing the applicants. Somehow, that particular detail helped Anthony enjoy the afternoon more. He put away his phone and looked at the tempting view ahead of him. Stash was truly quite alluring, and he couldn't wait to spend the night in his arms again. What they'd shared two nights before had been a quick taste of what he wanted to savor for the rest of his life.

Anthony was glad when the hostess of the restaurant he'd chosen didn't bat an eye when she saw Stash and led them to a private dining area. Anthony noticed a few heads turn as they were walking through the maze of tables, but other than that, they were completely ignored. As soon as they finished their meal and had their dessert, Stash begged exhaustion and requested they go home. After a quick consultation with Christian, he got the go signal that it was safe to go back. They arrived home at half-past ten and were greeted by Christian, who introduced them to the new butler and staff.

Stash didn't appear surprised at all to see the new faces. Anthony suspected Meggie had managed to tell Stash what was going on. That Stash didn't say anything to Anthony was revealing of his personality.

An errant thought occurred to him that he might have opened the door for Meggie to plant a spy in his home. What surprised him more was his reaction. He didn't mind. Maybe he was naïve not to feel alarmed, but Meggie's bullish manner as she hovered over Stash, and now him, proved he was in safe company.

Chapter Sixteen

Stash kept his eyes closed as he surrendered to Anthony's kiss and sighed when Anthony's tongue probed his mouth. Anthony's slow and sensual movements made his heart thump hard inside his chest. The hand on his neck was comforting rather than constricting. He couldn't help comparing the way he felt when Anthony made love to him. Where the others had used his body for their sexual release, with no consideration for him, Anthony always made him feel special.

"Why are you so different?" he whispered when their lips parted.

"What do you mean?"

Whatever explanation he might have come up with was swept away as Anthony's other hand moved down his back, wrapped around his waist, and held him tight. He couldn't help the moan that escaped when Anthony's mouth closed over his once again. He really liked the feel of Anthony's hard body pressed against his. Already aroused, his cock hardened even more when Anthony pushed him deeper onto the bed.

Urged by the pleasurable sensations running throughout his body, Stash reached out to remove the belt from around Anthony's waist. As if reading his mind, Anthony reached for his belt as well, and they worked to undress each other as quickly as possible. He looked up and met Anthony's gaze, feeling his body temperature rise at the naked need he saw reflected in Anthony's eyes.

Stash drank in the view before him. Anthony was a known workaholic, yet lean and muscled without an ounce of fat on him. He found that particularly incredible and felt a little jealous. His own body could never achieve what was obviously inborn genetics for Anthony. He ran his fingers over Anthony's chest, which was covered with a light down of brown hair, lighter than on his head. Another little detail Stash could never achieve. He traced the path of fur as it tapered down to his crotch, marveling at every inch he touched.

Anthony remained still while Stash explored. When he looked up, he caught Anthony checking out his body as well. He smiled at the desire he saw in Anthony's eyes.

"What are you thinking about?" Anthony said.

Stash smiled and gently pulled on the chest hair. Anthony hissed, and Stash quickly leaned over to kiss the sting away.

"I may be a little jealous of your muscles and chest hair," he said. He ran his hands up and down, loving the soft tickle on his palms.

"I guess we both are a little jealous of each other," Anthony said as he pressed Stash onto his back. "I love your skin, and you love my body hair."

Stash let out a husky laugh as he twisted his body to switch positions. "Don't ever shave or wax your chest hair. I can live vicariously through you."

Anthony barked out a laugh when Stash began to crawl on top of him. Stash silenced him by leaning down and kissing him. The feel of Anthony's hard body beneath him, and his body hair prickling his skin, made his cock leak with precum. He pressed his body down for more contact, and Anthony closed his arms around him, sighing into his mouth before spreading his legs open.

Anthony's hand slid up to the middle of his back, pulling him down until not even air separated them. Stash felt Anthony's cock, thick and long and hard, pressed against his groin, and he rotated his hips slowly. He smiled when Anthony moaned before going rigid from the friction.

Stash let out a moan of his own and reached down until his fingers brushed over the slick head of Anthony's cock. He circled it with his hand, gripping it firmly before pumping it up and down. Anthony moaned deep in his throat before he deepened their kiss.

Stash twisted away from the kiss, gulping air into his starving lungs. Anthony's breathing was ragged as he, too, took in air.

"Let me . . ." Stash had found his voice but wasn't sure what he was requesting. He ran his fingers down Anthony's side, making the man beneath him squirm from his touch.

"Come to me," Anthony growled.

Hearing his words, Stash looked up and saw the intense look on Anthony's face. He didn't see any hesitation in the passion-lit eyes, only burning need and desire.

Anthony's lids lowered a moment before he flipped Stash onto his back and claimed his mouth. This time, the kiss was harsher, and yet, to his surprise, it was a gentle kind of harshness, one he'd never thought to feel.

Stash's breath locked in his throat when Anthony's tongue invaded his mouth once more. He felt a knee press between his legs, so he widened them further, allowing Anthony's body to press against his groin. He grabbed Anthony's ass and pulled, urging him to get even closer. He needed to feel Anthony's hard cock rubbing against his own.

Stash shivered when Anthony rolled his hips and kissed his way down Stash's neck, nipping at the soft skin where his neck joined his shoulder. Anthony kept going until he reached Stash's ear, making him squirm at the tickling sensation on his earlobe. Every touch of Anthony's mouth and teeth sent currents of electricity from his spine down to his cock, causing it to jump in anticipation. His cock felt so full it was almost painful, but he didn't care. He wanted it all, to feel more of everything this man was offering.

Stash arched in surprise when Antony nipped at a nipple. When had he stopped teasing his earlobe? Anthony's wet, hot tongue laved on him a bit longer before it traveled across his chest and took command of his other nipple.

"Stash," Anthony murmured against his skin.

Stash closed his eyes when Anthony licked his way down to his cock. A hand slipped beneath his buttocks, and he pushed up in response. He knew what was coming and began to tremble. Anticipation had him pushing more against Anthony until he felt the wet heat as his cock was swallowed down a deep, tight throat. He lost himself to the sensation only to moan in disappointment when Anthony pulled back. The protest lodged in his throat when Anthony's velvety soft tongue brushed against the vein on the underside of his cock.

Stash couldn't help all the sounds that escaped him at every suck on his cockhead, or the tongue flicking on his foreskin before pushing up and sliding into his slit. Stash hissed at the stinging pleasure. Then Anthony rose to his knees and straddled him, trapping his legs. Stash gasped when Anthony bent to nibble on the skin where his leg joined his hips.

He lost track of time, his voice echoing in the room as Anthony's mouth drove him insane. Instinct took over, and he began to thrust into Anthony's mouth. Little moans escaped again when he felt the back of Anthony's throat close around his crown. Then he worried that he might be choking Anthony, so he forced himself to stop thrusting.

Stash opened his eyes when Anthony relinquished his cock and rose to his knees. Anthony placed his hands under his knees and pushed them up toward his chest. Before Stash could say anything, Anthony had a slick finger probing his hole. A groan that came from deep inside his chest escaped when the tip of that finger pushed inside. How Anthony had managed to grab hold of lubricant was beyond him, but he was glad someone had remembered.

"Don't move," Anthony said.

Stash breathed through his nose when Anthony dug deeper into his hole and hit the sensitive spot that drove him crazy. Raw passion coursed through his body, and he began to tremble. He reached out to grasp the back of Anthony's head, but his hands were gently pushed away.

Stash whimpered in dismay when Anthony removed his finger but stopped when he reached down, grabbed himself, and rubbed the tip of his cock against Stash's opening. Driven on instinct, Stash widened his legs as Anthony began to slowly enter him. The sting of his entrance made him hiss, and Anthony withdrew slightly, dribbling more lube where they remained connected. Anthony pressed deeper in small increment until he bottomed out. All thoughts fled Stash's mind at the feeling of fullness.

When Anthony began to move, it was all Stash could do to will his body to adjust to his girth. Anthony's size caused the first few thrusts to sting a bit, but Stash was enjoying every sensation running through his body. His senses whirled at what was being done to his body, centering on the nerve endings excited by the friction as Anthony drove in and out, filling him, completing him.

Stash leaned up to meet Anthony's kiss, loving every second of their connection. The change in position made him gasp, and he felt himself losing control. Anthony's cock felt bigger, stretching him to the point where he thought he would break in half. The realization that he was going to feel full after this encounter in the following days only made him smile with satisfaction. If there was one thing to boast about, it was that he had a man who really knew how to use his cock.

Anthony lifted Stash's hips higher and began to drive in deeper, again and again, creating a tingling heat that traveled down his spine. Anthony began to move faster, driving Stash's ecstasy higher. He winced, but a wide grin bloomed over his lips. He could feel his release approaching.

Time stood still until suddenly, like a band snapping mid-stretch, Stash felt his world explode. Above him, Anthony jerked and groaned as he, too, fell over the edge.

The tremors lasted a few minutes, and Anthony slumped on top of him as they tried to catch their breath. He didn't mind in the least. In fact, he liked Anthony's weight pressing against him. That was, until he began to itch where he'd come over his stomach. Stash pushed against Anthony's chest, but his arms were weak, and he flopped down on the bed. He began to laugh.

"What's so funny?"

"I can't move." Stash chuckled over his predicament. "You fucked me into the mattress. I need to pee."

"Right now?"

Stash nodded. "Unfortunately, yes."

"Okay." Anthony groaned, slowly pulled out of Stash, then fell to the bed on his back.

"You okay?" Stash said, pushing himself up on his elbows.

Anthony's eyes remained closed, but he gesticulated with his hand. "You can go first. I'll just stay here a while longer."

Stash grinned and slung his legs over the side of the bed. His legs tried to buckle underneath him, and he flung out his arms to regain his balance. It took him a minute or two, but he finally was able to walk to the bathroom without falling once.

When he was done, he flushed the toilet and thought it a good idea to take a shower. He was still toweling his hair as he stepped out of the bathroom and stopped at the sound of Anthony snoring.

A surge of satisfaction hit him then, pride that he'd managed to tire out his lover. On silent feet, he crossed the short distance to the bed only to stop when Anthony began to jerk and fling out his arms.

"Where is it?" Anthony cried.

Surprised by the question, Stash looked around the room. Nothing seemed out of place, so he turned back to Anthony again. "Where's what, Ace?"

"Where is it?" Anthony's voice sounded pained. He began to groan, and his arm kept reaching out for something on the bed.

"Ace? What's wrong?" Stash stopped toweling his hair. His frown deepened. Something was wrong.

"I can't find it. Where is it?"

Anthony's hand reached out and pounded on the sheets, yelling, "No!"

"What are you looking for, Ace?" Stash asked, beginning to panic. He approached the bed until he was standing over Anthony only to muffle a gasp when he saw that Anthony's eyes were closed.

It was only then that Christian's warning about watching out for nightmares came back. Was this what he was talking about?

"What are you looking for, Ace?" Stash repeated, this time in a softer voice. He sat beside Anthony and squeezed his shoulder.

Anthony stilled, and his breathing eased. Stash waited and watched. He couldn't help wanting to shake Anthony awake, but he knew he shouldn't.

A few minutes later, Anthony's eyes fluttered open, and he gazed up at Stash in confusion. "Hey, are you done in the bathroom?"

For a moment, Stash could only stare, but then he pasted on a smile and rubbed his hand up and down Anthony's arm. "Yes, I just got out. I took a shower, too."

"Okay then, my turn," Anthony said. "Give me a hand."

Stash stood and offered a helping hand. "You fell asleep."

Anthony grinned and dropped a kiss on Stash's lips. "You

wore me out. Anyway, it was just a nap, and once I get out of the shower, I should have my second wind."

Stash stood watching the bathroom door long after it had closed behind Anthony. Whatever pleasure and satisfaction he'd felt earlier had given way to worry. His brows furrowed as he went to get his phone. After one ring, his call was answered.

"Yes, Mr. Stash?"

"He was having a nightmare, but he wasn't sleeping. It was just . . . like a short nap. So, I'm not sure if it was actually a nightmare."

"Did he say anything?"

Stash nodded even though he knew Christian couldn't see him. "Yes, he kept asking, *where is it*, and that he couldn't find it. What is it he's looking for, Christian?"

"I'm sorry, Mr. Stash, I'm not entirely sure what it is he is looking for. I was never given the details of what his nightmares consisted of, only to watch out for them and report them to his psychiatrist."

"What's his psychiatrist's name?"

"Dr. Yvonne Smalling. She's based in Sacramento."

"Why Sacramento? Why not New York since that's his base?"

"I don't have the answer to that either."

"All right, thank you, Christian."

Stash ended the call and sat pondering what he'd just learned. He pursed his lips and thought over what to do. The pros and cons weighed heavily on his mind. The sound of the toilet flushing pulled him out of his thoughts, and he made his decision. He stared at the bathroom door as he made another call.

"Hello?"

"Ian? I need to know everything about an Yvonne Smalling. She's a psychiatrist based in Sacramento."

"What in particular?"

"She's Anthony's psychiatrist."

"Everything it is. Okay, Stash. I guess, if you're calling me, I shouldn't tell Meggie about this?"

"No, she is to know nothing. If she finds out what you're doing and asks for information, tell her I gave you the assignment and that you cannot tell her what you found."

"She's going to argue that point."

"Tell her she doesn't have the proper clearance."

"Oh, that's mean. Okay, anything else?"

"I don't want Anthony's people to find out." Stash began to pick at his skin. He stared as the area started to turn red.

"Noted, Stash."

"Good night, Ian. And thank you."

"No problem, Stash. Good night to you, too."

Stash threw his phone on the bed and covered his face with his hands. "What the hell am I doing?"

"You could just ask me, you know," Anthony said from behind him.

Stash jumped but kept his expression calm as he turned around. "You overheard? I hope you don't mind."

"Nope I don't mind. I take it, from your conversation with Christian, that I had a nightmare."

"Yes." Stash went up to Anthony and wrapped his arms around his waist. "What triggers them? Do you know?"

"Usually when I'm under a lot of stress."

"Stress from work or stress from learning that Lawrence is out on bail?"

"I think both."

"Should I cancel my request to investigate Dr. Smalling?"

"No, I think it'll be useful. I haven't been to see her in over a year."

"Shouldn't you instruct Christian not to report to her about your nightmares?"

"No, it's all part of a criminal investigation. That way, if Lawrence does something, we get to cover all angles."

"Okay," Stash said, but he was worried. His expression must have shown it, for Anthony kissed his cheek. Something wasn't adding up, but he hesitated to ask for the full story.

"Don't be troubled about all of this, okay?" Anthony ran his hands up and down Stash's back, comforting him. Stash closed his eyes and rested his forehead on Anthony's chest.

"I'm really beginning to like you a lot, Ace. I can't help being worried. What if Lawrence does something awful, and I lose you?"

"Hey, don't talk like that. I'm not going anywhere. Plus, I've got you by my side, and that means an increase in security. I'll be fine," Anthony said, bending low to peer into Stash's face.

Stash nodded and licked his lips. "I want chocolate mousse right now."

Anthony chuckled. "Is that your answer to everything? Chocolate?"

Stash nodded. He didn't feel guilty one bit. "Chocolate makes me feel better."

"Okay, let's go down and get some." Anthony chuckled under his breath. He flung an arm over Stash's shoulders and led them out the door.

As they descended the stairs, Stash couldn't help but look around to see where their combined guards stood. He made sure to keep count, and when he reached the appropriate number, he pressed himself closer to Anthony. Somehow, seeing the security detail manning their posts made him feel a little safer. He couldn't help but worry that danger lurked in every shadow, and he didn't like it one bit.

Chapter Seventeen

The following days leading up to the meeting kept Anthony busy with research and background checks on individual directors and executives. He also planned for the worse case scenarios. Fortunately, he hadn't suffered any more nightmares, and Stash hadn't mentioned him talking in his sleep.

Anthony ran his hand through his hair and breathed out a shaky breath as he went over the different files Meggie and Christian had prepared. Everything was coming to a head, but after spending three days preparing for what he wanted to discuss with the board of directors, he felt more confident. The overall picture was clear in his mind. He now knew which directors to trust and which to watch out for.

Meggie proved to be a skilled investigator and cunning planner. After working side by side with the woman, Anthony no longer had any doubts as to why Stash relied heavily on her.

On the day of the meeting, Anthony stepped out of the elevator, followed by Christian, Meggie, four other guards that Meggie had insisted accompany them, as well as two junior assistants. The additional security baffled Anthony, but Christian seemed to agree with the increased numbers, so Anthony shrugged it off. He took another step only to hesitate mid-step when he saw another four guards lining the hallway leading to the boardroom.

"Christian? We talked about additional security, but don't you think this is overkill?" Anthony asked, resuming his trek to the boardroom.

"Stash insisted," Christian said.

Anthony blinked at the unexpected response. "Meggie, what is this all about?"

"Your brother's whereabouts are still unknown. We discussed it at length and decided on what was best to protect you and Stash," Meggie said. She checked the watch on her wrist. "We are also running behind our scheduled entrance. Everyone important is in there except the senior Mr. Burcell. Schoffield arrived ten minutes ago."

Anthony pursed his lips. "Does anyone know what's going on with Adrien?"

"Not yet," Meggie said. "However, I'm not worried. If it's anything serious, I would have heard about it by now."

"How's his security?"

"In place," Meggie said. She made a gesture with her hand, and Christian hurried forward to open the doors. Meggie stepped up to Anthony's right, taking Christian's place.

"You jump to her command now?" Anthony whispered to Christian as he walked past him and entered the boardroom.

Anthony wasn't fazed when he was greeted with a few grim faces. He'd half expected to get greeted like that and was more than prepared. He pasted on a smile and joined the meeting.

Emergency meetings were typically intense because they were almost always borne from situations beyond their control—or lack thereof. Thankfully, the company was solid, so there were no jittery emotions one would normally expect. However, the agenda for the day was no secret, and discovering an unknown entity trying to make trouble was something no one welcomed. He shook hands with everyone on his way to his chair at the head of the enormous conference table.

"Who are all of these people, Anthony? Do we really need for them to be here?"

The question was startling in its arrogance and rudeness, but he expected nothing less from a man like Frank Schoffield.

"Now, now, don't be so rude, Frank," a voice chimed in from behind Schoffield. "I'm sure Anthony wouldn't be bringing them in if he didn't need them."

Schoffield turned around, and Anthony spotted Joel Byrd sitting at the table.

"What are you doing here, Byrd? You're not even a director."

"Oh, but I got a personal invitation from Mr. Eisemann himself. Didn't I, Anthony?" Byrd leaned slightly to his left to peer past Schoffield.

Byrd was only thirty-one but had already made a name for himself as an executive of a defunct internet media company, which he had formed with help from a few friends. Until three years before, he had also owned a successful dating site he'd set up on his own. That company had been bought out by one of Anthony's subsidiary companies, but Byrd had stayed on as creative director. He was invaluable to the success of the dating site that garnered Anthony billions of dollars annually.

"Yes, I did. Thank you for coming on such short notice, Byrd." Anthony extended his hand in greeting.

Joel Byrd stood up and shook Anthony's hand. "Thank you for the invitation. I can't wait to hear how you're going to deal with this debacle."

"What debacle?" Schoffield asked.

Anthony had already turned his back on them and returned to his seat. "Meggie and Christian are my personal assistants, Schoffield. You can introduce yourself to them after the meeting." He faced the rest of the seated directors and folded his hands over the table. "Shall we begin?"

"What happened to Gregory?" Schoffield demanded.

Anthony took a deep calming breath before giving Schoffield an intent look. "I fired him. Now, is there anything else in particular you need to know?"

A brief frown marred Schoffield's forehead before it was replaced by a bright smile. Anthony kept his face dead-panned, but there was nothing he could do about the chills that went down his back. He couldn't wait to get rid of the man, but Max had advised him to hold off. He only needed to be patient a few more hours.

"Oh, well, that's entirely your personal business, Eisemann. However, it makes me wonder about keeping your people loyal to you," Schoffield said with a smirk twitching on his lips.

Anthony opened his mouth to respond when once again, Byrd inserted himself into the conversation.

"I'm sure this is all interesting, Schoffield, but I did not cancel my golf tournament to listen to your prattling about Anthony's hiring and firing. Personally, I thought Gregory was a snake. Eisemann, please call the meeting to order." Byrd suggestively tapped on his watch.

"Of course, Byrd . . ." Whatever else Anthony was going to say died his throat, because the doors opened, and Stash strode in.

Stash wore a dark navy pinstriped suit with a pink shirt and purple tie. On his feet were a pair of strappy purple-buckled black stilettos. Wide-rimmed dark sunglasses hid his face, and in his hand, he carried a crocodile skin handbag. Anthony stood up so fast his chair fell over behind him, and he gaped like an idiot. It was only when Stash waved at him that he was able to break from his paralysis.

"Stash, what an unexpected surprise." Anthony quickly headed toward where he stood by the doorway.

"Who the hell's that? Has Eisemann hired a circus performer to entertain us?" Schoffield laughed at his own joke.

A chorus of clearing throats and gasps of disbelief followed Schoffield's words. Anthony didn't stop walking but shot the man a warning glance. In his peripheral vision, Anthony noticed that Christian had stepped forward, but he signaled for him to stay where he was. If it had been anywhere else other than a boardroom, nothing would have stopped him from punching Schoffield in the jaw. Unfortunately, as CEO and the name behind the brand, it would have been a bad idea.

He couldn't deny he was more than just angry at the rudeness displayed in front of the other directors and high-ranking executives. Schoffield would have to be dealt with properly, but he would have to wait a little longer. There were other ways to deal with those who overstepped themselves.

Anthony was close when Stash made a show of taking off his sunglasses. Stash cocked his head to the side and stared at Schoffield for a long moment as he nibbled on an arm of his glasses. Silence hung over the room, and Anthony hurried to his side.

"Stash, you should have told me you were in town," Byrd exclaimed, suddenly standing beside Stash with his hand on the small of his back.

But Stash didn't budge or change his focus.

"Frank Schoffield." Stash drawled out.

That Stash recognized Schoffield and called him by name surprised Anthony. Suddenly, whatever irritation he'd felt before gave way to curiosity.

"I am." Schoffield sneered. "And you still have not answered my question. Who are you? Are you aware that this is a private meeting? What business do you have here?" He approached Stash, glaring at him up and down.

What Anthony really wanted to do was sock the man, but his curiosity piqued when Stash's stance became relaxed and thoughtful. It was only when the outer corner of Stash's eye tightened briefly that Anthony knew Stash was going to deal with Schoffield in his own way.

Anthony folded his arms in front of him and widened his

stance. He couldn't wait to see what was going to happen. To his surprise, instead of a scathing rebuttal, a bright smile broke over Stash's lips, and he held out a hand to Schoffield in greeting.

"I'm surprised you don't recognize me, Frank. It's only been a few weeks since we last spoke to each other. But don't worry, I forgive you," Stash said.

Schoffield jerked back as if he'd been struck. Anthony could barely contain his glee when Schoffield paled and his eyes widened in sudden recognition.

"I must apologize, Mr. Burcell. You're right. I didn't recognize you," Schoffield said and extended a visibly trembling hand to shake Stash's hand.

Anthony's interest grew when Stash turned his back on Schoffield and faced Byrd.

"Joel, how are you?" Stash stepped closer, grabbed Byrd by the shoulders, and kissed the air on both sides of his face.

Jealousy clouded Anthony's vision, and he wanted to punch the man. He clenched his fists by his sides. How dare he touch Stash with such familiarity?

Byrd looked delighted and returned the greeting, but then he glanced at Anthony and must have seen the flash of anger there. Byrd's expression paled, but his attention was drawn back when Stash began to laugh. The corners of Byrd's eyes crinkled as he smiled. There was obviously a story there, and Anthony couldn't wait to find out what it was.

Schoffield slowly backed away from Stash, and Anthony reveled at the look of fear on his face. Was he just beginning to realize that his words and actions to block Stash's business from using Eisemann Foods would be a topic of discussion that day? Anthony glanced at the other directors and saw the same level of scrutiny aimed at Schoffield. He kept his satisfaction to himself. He had sent the other members an advanced copy of the file documenting Schoffield's questionable activities, and it looked as if none of them had liked what they'd learned.

All the directors, as well as their assistants, were staring at Schoffield. Except for Meggie. She was smirking. The suspense in the room grew palpable.

"It's good to see you, Joel." Stash practically purred his words.

Anthony gritted his teeth and closed his hands into tight fists. *Seriously? He's flirting with the guy?*

A blush spread over Byrd's cheeks. "How have you been? How is your father? I hope he is doing well," Byrd said as he straightened his tie.

"Thank you for asking. I'll give him your regards the next time I speak to him," Stash said. "Now, do excuse me. I came here for business, not pleasure." Stash turned his back on Byrd.

Stash's eyes were glinting when he directed his dazzling smile at Anthony. Unlike the one he gave to Byrd, this one was not fake or forced. Anthony placed a hand to his chest when his heart thumped hard against his ribs. "Stash, you didn't tell me you were planning on joining us today," Anthony said, smiling just as brightly as he closed the distance between them.

He ignored the gasps of surprise and mutters of disbelief when he placed his hands over Stash's shoulders and dropped a kiss on each of his cheeks. Stash's soft chuckle in his ear went directly to his cock. He tightened his hold briefly and gave Stash an admonishing look.

"I apologize for not giving you advanced warning, Ace. Dad called right after you left and instructed me to take his place in today's meeting," Stash announced. "Oh, and before I forget." He opened his handbag and pulled out an envelope, which he handed over to Anthony. "Here you go. It's only a printout copy, but I forwarded you the original. You know, just in case someone is curious about whether or not I have a proxy letter," he whispered conspiratorially before giving Schoffield a sidelong glance and grinning broadly at the man.

Anthony had a hard time containing his amusement. Conscious of the many eyes closely observing their interaction, Anthony cleared his throat. Another round of surprised gasps and comments went around the room when he placed his hand in the small of Stash's back.

"Jesus Christ, am I missing something here?"

"What the hell is going on?"

"So that is Stash Burcell. Interesting."

The last comment was made by Vincent Bean, but Anthony ignored all of them.

"That's all right. We were just about to start, so I'll take you to your seat." Anthony led Stash to the chair directly to his right.

Anthony helped Stash take off his coat and settle into his seat. It was also the one nearest to where Meggie and Christian sat against the wall along with the other assistants. That way, he didn't have to worry should Stash needed anything. He knew Meggie would take care of him.

"Now that we have everyone present, shall we begin?" Anthony said as he took his own seat. While everyone settled into their chairs, Anthony began the introductions, starting as casually as he could with Stash. Already he could feel the tension in the air mount.

Something Stash had never expected when he'd woken up that morning was to attend Anthony's emergency meeting. Although he knew he had been the start of it all, he'd done his part for his father's sake. Other than requesting to use some of the corporate facilities, Stash had felt he had no business knowing what went on behind the scenes. He had always tried his best not to listen in whenever the subject was discussed within his hearing. Now, thanks to his father's sudden request, he was in attendance and found himself sitting beside Joel Byrd. He hadn't talked to Joel for a while and hadn't known he'd managed to become a director of Eisemann Industries. Yet there he was . . . in the flesh.

No matter how Stash wracked his brain trying to figure out when Joel had become a member of the board, he couldn't come up with an answer. Speculating proved too much of a distraction, so he sent a quick text message to Anthony's phone and waited. He watched as Anthony took out his phone from his pocket, looked at it briefly, and set it down again.

Stash sat back into his chair and tried to pay attention to the discussion, but he could feel the curious glances cast his way. More than once, he caught some of them staring openly at him, but he ignored them all.

He recognized most of the attendees other than the five Anthony had mentioned before. When he was growing up, his father had made it a point to have Stash study the files of his acquaintances, so he knew their names, but they didn't know who he was. He doubted any of them had even known of his existence before he'd arrived, much less recognized him. Even Anthony hadn't known who he was the first time they'd met. Such was the result of decades spent hiding from society and their censorious eyes.

Anthony finally stopped talking and picked up his phone once more, tapped something on it, and set it back down on the table. Within seconds, Stash's phone vibrated. When he saw what Anthony had written, he nearly burst out laughing.

Byrd's not a member of the board, but he is a director for one of my companies. He's here in that capacity because we needed his vote on dealing with Schoffield. Also, I wanted to save time explaining about the illegal sale of company shares. There are six others here who I invited to attend. Is he a problem? Because I can send him out if you wish,

He bit back his smile as he typed out his response.

No, don't. He's an old friend, but I didn't know what he was doing here. I guess I better catch up with him at a later date. Thank you for clearing things up for me. By the way, you look sexy up there.

Anthony's eyes widened for a fraction of a second as he read Stash's reply. When he turned his gaze on Stash, Stash gave him a slow wink in response. Anthony shifted in his chair and went on as though nothing had happened, but Stash knew better. The telltale signs of Anthony's sexual arousal — that he'd gotten very familiar with — were plainly clear to him.

Two long hours later, Anthony was back in his office. He sat back and huffed out a breath of relief. Contrary to his earlier worries, he'd faced no real opposition to dealing with Schoffield and his dubious activities.

Anthony had found it hard to focus on the meeting every time Stash had paid attention to Byrd. Whatever Byrd's relationship with Stash had been, it had certainly improved his demeanor. In the past, Byrd had loved dichotomizing every single subject discussed, but not at this meeting. Instead, Byrd had made it a point to sit beside Stash and whisper in his ear, which drove Anthony to distraction.

Another cause for concern had been Vincent Bean.

As one of the original founding directors, Bean was someone Anthony thought he could rely on, but the meeting made him question his earlier assessment. The old man took a lot of time discussing every single point, and to everyone's surprise, it had been Mae Sutherland, another elder director, who had literally told Bean to shut up. Another director had quickly seconded the request, and that was immediately followed by a third.

Sutherland's actions had surprised Anthony the most. The woman usually attended board meetings without much participation, simply sitting in silence as she listened to the discussion.

After Bean had quieted, the rest of the meeting continued much smoother and faster. No one had raised an objection when Anthony had proposed stripping Schoffield of his rights as a director. Bean had suggested giving Schoffield a chance to redeem himself by selling back his shares to the company. Of course, Sutherland had immediately seconded the motion, but that was the end of his role as a director of one of the world's largest family-owned conglomerates.

Anthony's only regret had been when Stash had left as soon as the meeting was over. He had waved a hasty goodbye and disappeared through the door. Anthony still had too many things to do the rest of the day and had no other choice than to return the wave Stash threw his way.

A frown marred his forehead. What could have been so important that Stash didn't even have time to kiss him goodbye?

Anthony ran his hand through his hair and closed his eyes. There was no question that he would have to keep an eye on Joel Byrd. He would have to talk to Stash about what Byrd's story was. The man had proven to be a major distraction, and he didn't like it.

He was still sitting there about half an hour later when Christian entered the office with Meggie following close behind. She carried a tray with a mug and plate stacked with sandwiches. She carefully placed the tray on his desk.

"Stash called. He told me I would regret it if you don't eat, so you better do what he says." Not once did Meggie make eye contact, and when she finally did, her gaze was hard. "I like the extra money and all, but no way am I quitting my job with Stash."

Anthony blinked, momentarily speechless from Meggie's boldness, but quickly realizing she was just the messenger.

"I'll give Stash a call," he said instead.

"You do that." Meggie abruptly turned her back on him.

"Where did he say he was?" Anthony asked only to be ignored when the door closed behind her with a soft click.

"She's a bit impetuous, but I must admit, she's quite good at her job," Christian commented.

Anthony took a sandwich and started eating. "Keep your eyes and ears on Byrd, Bean, Sutherland, and everyone they're associated with. Report to me as soon as you're done." Anthony chewed on his food thoughtfully. "Find out what you can about Byrd's history with Stash and his father."

Christian nodded briefly. "Understood, sir."

"Also make arrangements for the plane to take us back to Limoges for whenever Stash prefers to go. I'll let you know tomorrow after I've spoken with him. Just make sure it's for tomorrow. We all deserve a long vacation after this week."

"I overheard Stash mentioning going to Italy."

"What for?"

"I'm not entirely sure, but I think it's something to do with makeup."

Anthony nodded. "Find out from Meggie and make sure our flight plan includes Italy. After that, I think Stash would prefer going back to Limoges."

"Noted," Christian said. "Anything else?"

"Yes. Call the chateau and ask them how Flossy is doing?"

Christian's only response was to nod as he continued to take note of Anthony's instructions on his tablet. There was a knock on the door, and Meggie entered before Anthony could give his permission. She closed the door behind her and walked over to stand beside Christian.

"Joel Byrd is outside, says he wants to talk to you," Meggie said, pointing her thumb to the door behind her.

Anthony cocked his head to the side and swallowed his food. "You know Byrd," he stated.

"I do, but for once, I can honestly say I don't know much about him outside of what he allows people to know. He's been good friends with Stash since our school days," Meggie said, twisting her mouth to one side. "Do I bring him in, or do you want me to make up an excuse and get rid of him?"

Anthony took two big bites out of the remains of his sandwich and dusted his hands over the plate. "No, I'm just as curious as you are. Let him in."

"Don't talk with your mouth full," Meggie said.

Anthony glared up at her, but she was already out the door. A suspicious noise came from Christian, who quickly covered it with a cough into his fist.

"I'll get this out of the way," Christian said, picking up the tray.

"Maybe I should fire you." Anthony took a drink of water. "Meggie, too."

"No, you won't," Christian retorted.

"Cheeky," Anthony grumbled. "Is that what you're learning from her?" He was going to add something more, but the door opened once again, and Meggie led Byrd into the office.

"Byrd, what can I do for you?"

CHAPTER EIGHTEEN

When the meeting was finally adjourned, Stash quickly took to his feet and picked up his bag. Meggie was by his side within seconds.

"Where are you going?" Meggie whispered.

"I had to reschedule my appointment earlier. If I don't go now, I'll miss it."

"What appointment are you talking about?"

"I'll let you know later," Stash said, already turning his back on Meggie. "Don't worry, I've got Ian and his men with me."

Stash hurried to Anthony's side to lean in and whisper in his ear. Anthony was still seated, signing documents that had been passed around earlier.

"I've got to go, I'll see you later, okay?" Stash said, patting Anthony's shoulder. He didn't give Anthony a chance to respond, just threw him a wave, and hurried out of the room.

Stash could feel the eyes burning in the middle of his back as he walked past the men and women, who all wanted a word with Anthony. His breathing quickened as did his steps, completely ignoring Anthony calling out after him. He stepped into the elevator and closed his eyes in relief as the doors began to shut.

"Stash, wait up," someone called out before a hand blocked the jambs from meeting.

Stash let out a curse when the doors parted, and Joel Byrd stepped inside.

"You're in a hurry," Joel said.

"I'm late for an appointment," Stash said, closing his eyes once more.

"Where to? I have my car downstairs. I can take you."

Stash opened his eyes and smiled gently at Joel. "Thank you for the offer, but it's only a building away. I can walk."

"Where are your people, Stash? Do you intend to walk over there without your security?"

"Jesus, Joel, not you, too," Stash said. "Look, if you really want to know, Ian's downstairs waiting for me, along with two others. I'm safe enough in here with Anthony's detail keeping watch. I bet they can see me now." He looked up and waved at the camera.

"So why are you here alone with me?" Joel looked up, grinned broadly, and gave the camera an exuberant wave, too. He lowered his arm and faced Stash. "How close are you with Eisemann?"

"Stop it," Stash warned, keeping his tone gentle but firm.

The elevator doors opened, and Joel stepped out ahead with Stash, holding up a hand to stop him from going any further.

Stash gestured toward Ian and his companions. "See, Ian's right here. You didn't need to worry."

"Hey, Ian, long time no see." Joel completely ignored Stash and held out his hand to Ian.

Ian answered with a grin of his own. He shook Joel's hand. "Hello, Mr. Byrd. How's Michael doing?"

"He's doing quite well. Now that I know Stash is in town, maybe you can bring him over for lunch sometime?"

"If their schedule permits it, sir," Ian said.

"*Their* schedule?" Joel gave Stash a side glance. "What is Eisemann to you, Stash? You still haven't answered my question."

Stash rolled his eyes. "I said, none of your business, but lunch would be good, just not anytime this week. I'm flying to Italy tomorrow and then back to Limoges for about a month, maybe two. I promise to give you a call when I get back."

Joel shook his head. "Okay, I get it. Stay out of your business. No asking about your boyfriend."

Stash beamed and leaned over to kiss Joel on his cheek. "It's good to see you again, Joel. I'll make sure to send Michael a present for his birthday."

"I'll tell him his favorite uncle is in town. Okay, I'll let you go. Now, are you sure you want to walk?"

"Uncle, oh my. That makes me sound so old. But yes, I'm not taking a car when the building is literally just around the corner. Now, get on back upstairs. I know you still have a few things to discuss with Anthony."

Stash waved goodbye to Joel and hurried toward the exit of Eisemann Tower. He checked his watch and saw he only had ten minutes to make it to his appointment.

"Ian, let's hurry, shall we? I refuse to miss this appointment," Stash urged.

"Don't worry, you have enough time. But I went ahead and called Colleen earlier and told her to give you another half hour." Ian pushed the revolving door so Stash could get into one of the slots.

"You're the best, Ian." Stash grinned up at him. "What would I do without you?"

Two hours later, Stash twisted his head from side to side as he scrutinized his reflection.

"As usual, Colleen, you are a brilliant artist," he said. "My roots were beginning to get on my nerves. Now I don't have to deal with wigs for a while. And my nails look fabulous."

"It's my pleasure, as always." Colleen stood behind him with the scissors, making last-minute adjustments to his hair. "I've trimmed out the ends, so you should be good to go.

Don't forget to use a keratin conditioner. Last but not least, please remember to come back in three weeks. I'll give Meggie and Ian a call about a week in advance to remind you."

"I'll try my best, but I don't exactly know when I'll be getting back. Why don't we compare notes, so I can write you into my calendar? That way, I can't forget," Stash said.

Colleen dropped her hands over his shoulders and peered at him in the mirror. She gave a nod of satisfaction and lowered her arms.

"You're too pretty for your own good. Makes me enjoy my work too much. Now go."

After signing up for a scheduled appointment in three weeks, Stash paid for the services, adding a considerable tip for each of the Fringe Studios technicians who had serviced him. Getting an appointment with Colleen Sterling took careful planning and a lot of patience. Luckily, Stash had known her before she had hit it big and had been one of the first to invest when she first pitched her dream to him. He had followed up with a little push and a gentle shove in the right direction, and it didn't take long for Colleen's talent to become one of the most sought after in New York. Her time was very expensive, so missing an appointment was something one shouldn't do.

As he walked into another mall he frequented in the city, he began to wonder what was keeping Anthony. Earlier, when his hair was baking, he'd asked Ian to have food delivered to Anthony's office so he, Meggie, and Christian could have snacks. But other than Ian reporting that Anthony had eaten what had been sent over, he'd heard nothing. He entered a favorite French luxury boutique, and his gaze immediately fell upon a beautifully bejeweled French watch.

Stash leaned over the glass display counter to look at it closer when he felt something pull on his coat. He looked down, and to his surprise, a boy of about four or five years of age was looking up at him. Ian was immediately there and was about to take the child away when Stash put up his hand to stop him.

"No, it's okay, Ian. Leave him alone. I think he just wants to talk to me. But go ahead and have someone in management look for his guardian, please," Stash said. He crouched down to the floor and gave the child a gentle smile. "Hey, dude. You wanted to talk to me?"

The boy held out a grubby hand. Stash looked down to see a piece of candy sitting in the middle of his tiny palm. He frowned down at the offering.

"Is that for me?" Stash asked, pointing to himself.

"You's pretty. Pretty eyes," the little boy said.

Stash briefly ran his gaze up and down the boy before carefully picking up the candy from his hand. Something told him not to make sudden movements, so he made sure to only touch the wrapper and not his skin. Once the candy was in Stash's possession, the boy turned around and ran out of the store. Stash stayed where he was, still crouched down on the floor, when he caught sight of Anthony walking in.

"What do you have there?" Anthony asked in a low voice.

"I think it's taffy." Stash stood up and started peeling off the sticky wrapper. He popped the candy into his mouth and was immediately hit with memories from his childhood.

"It's salted taffy. I haven't had these since I was a little girl." Stash began to suck on his candy. "Are you done for the day?"

Anthony nodded. "I could have joined you earlier, but guess who came to see me?"

Stash smiled. "Joel Byrd. I thought he might do that. What did he talk with you about?"

"Nothing much. He basically just told me to stay away from you."

"Typical. And what did you say?"

"That you're none of his business," Anthony shrugged.

"Oh, you shouldn't have done that." Stash sighed. "He's going to call Dad."

"Okay, you got me. What's Byrd to you?"

Stash shrugged. "Nothing really. We just slept together once."

"So, he's an ex?"

Stash gaped. "Eww . . . he's definitely not an ex. Excuse me, ugh . . ." He shimmied off his discomfort. The thought of Joel as a lover creeped him out.

"Look, I just came over to apologize for my son," a woman said from beyond the store entrance.

Stash glanced in the direction of the doors and saw one of his men blocking a woman's way.

"I'm sorry, ma'am, but can you wait outside until after Mr. Burcell is done shopping?"

"Stay here, let me talk to her, okay?" Anthony murmured.

Stash nodded and watched as Anthony walked over to the entrance. The commotion was attracting a few people who stopped to watch what was going on. When Stash saw a man at the back of the crowd take out a phone and hold it up like he was filming the scene, he moved back until he was hidden behind one of the upright display stands. He pretended to examine elaborately designed bangles as he peered through the glass to see what was going on.

"Please, I just want to talk to whoever my boy spoke to. I need to explain," the woman was saying.

Anthony nodded to the guard blocking the way, and the man lowered his arm. The woman walked into the store, and Anthony met her halfway.

"Hello. You must be the mother of the boy from earlier," Anthony said.

"Hello, yes. Look, I came to apologize. Are you the man my boy spoke to?"

"No, not me. That man over there." Anthony pointed at

where Stash was standing.

"Oh, please, do you think you can take me to him? Please?" The woman was practically begging.

Anthony looked torn over what to do. Stash looked at how the woman was dressed and determined that she seemed harmless enough. If what he suspected about the boy was correct, she would want to know every detail of his interaction with a stranger.

"Ace? What's going on?" Stash stepped out from behind the display stand.

Anthony let out a sigh of relief. "This is the little boy's mother," Anthony began but then stopped and turned back to the woman. "I'm sorry, but I didn't get your name."

"Hello. I'm Loraine Smith." Loraine held her hand out in greeting. "I just wanted to apologize for my boy. The store security told me he came in here without adult supervision, and that he'd talked to you."

Stash took her hand and shook it. He studied her carefully, looking for warning signals that she might cause him harm, but she looked genuine and safe.

"Yes, he's so sweet. He said I was pretty and then gave me a piece of salted taffy." Stash let go of Loraine's hand pointed at his mouth. "It's really delicious. Reminds me of my childhood."

The woman's eyes widened, and she covered her mouth with her hands. "He spoke to you? He actually spoke words? To you?"

Stash gave her a gentle smile. So, he had been right. The little boy was special.

"Yes, he did. I hope I didn't do anything wrong?"

"No, no. Of course not. It's just that he never speaks to strangers. Never. This is great. I can't tell you how I feel right now. Thank you," the woman said excitedly.

To Stash's horror, her eyes filled with tears.

"It's okay, really. As I said, he really is a sweet boy. I take it he's a special child?"

"Yes, he's autistic, and it's been difficult." The woman took out a handkerchief and wiped her eyes with it.

"Oh, I'm so sorry to hear that."

"May I ask what his exact words were?"

"He said *you's pretty*. That's all."

"Oh, my goodness. That's like . . ." she sobbed harder. "That's so good to hear. And he's got great taste, you are beautiful."

"Thank you, ma'am," Stash said graciously but felt his cheeks heating up. He always got embarrassed when people said things like that to him.

"No, he said something else," Anthony interjected.

"Something else other than *you's pretty*? Oh, my goodness." Loraine looked like she was about to cry harder.

"He said Stash had pretty eyes." Anthony smiled. "Your little boy's got good taste."

Loraine looked from Stash to Anthony. "Are you his boyfriend?"

At the mention of boyfriend, Stash bit the inside of his cheek, but to his surprise, Anthony held out his hand and shook the woman's hand.

"Yes, I am," Anthony said.

"Well, you're so lucky to have him in your life. Thank you both. Again. I know I'm repeating myself, but you can't imagine how hard it's been raising a special child." Loraine took both of Anthony's hands in hers. "You just don't know how fortunate you are. Your boyfriend is a good soul, and my boy recognized that in him. He loves salted taffy and never offers it to anyone but his dog and me. You must love him very much."

To Stash's complete surprise, Anthony took his hands from the woman, and instead, enveloped hers in his larger ones.

"I do know, and yes, I am *very* lucky. Stash and I wish you and your son well."

"Oh, my God, wait. Hold on." Lorraine looked back and pointed at the guard standing at the front door before turning back around. Her mouth opened and closed several times. Stash thought she would have a fit. The next words she uttered were a shock to his system.

"Did you just say his name is Stash? As in Stash Burcell?"

Lorraine didn't wait for Anthony's answer. She took out her phone and started to frantically tap and swipe on its surface.

"Oh, my God. You should have said something before I took pictures." Lorraine was speaking so fast her words were almost stumbling one on top of the other. "When my little Johnny does something like this with strangers, I send pictures to his doctor. To check if there is a pattern he may be following. Something that triggers him. Don't worry, I'm deleting everything. Stash, I know you wouldn't like to see your picture uploaded online. The stans would kill me if they found out. No wonder Johnny went to you. He absolutely loves your pictures on social."

It was Stash's turn to drop his mouth open. He tried to say something several times, but nothing came out. Anthony stepped closer to the woman.

"Excuse me, but what are you talking about?"

"You said *Stash*, and the man over there said *Mr. Burcell.* So I figured, his name's Stash Burcell. We don't know your name, but everyone knows he had someone special because he posted a series of Easter Egg hints a few days ago. If you hadn't mentioned his name . . . Okay, there. Your security men can check my gallery. Here." Lorraine handed the phone over to Ian.

He took it and checked it out but probably found nothing because he handed it back to her after a minute.

"Stash, I promise no one will know I talked to either of you," Lorraine said in earnest. "You're such an awesome guy, and I know you wouldn't want your secret out. Oh, and please, we're all waiting for the next collection and can't wait to buy them. I have to go. I won't waste more of your time, and my boy's waiting for me. Oh, my God, I talked to Stash Burcell."

Lorraine turned around, squealing excitedly under her breath, leaving Stash to gape after her.

"What the hell was that all about?" Anthony said to no one in particular.

"Apparently, that was one of my stans." Stash finally found his voice.

Anthony was not the only one who was astounded over what had just happened. Stash had never thought to be recognized by anyone. He'd made sure to only post makeup related pictures of his eyes or makeup swatches, never showing his entire face. That little Johnny had actually recognized him just from his eyes was truly unexpected.

"Stans? What the hell's that?"

"My extremely devoted fans. As in they stand by my side through thick or thin and will defend me online until they defeat the enemy. My stans."

"But I check your social every day. There's no way anyone could recognize you. How did Johnny do that?"

"I don't know, but one thing is clear to me, now that I've met Johnny."

"What is it?"

"He truly *is* a special child."

Chapter Nineteen

The flight to Italy went smoothly and without incident. The trip to the cosmetic packaging company in Capergnanica had excited Stash, even if he had only stayed long enough to discuss his vision for marketing his cosmetic and fragrance lines. Although it had all been very professional and straight to the point, some of their early proposals had Stash looking forward to the final results.

After the marketing manager had promised to send the samples to Stash at Limoges, Anthony hadn't wasted any time. He immediately arranged to fly them all back to Paris.

"What did you think of the packaging ideas they showed us?" Stash asked. He was sitting next to Anthony in the plane, enjoying the snacks they'd been served, busily typing up an Instagram post to update his fans. He wanted to share what was going on with the collection.

"I think you won't go wrong with the company. Italian packaging is up there when it comes to technology, creativity, and quality," Anthony said. "I especially liked the blown glass bottle for the perfume. That one was truly unique."

Stash nodded. He looked over what he'd written and then went back to the picture he was thinking of uploading. It was a simple image of his hand holding a flute of champagne he'd been served at the packaging company. The flute was also designed by the craftsmen who'd created the perfume bottle he had been drawn to. After careful consideration, he finalized his post and put away his phone. The day had gone smoothly, and he couldn't wait to get back to Limoges and Flossy.

"Do you want to stay in Paris for a few days, or do you want to go home as soon as we land?" Anthony pierced a pickled olive with a metal picker and offered it to Stash.

Stash leaned forward and bit the olive with his teeth before relaxing into his seat once more.

"I don't really know. I've got everything I needed done today." Stash shrugged and leaned forward once more. "I want some more."

He met Anthony's gaze and held it.

A smile curved the corners of Anthony's lips, broadening until the corners of his eyes crinkled. "You're so sexy, you know that?"

"I am? Why do you say that? I'm just asking for more of those delicious olives." He flashed an innocent smile. He didn't know what was going on with Anthony, but the way the man was looking at him right then was kind of discomfiting, and it made his cock jerk to attention.

Anthony didn't respond immediately. He looked to be taking his time choosing an olive before he finally settled on one, pierced it, and offered it to him.

Stash narrowed his eyes. "What are you thinking about?"

"Why do you ask?"

"Why are you talking like that?" Stash leaned back and scrutinized the way Anthony was smiling at him. "Are you flirting with me?"

"I can't wait to get you into bed."

Anthony's voice was so quiet, Stash had to strain his to hear.

Heat bloomed all over his body. He wondered how he was going to keep himself from jumping Anthony and riding him until they landed.

Instead, he hissed, "Stop it," the words slithering between his teeth. "We're on a full plane, and everyone can hear you."

Stash glanced over his shoulder to check whether anyone

had heard Anthony's comment. Fortunately, Meggie, Christian, and their combined detail were busy eating and conversing amongst themselves.

He turned back to Anthony, stabbing a finger at him. "You keep your voice down, Ace. I swear, you're incorrigible."

"You've called me that before." Anthony chuckled. He looked to be enjoying himself.

"Well, it's true." Stash huffed. He wanted to add something else, but he decided against it. "So? Paris or not?"

"We'll be there in about half an hour," Anthony said. "It's seven-thirty now. We can take a drive directly to Limoges, or we can stay the night there, have dinner and continue tomorrow at our own pace. What do you think?"

"I love the thought of being home tonight, and I do miss Flossy, but I'm tired and hungry. We can go home tomorrow after lunch, or maybe earlier."

Anthony nodded. "I'll have Christian make arrangements for a hotel."

Stash dismissed Anthony's suggestion with a wave of his hand. "I'll call Joel and tell him we're imposing on his good graces and stay at his house. Give me a few." Stash was already tapping on his phone.

Joel answered on the fifth ring. "Stash, this is a surprise. I thought you were flying to Italy?"

"We just left and are now on our way to Paris. Anthony and I were thinking of driving to Limoges directly, but frankly, I'm tired. Can we impose on you and borrow your house for the night?"

"Of course, you don't even need to ask, Stash. You know my house is at your disposal anytime you need it. What time are you arriving there?"

"In about half an hour, plus the usual deplaning process, so we'll get there about nine tonight."

"Sounds good. I'll make the arrangements with the

housekeeper and have your dinner ready by the time you get there. How many are you?"

Stash and Joel discussed the details of their stay and ended the call after they agreed on a menu. But not without Joel asking one last question.

"I take it you and Anthony are sharing a room?"

"Shut it, Joel. Seriously," Stash huffed.

Beside him, Anthony chuckled. Stash bared his teeth and threatened to kick him with his slippered foot. To his surprise, Anthony caught his leg and held it. He tried pulling away, only for Anthony to tighten his hold.

"All right, I get it," Joel said. "None of my business. You two must have talked about me, because I seem to hear a pattern here. Have a good night, Stash. And call me when you get there."

Stash ended the call and glared at Anthony. "That wasn't funny. Now let go of my leg."

"You were the one wanting to kick me." Anthony pouted but was still chuckling as he did as requested. "You never did tell me. How well do you know Joel? And what is this about you sleeping with him?"

"You're still stuck on that?" Stash winked and smiled. "We were in school together, and our class had to go to this camp for a weekend field trip. It was a first for all of us, but Joel was small for his age and got bullied by the bigger boys. Anyway, I found him outside the tent he was assigned to, braving the rain. So I took him into mine and introduced him to the other girls there. We made a bond and promised to tell no one he was sleeping in the girls' tent for the rest of the week."

"Wait, so you've known him since you were still considered a little girl? How old were you at that time?"

"It was just before my thirteenth birthday, and he was eleven at that time. He married one of the girls in that tent with us. She died from complications when she gave birth to their son, Michael, two years ago. I happen to be Michael's godfather," Stash said with pride.

"So you're good friends," Anthony said.

"Yes, but we're not as close as we used to be. I mean, I didn't even know he'd sold his company to you."

"Don't take it personally," Anthony admonished.

Stash couldn't help but laugh at the disgruntled look on Anthony's face. "Hey, there's nothing to be jealous about. Joel's one of the few who accepted me as a girl and then as a boy. His wife, Miranda, was one of my better friends."

"She died?"

Stash nodded. "It was all so tragic. Everything was going fine until after she gave birth to Michael. Joel was with her when she died. They said it was a blood clot and couldn't be stopped."

Anthony shook his head. "Maybe I should go easy on the guy."

"He's a good friend, Ace. Plus, he's loyal. He won't be involved in any illegal sale."

"Now that you've told me about him, I think I can trust him."

"There's something else you should know. He's really good at marketing. In fact, he was the one I first approached when Anastasia Beauty was still just starting."

"What are you getting at?"

"It didn't come from me, but you can ask him to look around for notices of a sale. He's got an ear to the pulse of the market and an even longer reach online. He may just surprise you."

"I'll take your word for it. All right, I think we're about to land." Anthony looked toward the cockpit just as the door opened, and the captain came out to announce they were landing earlier than anticipated.

Stash sighed and closed his eyes. The fluttering in his

stomach tightened, and his heart started pounding in his chest. He began breathing through his mouth and counting to quell his panic. A warm hand covered his as they began to descend. He didn't have to open his eyes to know it was Anthony holding his hand. When the plane jerked and the gears shifted, Stash hissed and held his breath.

Anthony squeezed his hand. "Breathe, baby, or you'll pass out. It's okay, we're already beginning to touch down."

Stash could only nod his head and pray. He always enjoyed flying but hated the landings. When the plane was on the ground, he figured Anthony would let go of his hand and was surprised when he didn't. Anthony never let go of his hand, even after they'd entered their car and it began to move. Only when they had reached Joel's house did Anthony let go. For some reason, Anthony's actions warmed Stash's heart.

Chapter Twenty

Stash stirred, caught in the twilight between sleep and wakefulness. Something was off. He reached out to his side and encountered an empty space.

"Ace?" Stash sat up and peered into the darkness. He called out again, but he still heard no response.

Concern had him worried. Ever since Christian had told him to watch out for nightmares, Stash had kept close observation on Anthony's sleep patterns. Already, he had woken up twice that night to hear Anthony speaking in his sleep, repeating the same words, over and over again, just as he'd done that first time.

"Where is it?"

"Where the fuck is it?"

This time though, Stash was alarmed to find Anthony was no longer beside him in bed. After a moment thinking over what to do, he stood up and shrugged into his robe. He slipped his feet into his slippers and opened the door. From the bed, Flossy whined sleepily.

"Shh, go back to sleep," Stash said. He didn't wait to find out how Flossy would react and closed the door behind him.

"Ace, are you down there?" Stash leaned over the banister and peered into the darkness below. When there was no response, he looked around and realized he was alone in the house. For a moment, he couldn't decide what to do. Where were the guards? Once more, he looked around but couldn't find anyone. Had the orders been changed, and he'd missed the memo? He jumped when a crash sounded from below in the direction of the kitchen. From the bedroom, Flossy's shrill barking filled the air.

"Ace? Where are you?"

When he was met again with dead silence, Stash decided enough was enough. He would deal with the security later, but first, he had to find Anthony. He went back inside the bedroom and took out the gun he kept in the drawer of the bedside table on his side of the bed. Flossy barked at him, but Stash ignored her. After checking that the gun was loaded, he picked up his phone with his other hand and went out the door again. He pressed the speed dial that would connect him to Meggie. She answered after the first ring.

"What's wrong?" Meggie said, sounding wide awake.

"I can't find Anthony, there are no guards inside the house, everything's dark, and I just heard a crash coming from downstairs." Stash started slowly down the stairs. He didn't meet anyone there, but he could see a sliver of light coming from somewhere to his right.

"Stay where you are," Meggie said.

"I'm already downstairs and on my way to the kitchen. I'm outside the kitchen door. I don't see anyone—" Stash stopped mid-speak at the sound of chopping.

"Stash, keep talking," Meggie said, her voice raised and alarmed.

"Shh, don't speak too loud," Stash whispered. He slowly walked further into the room. Other than the open fridge door where the light was coming from, the kitchen was dark. Anthony was standing naked in the middle of the kitchen. In his hand was a butcher knife that he was using to chop onions.

For a moment, Stash didn't know what to do. Anthony looked awake, but something was terribly wrong about the way he was moving. It was almost mechanical, as though his actions were controlled by someone else. What scared Stash was that Anthony didn't look at what he was doing. He was wide-eyed, staring into space while his hands moved through the motions.

"Oh, my God, I think Ace is sleepwalking," Stash whispered low into the phone. "No, make that sleep cooking."

"Sleep cooking? What the actual fuck?" Meggie said something to someone on her side of the line.

Then Christian's voice came on. "Can you confirm what Mr. Eisemann is doing, sir?"

"He's cooking an omelet," Stash said. He kept his gaze on Anthony as he began to slowly walk backward in the direction of the door. "I'm afraid to speak any louder, or I might startle him, and he'd hurt himself. Christian, where are the guards?"

"We're coming right over," Christian said.

And then Meggie's voice came back on. "Don't startle him."

"I'm not," Stash said. "He has this butcher knife, and earlier he was slicing onions. Oh, my God, he's lit up the stove. What do I do?"

"Don't do anything. Wait for us until we get there. We can't afford to startle him."

Stash nodded. "Okay. He's now going to the fridge. He's taking out butter. Oh, that's good, he knows how to cook. Oh, now he's frying up the onions. It smells wonderful."

"Seriously, Stash, I don't need a cooking show. This is an emergency," Meggie sounded irritated.

"I know that. I'm just giving you updates on what he's doing. Don't worry, I'm staying far away and standing by the doorway. He can't hear or see me. Oh, he's beating the eggs. He only used three. Not four. Oh damn, Ace. Add another one."

"Stash!"

"Sorry, but he really should. Oh, he added another and—"

"Can't you keep quiet?"

Stash slapped his phone over his mouth to muffle the squeal of surprise at Meggie's voice suddenly right next to his ear.

"Ow, ow. Meggie, I told you never to do that," Stash admonished. He touched his lips tentatively and winced. "Where's Christian?"

"He's going in through the other entrance. Where the hell are the other guards?"

"That's what's worrying me. Were there any changes I missed somehow?"

"Not that I know of. I'm going to kill them. We promised we would keep you and Anthony safe, and now look at what's happened."

"Shh, look. Ace is done cooking. What is he doing? Why is he just standing there?"

"I think he went back to sleep," Meggie said. "Stay here, I'll go in and check him out."

"No, you're not." Stash pulled Meggie back to his side.

"Why not?"

"Let Christian do it. Also, he's naked."

"So what if he's naked?"

"You shouldn't see him undressed."

"Oh, for heaven's . . . Okay, I'll go get a blanket to cover up his butt."

"There's a throw over the chair in the living room. It's closer," Stash said.

Christian came into view. He quickly assessed Anthony's state but didn't touch him. He waved his hand in front of Anthony, who didn't appear to react to the stimulus. Meggie came back. Stash handed her his gun and took the blanket from her.

"Let me do that," Stash said. He went over to where Anthony and Christian were standing and met Christian's gaze.

"Is he asleep?" Stash whispered.

Christian's lips thinned, but he nodded. "I'll help you get him back to your bedroom."

"Okay, but let's put this around him, first," Stash said, lifting the blanket so Christian could see it. "No one should see him naked."

Christian shook his head. "No, it might startle him awake. Let's take him as he is back upstairs and put him to bed."

Stash briefly thought over the suggestion and grudgingly agreed it was the best course of action. This was no time for modesty.

"How do we do this?" Stash asked.

"I don't know," Christian said, frowning. After a moment, his eyes lit up. "Whenever you call him on the phone, he drops everything. Why don't you talk to him and ask him to go with you?"

"He does? Oh, that's nice to hear. Okay, let's do this." Stash sent a quick prayer for success before stepping up in front of Anthony. He reached out and took hold of Anthony's wrist.

"Hey, sweetie, why don't we go to bed, hmm?"

Stash didn't expect a response, but to his surprise, Anthony straightened, and a sweet smile curved on his lips. He took a step forward until he was face to face with Stash.

Stash immediately took a step back to give Anthony space. Now that he knew Anthony was receptive to his voice, Stash patiently cajoled him out the kitchen, then up the stairs and all the way back into their bedroom. Anthony automatically went to his side of the bed, lay down, and closed his eyes.

Stash stared down at Anthony for a long while, his thought replaying the entire incident like a video caught in a loop. His Ace. His man.

The man he loved.

When had he fallen for this guy? What had been the trigger that had sealed the deal for him?

Love shouldn't hit someone as paranoid as him this hard

and sudden, should it? Could it?

From his realization came hindsight.

He'd nearly lost his man tonight. Not from the hands of a murderer or a bullet shot from a gun, but from a nightmare. One that Anthony had lived with for God knew how long.

A nightmare that had taken control of his unconscious mind and made him get up and go down those stairs.

He could have missed a step, fallen, and broken his neck. He could have cut himself with the knife. And where had the security been? Why had he and Anthony been left alone in the house?

From hindsight came simmering anger that threatened to boil over. The overwhelming sense of panic made tears fall, and his body moved on its own volition. Before he even realized what he was doing, he slammed open the door and walked out of the bedroom. That was when he saw them.

Meggie and Christian were talking to each other in the hallway. Six guards stood with them, and they all appeared to be discussing something between them. When Meggie looked up and saw him, she gave him a smile. He knew it was meant to reassure him, but his vision was blurred by a red haze of fury. Something inside him snapped, and he walked over to the group. When he neared Christian, he raised his arm to slap him, but Meggie intervened.

"No, Stash, don't." Meggie grabbed hold of his arm and pulled him back.

"Let me go," Stash growled. He wrenched his arm from Meggie's hold and glared at Christian.

Meggie, however, would not be swerved.

"You're not going to hit Christian, Stash. That is not how to deal with this problem."

Stash turned his glare on her. "Shut up. Where were my guards, Meggie? Where were Anthony's guards? Where were any of you when this was happening? We were alone in the house, Meggie. Alone. In the dark. You know how I feel about being in the dark."

Both Meggie and Christian flinched as he yelled the last word out.

"Stash, look, that's what we're trying to figure out," Meggie said. "Christian was with me, and we both thought the guards were in the house. We think someone hacked into the system and somehow called them to check outside. *Someone* changed the orders on us."

The words were like a bucket of ice water thrown over his head. "Hacked? How is that possible?"

"We don't know yet, but don't worry, I'll have our people check into it."

"Do it. I want the answers within an hour. As for you, Christian," Stash turned, pointing his finger at Christian's nose. "I thought you knew the risks involved with Anthony's brother, especially as you have yet to discover his whereabouts. Yet your men failed on a very basic principle. They abandoned us."

"Yes sir, I completely understand," Christian said.

But Stash refused to listen. He was on a rant. "I want answers from the both of you. I don't care how you do it. Look into this breach. I want everything scrubbed, from the attic down to the basement. No one sleeps tonight. Do you understand me?"

"Yes sir," Christian said, his cheek muscles jerking spasmodically.

"Completely," Meggie said in a tight voice.

"Get out of my sight," Stash said as he stared Meggie and Christian down.

Christian bowed his head stiffly, did an about-face, and walked away. The other guards briefly gave Stash a low bow and hurried after Christian.

"Was that all really necessary, Stash?" Meggie said.

Stash whirled around, holding up a finger. Meggie's eyes widened, and she took a step back.

"Don't," Stash growled. "Help Christian if you have to, but don't you dare lecture me on this one, Meg. Just don't." He drew in a stuttering breath, and his eyes burned with the threat of tears. Pulling in what was left of his tattered dignity, he lowered his arm and straightened his back.

"I'm going back inside to watch over Anthony. Update me if you need to. Otherwise, I don't want to be disturbed. Get those guards back in here and tell them to turn on the goddamned lights. Good night."

Stash turned his back on Meggie, ignoring her call for him to stay and talk to her. Although tempted to slam the door shut, he didn't. He quietly pushed it into the jamb. When he heard a soft click, he turned around and pressed his back against it. Taking deep breaths, he waited until his heartbeat slowed down.

His hands started trembling uncontrollably as he grabbed his phone. It took him three tries before he was able to settle on a message he was satisfied with. After he pushed send, he placed his phone on the nightstand and got into bed beside Anthony. But he didn't sleep.

Anthony shifted in his sleep and reached out toward him. But he didn't move, too afraid to he would startle Anthony. When Anthony's hand gripped his wrist and pulled on it, he had no choice but to move closer. Anthony turned onto his side, hugging Stash's arm close to his chest.

"Stay," Anthony breathed out.

Tears welled in his eyes, yet he didn't wipe them away. "I'm here, Ace," he whispered.

"'Kay," Anthony said. "Love you."

Dawn broke through the mountains, bringing with it the sweet calls of twittering birds. Stash stood, looking out, but saw none of the beauty. His message had been received, and the response was one simple word. *Noted.* Although he wanted to know more about what it meant, he knew he couldn't ask for anything more.

A sleepy sigh came from behind him, and he twisted to see if Anthony was awake. When there was no other sound or movement, he turned back to the view outside.

A thud from beyond the bedroom door broke the impenetrable silence that had taken over the house after he'd dismissed Meggie. He really should be mortified by his actions, but he was still too angry. Anyway, he knew he was in the right. Both his and Anthony's security had failed.

The phone in his hand began to vibrate. After checking who the caller was, he walked into the bathroom and accepted the call.

"Talk to me," Stash said as he quietly closed the door.

"We traced the hacker, but it's a dead-end," Meggie said. She sounded tired as though she hadn't slept the whole night.

"What about the guard assigned to communications?"

"He claims it was Christian who called him, but as we well know, that's not true. He's been relieved from his assignment with us."

"I want his file handed to me by breakfast," Stash said. "What else do you have for me?"

"Christian wants to apologize to you personally, that is, once you've calmed down a bit. I told him not to push it, and he'll just have to wait until you're ready."

"Ask him to join us at breakfast, then he can apologize to me and Anthony. What else?"

"That's about it," Meggie said, sounding defeated.

"I'm not that mad anymore, okay, Megs? You know how I am."

"Yeah, your bark is worse than your bite, and all that bull crap." Meggie sighed. "But I saw how frightened you were last night, and I'm the first one to admit this was a failure on my end.

"Say what you mean. I panicked," Stash said and then yawned loudly."

"Did you even sleep at all?"

"Nope. I was too scared for Anthony."

"I'm so sorry, Stash," Meggie said, sounding forlorn. "But I swear to you, neither of us knew about what was happening."

Stash tightened his lips and shook off the excuse, for it was an excuse. One that could have cost Anthony's life. Or his.

"We can talk about that later," Stash said instead.

"I know you too well. You think I'm making excuses."

"Yes."

"You're right, and that was wrong of me. Christian did say it would never happen again."

"I hope he didn't take it out on anyone, but if he did, good for him. It could have been worse."

"Oh, he definitely knows, but no, he didn't punch anyone."

Stash nodded. "Good to know." He let out another tired sigh. "Look, I'm going to wake Anthony up, so please advise the kitchen staff to get breakfast ready."

"Will do," Meggie said softly. "Please, do me a favor?"

"Depends on what the favor is. Ask away."

Meggie moaned through the phone. "Never mind. Forget I asked."

"You wanted me to talk to Anthony about Christian, right?"

"It was just a thought."

"I'll see how things go, otherwise, no promises." Stash ended the call and stared at the bathroom door for a long minute. No matter what had transpired, he meant what he said. Now that he was in a calmer mood, he knew the fault hadn't all been because of Christian. Someone had maliciously sought to harm Anthony or both of them. Not far from his mind was the mystery of Lawrence's whereabouts.

Stash hung up his robe on a hook behind the door and stepped under the hot shower. Under normal circumstances, he would have spent at least twenty minutes in the cubicle to complete his routine, but that morning he was too impatient. He was toweling his hair dry with one of his special bamboo viscose hair towels when a knock came on the door.

"Stash? Are you in there?"

"Coming right out, Ace. Hold on." Stash gave his hair a final swipe before dropping the towel into the laundry bin.

"Hey," Anthony said. He was leaning against the wall outside the bathroom.

"Had a good sleep, sweetie?" Stash ran his gaze over Anthony's features.

"The best," Anthony said. "I think it's because you're with me."

Stash chuckled under his breath. "You're so sweet, do you know that?"

"I like to think I am. But don't tell anyone, okay?"

"Of course. Reputation to protect and all that." Stash smiled brightly, but he could feel his lips tremble. He shook his funk away and cupped Anthony's face in his hand. "If you don't mind getting ready, I'm really hungry. I ordered for an early breakfast downstairs."

Anthony frowned. "But you ate a full dinner last night. Did you go for a run or something?"

Stash shook his head and soothed Anthony's frown away with a kiss between his eyes.

"No, I just have an energetic metabolism, that's all. So, go on, get ready."

Anthony shrugged. "Okay, early breakfast it is."

"Thank you, sweetie."

"Anything for you, babe." Anthony dropped a kiss on

Stash's lips and closed the door behind him.

Stash closed his eyes and ran his fingers through his damp hair. Keeping things from Anthony was something he didn't want to do, and he knew he'd never be able to get through the day without telling him about what had happened. Might as well get it over with. He began to pace as he thought over how to approach the subject. Sleepwalking was a sensitive topic, and he still knew too little about Anthony's personality or how he would react. His time ran out when Anthony exited the bathroom.

"Hey, before we go downstairs, sit with me for a minute. I need to tell you something." He patted the bed to his side. When Anthony sat down, he shifted so they were face to face. "First, I asked Meggie and Christian to join us at breakfast."

"Is that all? Why so serious about it?" Anthony laughed quietly under his breath. When Stash winced, Anthony's expression sobered. "Did something happen last night?"

"You were sleepwalking last night," Stash murmured. "Christian had warned me that you might have nightmares, so I'd been keeping a close watch. I didn't expect what happened last night."

Anthony rubbed the back of his head. "Why do I get a bad feeling about this?" He took in a deep breath through his nose and held it. "Okay, tell me what happened. What did I say?"

"Well, earlier in the night, you kept repeating the same thing like before, but then you went back to sleep. Later, I woke up, and you were gone. I went searching and found you in the kitchen. You were naked, with a knife in your hand, and cooking an omelet. What I didn't like was that no one was around, and I was the one who found you. I'm sorry, I panicked. If you had fallen down the stairs or cut yourself, I don't know what I would have done."

"I was sleepwalking? Where was our security?"

"Christian didn't know about the sleepwalking. Also, it

looks like there was a breach in my communications system. I'll let Meggie and Christian tell you all about it over breakfast. Anyway, I called Meggie when I didn't see anyone on the floor. I'm sorry, but I lost my temper with Christian. And Meggie, too. She's head of my security, and it wasn't just your men involved, mine were, as well. I said some things maybe I shouldn't have, but we were on our own. You could have gotten seriously hurt."

"No, don't apologize." Anthony rubbed his palms over the back of Stash's hands. "If it had been me, I don't think I would have limited myself to harsh words."

"Thank you," Stash said, relieved Anthony was on the same page as him.

"Were you alarmed over what happened?"

Stash scoffed. "When I said I lost it, I meant I totally lost it. I panicked." Stash shook his head and held his stomach in. "You had a knife in your hand, and you were prepping food while you were asleep . . . I was so scared that if I made the slightest sound, I'd startle you, and you'd cut a finger off."

"I'm sorry you had to go through that. I've not sleepwalked since I was maybe six or seven." Anthony sighed and shook his head.

Stash didn't know how long they both sat on the bed. Neither of them spoke until Stash's stomach growled.

Anthony twisted his neck as though it was sore and stood up. He held a hand toward Stash and gestured for him to get up.

"Come on, let's not keep Meggie and Christian waiting."

CHAPTER TWENTY-ONE

Anthony looked up as a burst of fluttering wings broke from the canopy of trees. The fresh air was a great improvement from the closed confines of the chateau. Breakfast had been uncomfortable, so he was glad when Stash suggested taking Flossy out for a walk.

The first time he had been here, he hadn't had the chance to look around, but now that he did, he couldn't help but envy Stash for owning such a treasure of a property. The woods surrounding the chateau fortress were quite extensive, and it had taken them over an hour to circle back. They were entering through the stone gatehouse while Flossy ran ahead across the wooden bridge over the moat.

"I think it's time you told me everything," Stash said. "I can't help you if I don't know anything. And I really want to help, Ace. Let me in. Please."

Anthony had been expecting Stash to ask him about Lawrence ever since news broke out about his release from prison. Expecting was far different from actually hearing the words, and to his horror, he began to feel anxious. He knew he owed Stash an explanation, but it was difficult—mainly because he didn't know how Stash would react when he learned the truth.

He took a deep, trembling breath before slowly releasing it. After all this time, he still could not get over his panic. The doctors had diagnosed it as PTSD, and Anthony accepted that. However, accepting it and getting past it were two very different things, and he doubted he ever could.

"Lawrence was diagnosed as a sociopath. I think he was seventeen or eighteen at that time. He's also a homophobic bastard. I'll leave it to your imagination as to how he'll react when he finds out you and I are even talking to each other. When he learns we're sleeping together . . ." Anthony let out a derisive laugh. "He'll go bat shit crazy."

Stash began to blink rapidly and shake his head as if he couldn't believe what he was hearing. "Why was Lawrence sent to jail? I remember you saying he murdered somebody?"

"Lawrence was nineteen when he killed our Uncle Robert, Dad's younger brother. Although we didn't find out about it until much later. At the time it happened, the police had no idea who'd done it. Lawrence wasn't even on the suspect list. At twenty-one, he was caught stealing into the bedroom of one of our guests. Lawrence later said that it was a birthday gift to himself. That unfortunate guest happened to be a senator. Lawrence had a knife to the senator's throat, but our security was able to talk him down from killing the man. They couldn't stop him from nicking the man's neck, though, so by the time the police arrived, the senator was bleeding all over the place. Dad asked Lawrence why he did it, and Lawrence said he was curious about how blood would flow if he cut a jugular."

"Oh, my God. That's insane," Stash said. "Go ahead. What happened next?"

Anthony nodded. The words were getting easier to get out. He didn't know if it was because of Stash's reassuring presence beside him, but he appreciated it.

"Dad tried to talk the senator out of pressing charges, but the senator didn't listen."

"Of course," Stash said.

"Exactly. The senator didn't waste any time, and soon Lawrence was arrested and charged with attempted murder. My dad didn't do anything to stop it or protect Lawrence after that point. It was either protect the rest of the family and the business or lose everything. We'd also known for some time that Lawrence had been using drugs and was involved in other illegal activities. Long story short, through the course of his trial, Uncle Robert's death came up, and that was the beginning of the end for Lawrence in Dad's eyes. For all of us. My mother was devastated. At first, Dad was in denial, but when he learned how his younger brother had suffered at Lawrence's hands, he couldn't forgive him. After his sentencing, Dad disinherited him from both the family and the company."

"What did your mother say? What did your Uncle Robert's family say?"

"Mother had started drinking and had given up on Lawrence long before that. As for my cousins, they were angry and unforgiving. I don't blame them."

"Did it affect your relationship with your cousins?"

"Not on the surface. We're all polite and charming with each other in public."

"Otherwise?"

"In private, we hardly speak to each other except when we have to. We did discuss Lawrence at one point, and none of them blamed me or Dad for what he'd done. It's just that they can't look at us the same."

"That's understandable." Stash merely nodded.

They were silent for a long time, Anthony taking in the beauty of the countryside and Stash looking thoughtful beside him.

After a while, Stash broke the silence. "What about you? How do you feel about Lawrence?"

"I'm scared of him. Always have been. He's my big brother. There's ten years between us, and he never let me forget it."

"Did he ever hit you?"

"You might say he had a mean streak and didn't like me hanging around him that much. I learned to stay away from him."

Stash didn't say a word, but he gave Anthony's arm a gentle squeeze, as though it was the only way he could give his support.

"Lawrence is the bane of my existence, and yet I can't think of hurting him."

"Of course not. No matter what, he is your brother and a human being. It's not in you to be evil, not like him."

"I heard my mother call him *the devil incarnate*."

"When did she say that?"

"After Dad died," Anthony said. "It was a bad time for all of us, but at least I was able to immerse myself in the company. My mother had no one. In the end, she just . . . died. It was as if nothing was holding her here, and she just stopped living."

"There are so many levels of grief, and dealing with it depends on the person who experienced it. My mother left me because she couldn't accept what I was. Your mother died because she couldn't accept the horrors one of her sons committed. So no, there's no need to feel embarrassed. We both have our demons," Stash assured.

A gust of wind disturbed the trees above them, and a cascade of leaves fell over them.

"This is not the first time he's escaped jail. Five years ago, he got out. That's when he killed Dad." Anthony stated. "It was supposed to be me, but Dad got in the way."

"What?" Stash stopped walking and pulled on Anthony's arm until he, too, stopped. "I thought your father died of natural causes."

"One of the perks of having all the money I do is I can make a story go away," Anthony said derisively. "My father's death and the story behind it were kept out of the media, and it will stay out."

"What happened?"

Anthony couldn't face Stash, so instead, he looked toward the copse of trees they had recently come out from. The words started hesitantly, but the more he spoke, the faster and easier it became. He didn't hear his words or listen to his voice, though. Instead, his mind relived the terror as he'd experience it.

The sound was loud enough to break through the noise of an action scene he and his father were watching. He went ahead to investigate, telling his dad to call the police. Curiously, the security alarm had remained silent. That could only mean one thing — the intruder knew the codes or had cut the wires. Either way, whoever the intruder was had managed to disable their security system. He turned the corner at the top of the landing, only to be caught by surprise when a dark form leaped out of the shadows, and something hard struck his hand.

That was the first of many cold, numbing slices of what could only be a knife cutting into his flesh. The gun he'd been holding must have fallen then. After the fifth stab, he stopped counting, and his instinct took over. He fought back, trying to fend off the many strikes that continued to rain on his body. He escaped further injury only by accident — he slipped, stumbled down the stairs, and lost consciousness. He didn't know how long he'd been out, but it mustn't have been very long, for when he opened his eyes, he was lying face up, and a dark, blurry shape of a faceless man was walking toward him. Suddenly, his father lunged from behind the intruder.

The horror unfolded above him as he lay sprawled at the foot of the stairs, dazed from loss of blood. His dad, grappling with the intruder on the landing, grunted in pain when a stolen move sank a mean-looking knife into his father's side. Anthony's vision blurred, and he licked at his dry lips only to taste a vile pungency. The sickeningly sweet metallic smell clung to his nose. It was so strong it smothered his senses, making him gag and fight for every pain-filled breath. Exhaling was even more painful, and the blurriness turned to dim fog. He blinked the darkness away. Thankfully, his sight cleared. So did his hearing.

"Son. The gun. Get the gun," his father said.

The words were followed by a loud gurgling breath before he watched in horror as his father's form fell onto his knees. The hand holding the knife drew back, revealing the dark blade before it lunged forward and sank into his father's abdomen.

For a brief moment, he didn't understand what his father meant. What gun? The cold crept up his limbs, and he knew he was going to faint, but somehow, his father's words finally registered, and it gave him the strength he needed.

Gun. He must get to the gun.

Where is it?

Shivers wracked through him as he attempted to sit up. The hot, thick, liquid pool he was lying in made him slip, but he finally did it. He rose to his knees and panted before pushing himself up. For a moment, he was swayed to settle back into the warmth of before, but he shook the temptation away. He recognized his weakness as blood loss.

Where is it?

His eyes stung as blood dripped down his forehead. Blinking the sting away, he checked around him. It was too dark where he was, but he recalled taking it out of the drawer soon after he and his dad had heard the glass shatter on the second floor.

A dull thud made him look up once more only to see his father fall face-first on the landing. The intruder turned back to him, the distinctive shape of a knife still in his hand. In spite of the dim light, he could clearly see the dark liquid dripping from its point. In quiet desperation, he frantically began to scan his surroundings for the gun.

Where the fuck is it?

He breathed out a harsh, ragged, gurgling breath, but he finally spotted the dark metal lying by his right foot.

Everything went in slow motion, but finally, he had the gun in his hand. He tightened his hold on it, the grip lending him courage. A surge of renewed energy swept through him as years of security drills suddenly kicked in. He'd resented his father for the hours of enforced training while he was growing up, envious of his peers who'd spent the same time partying while he'd had to stay at home. He thanked his dad now for the tutelage as his mind began to automatically work out what method would work best to save them both. His arm trembled, but he was able to raise the gun and lock his sights on his target.

Beyond the weapon, his gaze met the wild one of his brother's. Tears merged with sticky blood, but he blinked the sting away. Lawrence let out a roar as his face twisted into something unrecognizable. Something evil.

With his finger on the trigger, he took a steadying breath and aimed.

"Lawrence," he said. "Please. Don't do this."

Lawrence continued down the stairs, his loud breathing ragged, his hair flattened over his forehead by sweat.

"Stop. For God's sake, Lawrence. Please stop." He could only manage to whisper the words.

Whether or not Lawrence heard him, he had no clue, for his brother's expression didn't change. Instead, he raised the knife over his head.

Lawrence didn't leave him any other option. Instinct forced him to pull the trigger and fire two shots in quick succession. The seconds passed, his ears rang, and his fear went up another notch. He couldn't look away from the incredible sight of Lawrence remaining upright, the knife held over his head. Lawrence took another step toward him, leaving him no room to hesitate. His hands trembled at what he was about to do. He closed his eyes and pulled the trigger again.

"The last thing I thought of as I fell on my back was the pain in the palm of my hand, and that I'd basically failed. I hadn't planned on it, blame it on an unexpected flinch, but in retrospection, I knew I'd done the right thing. I couldn't do it. I couldn't kill him. But now, I question my decision."

Stash took hold of Anthony's hand and traced the glossy, whitened skin shaped like a V that stretched between thumb and index finger where the gun had kicked back and torn the flesh. Even in the light of day, it was barely discernible, but Anthony knew it was there.

"I didn't even notice you had a scar here. I haven't seen any scars on your body. Was it plastic surgery?" At Anthony's nod, Stash closed Anthony's palm and gazed at him. "At the end of the day, Lawrence is your brother, and no matter what you want to think or feel, I don't see you as a killer. Not like Lawrence is."

"He's not going to stop. He's going to come after us until he's killed us both."

"Which is why we're increasing our security protocols. Both of our teams are working together to ensure no harm comes near us."

"And yet he managed to hack into our system and change the orders. Worse, no one questioned it."

Stash bit on his lower lip. "I forgot to mention that I sent Paul an SOS. I'm sorry if I stepped out of line, but I was just so mad about the breach."

"We could use Paul's expertise, or rather his people's. Christian is just as angry and is investigating who was lax in their duties. He's teamed up with Meggie." Anthony dragged his palm over his face. "What a mess."

"Did I tell you he was with Meggie last night? They were in her room."

Anthony pinched the bridge of his nose. "Another potential complication waiting to happen." He opened his eyes and gazed at Stash. "None of our business, it's their life."

"I have to agree." Stash wrinkled his nose and chuckled. "Know what?"

"Not yet."

"Prick," Stash slapped Anthony's upper arm. "Quit it, I'm warning you."

"All right, all right," Anthony wrapped his arms around Stash and dropped a kiss on his forehead. "Forgive me?"

Stash grinned broadly. "You're forgiven. Remember when I said you were cooking an omelet while you were sleeping? Well, I'm craving for some omelets right now."

Anthony threw back his head and laughed out loud, the sound echoing across the park. He slung an arm around Stash's shoulders and started walking.

"We just had breakfast." Anthony narrowed his eyes.

"I've got a fast metabolism. The walk made it burn faster." Stash smiled playfully.

Anthony looked up and down the lean—to the point of thin—body next to his and had to admit the truth of Stash's statement.

"Okay, I guess I can do that." Anthony chuckled, suddenly feeling as if a heavy weight had been lifted off his shoulders. The more he got to know Stash, the more he had come to realize that Stash was the one who he could talk to or just be with.

"I want green peppers, cheese, and ham in it." Stash placed his hand over his chest and closed his eyes. "Oh, my God, I'm drooling just thinking about it."

"How about you make that tea we had over at Howell's place—the one with the berries in it?"

"I can do that."

Stash pressed close enough against Anthony that their thighs touched. The position made the walk back to the house more difficult, but Anthony didn't mind. This was a moment he would cherish forever in his memories, time-stamped in his heart as the minute he realized he had fallen in love.

CHAPTER TWENTY-TWO

Anthony studied the latest reports from his head office. Not a single stock had been illegally sold since the emergency meeting two weeks before. Schoffield had surrendered all his shares, but not until after filing a retaliatory lawsuit against Eisemann Industries.

The week before, Max had called to let him know he had taken the lead for their defense. Anthony wasn't worried and didn't doubt Max's capabilities. What concerned him was the time involved. Legal battles like these could stretch from weeks to years before everything was settled. And Schoffield would fight every step of the way. He was not one who would take his humiliation sitting down. But the law was on the company's side, and the internal bylaws were very clear on how shares were to be dispensed. Knowing that should have satisfied him, but somehow, he had a feeling this wasn't the end of it.

Anthony grimaced. He hated complications. They were too distracting and kept him preoccupied. A beeping sound indicating an incoming call made him check his phone.

"It's mine," Stash said, waving his phone in front of him. "It's Dad."

Anthony gestured to ask if he should go out, but Stash shook his head. When Stash started talking, Anthony went back to studying the figures on his excel spreadsheet, pushing Stash's voice to the back corner of his mind. He found he enjoyed listening to Stash's voice, but quickly changed his mind when the man started yelling in falsetto. It was so loud that

Anthony literally jumped in his seat and gape at Stash.

"What do you mean, get out of the room? Why the sudden secrecy?" Stash began to breathe rapidly.

Concerned, Anthony set aside the files and went over to where Stash was sitting.

"Hey, what's going on?" Anthony whispered.

Stash took away the phone from his ear and pressed the mute icon. "Dad wants to talk to you. In private."

"Did he say what it was about?" Anthony asked, folding his arms across his chest.

"No. I'm pissed." Stash stabbed at the phone with a long fingernail. "He's keeping secrets from me."

Anthony let out an exasperated sigh and gestured for the phone. He had a feeling his quiet time with Stash was coming to an end. After spending three weeks getting to know each other, he wasn't looking forward to entertaining people, be they family or friends. Stash tightened his lips and placed the phone on his hand. Anthony took it in silence, and when Stash made a move to step away, reached for his wrist.

"Stay with me." He gave Stash a wink.

Anthony couldn't help feeling amused when Stash settled by his side and pouted. Taking a deep breath, he pushed the mute icon.

"Adrien, it's Anthony. Stash said you wanted to speak with me."

"Tell my son to leave the room. I need to talk to you in private," Adrien replied in a gruff voice.

Anthony thought over the request and decided he was more than curious about what the older Burcell wanted to speak with him about.

"All right, I'll let him know. Give me a few minutes so I can transfer your call to my phone."

"No, that won't do. Are you in Paul's house?"

At the abrupt tone, Anthony's curiosity turned to caution.

"No, I'm in Limoges."

"Why aren't you at Paul's place?" Adrien barked.

"It's a long story, but Stash felt it safer to be here. We've been here since we got back from New York."

"I see," Adrien drawled. "You're telling me that you and Stash have been staying in his house over the past month?"

Anthony tensed at the suspicious tone in the older Burcell's voice.

"Yes."

"Put down the phone," Adrien ordered. "I'm calling the phone in the study in about five minutes. Get Stash out of the room."

The call abruptly ended, leaving Anthony to stare at the phone in confusion. The conversation left him feeling like a schoolboy who had been caught with his hand in the cookie jar.

"What did he say?" Stash asked.

"It was kind of strange. He said that he has to speak to me in private, and to tell you that he'll be calling in five minutes."

"Oh, well now, I guess he's calling here then." Stash huffed. "Why do friends and relatives insist on inserting themselves into our business? We're mature adults here. Plus, I'm older than you by two months." Stash twisted his lips. "Come, I'll show you how to answer a video call."

Stash swiped at the surface, and a control panel appeared. Anthony was familiar with the app, but it took him a few trials to learn the commands. He usually had an assistant who took care of such things.

"Five minutes is almost over, and if I know my father, he will call any second. I'll leave you to it." Stash headed to the door and opened it just as a loud beeping sound echoed inside the office. He smirked and closed the door behind him.

Anthony sat on the chair and touched the controls Stash had showed him earlier. As soon as he did, a monitor rose from the opposite edge of the desk, and he was face to face with Adrien Burcell.

"Hello, Anthony. It's good to see your face," Adrien said before the monitor had stopped its ascent.

"Good morning, Adrien. You wanted to talk with me."

"I'm proposing a merger," Adrien said in a brusque tone. "Between Burcell and Eisemann Industries."

Momentarily struck speechless, Anthony stared, wondering if he'd missed out on a joke. When Adrien's serious demeanor didn't change, he slumped back into his chair.

"This is shocking, Adrien. Why the sudden offer? What's going on?" Anthony had read the financial reports on the Burcell Group. It was in the black and had reported an increase in revenues and stock values. Clearly, there was something he had missed.

"I want to begin the process of merging my company with yours. Bring it under one umbrella."

"Are you in trouble? Do you need money?" Anthony grew even more puzzled. What could the old man have done to get his company in the red after reporting a sixty-billion-dollar revenue for the year alone?

"No, the company's in a good position right now, thanks to Stash and his modern ideas." Adrien waved a dismissive hand in front of him.

"Then why?"

"Because of Stash," Adrien said. He cleared his throat and bowed his head as though in shame or embarrassment.

Anthony didn't know why, but his worry kicked up a notch.

"Adrien, what are you saying? Talk to me, because frankly, I'm confused."

"Let me ask you a question, Anthony. Just answer me truthfully, that's all I'm asking for."

"What is it?"

"When you first saw Stash, what did you think about him?"

Anthony deadpanned his expression. He had absolutely no intention of telling Stash's father that he lusted after his son at first sight and obsessed over his flawless skin. Or that they were basically living together for over a month and having sex on more than a regular basis. Sometimes twice in one afternoon.

"Uhm, in what sense, exactly?" Anthony said carefully.

"His sexuality," Adrien said, raising his voice. "What was he wearing when you first saw him?"

Oh, no, they were not going there. Anthony balled his hands into fists and rubbed his knuckles over his thighs. He hoped Adrien wouldn't notice his discomfort, but he doubted it. The man didn't miss anything.

Flashes of a red wig and a delicious derriere came to mind, and he was suddenly sweating under his sweater. He forced the vision aside and maintained his professional manner.

"I have no comment on that matter, Adrien. What I've learned since then is that he's a great guy, intelligent, and an astute businessman." He gave himself a mental pat on the back.

"All right, I'll give you that. But let's be honest with each other. What do you think the board members or stockholders will think about him? I've helped keep his privacy to almost a lockdown, and any pictures or articles written about him are killed instantly. We both know how bigoted some of our stockholders are. Do you honestly think they would give Stash the chance to take the reins of my company?"

"I admit that your fears are not unfounded." Anthony cautiously chose his words. "However, that's what CEOs are for. He can designate operation without having to show his face. We personally know two men in our circles who are eccentric that way. Stash could always plead eccentricity if he wanted to, but I highly doubt he would."

"Yes, I agree. But does that give him the stability of say, what you or Howell enjoy? Will they allow him to lead them, or will they make him a puppet and possibly vote him out of the company my grandfather built?"

"I may be friends with Howell, but we're not that close. However, I just learned you and he are related in some way. But that's beside the point. Why are you telling me this, Adrien? It's now your turn to tell me the truth."

"I need to settle my affairs before I go, Anthony."

Anthony slowly straightened and studied Adrien's face in the monitor. The man was in his sixties, and other than the heavy bags under his eyes, appeared to be in good health. Then again, there were many illnesses categorized as silent killers because they typically didn't present any symptoms until after it had done significant damage to the body.

"What's wrong with you?"

"Stage four, pancreatic cancer. I have four, six months, tops."

"Dear God, I'm so sorry, Adrien. Clearly, Stash doesn't know, for he never once mentioned you were ill." Anthony thought about how Stash would react should he find out that Anthony heard before he did. He obviously had no idea what was going on and would be more than a little upset if Anthony kept the information from him. He closed his eyes and pressed the heels of his hands on them. Things were getting complicated.

"Meggie called me last night. It was quite an interesting conversation we had," Adrien continued.

"What did she tell you?" Anthony said, dropping his hands to the table. His eyes burned after the release of pressure, but it helped him keep control of his emotions as worry over how Stash was going react to this news ate him up inside.

"That you and Stash have hooked up."

Anthony let out a long breath and gritted his teeth. "Is that why you came up with this merger proposal of yours?" Whatever empathy he had for Adrien disappeared, and all he wanted to do was end the dialogue and leave the room. The conversation had gotten way out of hand.

"You'd be surprised, but no. I had been thinking about this for some time. Your father and I even talked about it once. Get you two married when you both came of age. We dropped the idea when we thought it would be impossible after we found out Stash was a boy. But then I talked to Meggie last night."

"I see."

"No, you don't. I've upset you, so I know. Look, Eisemann. I've watched my child bullied as he grew up. It didn't help that the doctors didn't know what he was. That was a whole other confusion I never want to wish on any parent or child. Stash's mother left us as soon as she learned of his condition when he was just six days old. She didn't give a damn and called him a *thing*. Left me to deal with everything. I have made it my life's work to protect Stash. All I'm doing now is to make sure he will continue to enjoy that protection once I am gone. Now, I need to know. What is it to be? Do we have a merger or not?"

"I'm sorry, Adrien, but I can't agree to your proposal," Anthony said. He felt sick to his stomach that a father would go to the extent that Adrien Burcell had, but a merger was not the answer.

"Why not? And don't give me excuses, boy."

"Why are you selling out on Stash? That's what I'd like to know."

"I am not selling out on him. I'm trying to protect him."

"You can do that without a merger. If you go that route, he'll think you don't trust him or something much worse."

"I know you've wanted Burcell Group for a long time,

Eisemann. Hell, your father was my friend, and I didn't hand it over to him."

"So why hand it to me now? If you insist on this merger, Stash will be on the losing end, and I can't . . . I *can not*, and will never hurt Stash that way."

"You're only hooking up with him because you can take advantage of my boy. Well, you can stop wasting your time. I'll give you the company, just leave my boy alone."

"I'm sorry, Adrien, but I can't do that."

"Bah, don't tell me you're in love with him."

"I am."

"Then you're stupid, boy." Adrien laughed contemptuously.

"I am not."

"What will it take for you to leave my son alone, Eisemann? Name your price."

"Stash is an adult, Adrien, so nothing you say counts for much, especially as Stash can stand on his own without your company to back him up. If you sell your company to the highest bidder, all you'll end up doing is to hurt Stash. If you care about your son, then you won't do that. As for buying me out, go ahead and try. I don't think you can afford me."

"You impudent young man," Adrien grumbled.

To Anthony's surprise, Adrien shook his finger at him, and his shoulders began to shake with laughter.

"What's so funny, Adrien?"

"You really think you love my boy, Eisemann?"

"I know I do."

"Then, let me ask you another thing."

Anthony threw up his hands. "Go ahead, what do I have to lose at this point."

"You're straight."

Anthony chuckled and shook his head. "We're not going there, Adrien. I don't care if you're Stash's father or a member of my board. You don't talk to me about my sexuality."

"My son's gay. It took me a long time to get used to seeing him as a boy, but then he was also gay. But he's my son, and I accept him for who and what he is. But you? You concern me. Far as I know, you've only dated women. When did you become gay?"

"Look, Adrien. I don't really want to be rude about this whole issue of yours about my being gay or not. Frankly, I don't care if you believe me or if you think I'm a straight male or maybe bi-curious, there's nothing I can do about it. I won't waste my time trying to convince you."

"Why date Stash? Explain yourself," Adrien said, gesticulating his impatience.

"It's true I'm attracted to women, but I've also been attracted to androgynous men. But I never met anyone, male or female, I wanted to have a relationship with. Until Stash. He just has everything I wanted and needed."

Adrien grumbled. "Did you ever think about how your actions would affect your company? If people find out you're gay, they may boycott your products. How do you intend to explain it to your stockholders?"

"At first, I hesitated to pursue it," Anthony said, giving his reluctant assent with a curt nod. "I thought about what people would think, but that didn't last long. I just went for it. I don't intend to let everyone in the world know about my private affairs. Should news of our relationship get out, I'll get PR to handle it. That's what I hired them for. Or I can keep all private affairs out of the media. I think that's simpler and more effective. My personal life is not owned or controlled by my companies."

"I see you've actually thought about this." Adrien narrowed his gaze at Anthony through the screen.

"Look, Adrien. I fell in love with Stash, and it's the best feeling in the world. I decided long ago that if I wanted to live my life happily, I cannot let others ruin it for me. I would advise you to get out of my way."

"Are you going for it? Like what Paul did?"

"Get married, you mean?"

Adrien nodded slowly with a small smile. "And we're back to the subject of a merger."

Anthony let out a derisive laugh and rested his chin on his steepled fingers. "You sly old man."

"Thank you."

"Oh, no, don't get me wrong, Adrien. I'm still saying no to the merger. I think Stash is a more than capable of handling Burcell Group on his own. Have faith in him. He may just surprise you."

Chapter Twenty-three

Stash hummed under his breath as he composed one of his daily updates on social media. Almost a month had passed since he'd approved the samples sent to him by the packaging company in Italy, and two weeks since he'd finalized the finished product.

He and Anthony had gotten to know each other better over the past three weeks, and it was one of the happier times of his life. They had a lot in common, one of which was their hatred of the dark. Another was their love for dessert.

In their time together, they'd hardly been apart except for the previous week. Stash had driven to Paris for a meeting with his marketing and finance teams. Although he'd hoped to return on the same day, unpredicted heavy rains prevented his trip back. Anthony, of course, had taken the opportunity to teach him a thing or two about online sex. That experience had been an unexpected pleasure. He'd been welcomed back to Limoges by an overly excited Flossy and a demanding Anthony. Needless to say, Stash felt his life was set on a more positive course, and he couldn't be happier.

Done with his post, he hesitated for a second before pushing the post icon. The release date was imminent, but he still hadn't revealed it yet. Everything depended on the post he had just uploaded and the response of his fans. If he didn't hit the one million likes within the next half hour, he would have to rethink his marketing strategy and probably push back the release date. Now that the teaser was out there, all he could do was wait. And if there was one thing Stash hated the most, it was waiting.

Speaking of which, Stash glanced at the bedroom door. It had been about an hour since he'd left Anthony to talk to Adrien, and he still hadn't come out. Stash wasn't anxious, though. His father had a habit of inserting himself into Stash's life, whether he was welcome to or not. Stash understood his father's concerns, especially as he'd depended on his father's approval and protection for much of his life. But what did he want to talk to Anthony about that was so secret that Stash had been told to get out of the room?

He was tempted to eavesdrop, but that would be just rude, and he didn't want to get chastised by either Adrien or Anthony. He sighed. Most likely they were talking company business, which was none of Stash's business. Feeling restless, he picked up his phone to call the one person he knew he could talk to. Meggie picked up after the third ring.

"Yello," Meggie said.

"Girl, what took you so long?" That wasn't the only question he wanted to ask, but then he remembered Meggie might be working, and Christian was most likely listening in.

"I'm busy," Meggie said.

"What are you working on?"

"Well, let's see, your dad's talking to your boyfriend, and he asked you to get out. Of course, I wanted to know what was so secret so I could tell you."

Stash sat up in bed. "You're not listening in, are you?"

"I just told you I was."

"Oh, you dirty, dirty girl. So, what're they talking about?"

"Your dad's up to his old jokes and just told Anthony he's got pancreatic cancer."

"He did what?" Stash jumped to his feet. "That bastard."

He ended the call and hurriedly put on his slippers. Within seconds he was out the door and running down the hall. He skidded to a stop when he looked out the window and saw two black SUVs in the distance.

"Who the hell?" Stash turned and ran down the stairs to the security office. Two men who ran the monitors stood up when he entered, but he didn't give them time to speak.

"Find out who those vehicles belong to."

"We've already dispatched four men to meet them, Mr. Stash. We've also sent word to Christian and Meggie."

"Don't let anyone inside the house until they find out who those people are," Stash commanded, his gaze glued to the monitor.

The cars slowed down, and he watched as four guards walk into the scene. In perfect synchrony, the doors of the first vehicle opened. When Stash saw the two men who'd gotten out, he closed his eyes and muttered several expletives.

"Tell security to let them in." Stash headed out of the room, calling over his shoulder, "And call housekeeping. We need more rooms opened up."

He strode to the front door and flung them wide open. He crossed his arms in front of him and glared at the guests.

"I would welcome you with open arms but seeing as you never bothered to call before coming for a visit, maybe I should just let you stand there under the sun," Stash said.

"I didn't raise you to be impolite, Stash Burcell," a woman's voice said from the other side of the car.

Stash's eyes bulged as the voice registered. "Aunt Irene? What are you doing here?" He turned to Paul Howell and his husband and pointed at them. "Why didn't you say something? You don't keep Aunt Irene under the sun. She might get a heat stroke."

"I remember quite clearly how you wanted us to suffer," Paul said, adding a brilliant grin. "How are you Stash? I hope everything's all right with you?"

"A little sun would do me some good, Stash. Vitamin D is an absolute must for people my age," Irene said as she approached slowly, leaning heavily on her cane.

Stash rolled his eyes and gestured for Paul to come nearer. "Help get Aunt Irene inside, will you?"

"Why don't you come out and help her yourself?" Paul quipped, but he was already holding Irene's elbow and leading her toward the house.

Irene glared up at Paul and pulled her arm away. "I'm not that old, young man."

"I don't want to ruin my bedroom slippers, and I'm sure you remember how independent she is," Stash said, flinging his arms open. "Welcome, Aunt Irene."

"Sorry, I completely forgot." Paul threw his arms up and shook his head.

"Hello, my darling." Irene smiled warmly and accepted Stash's hug. "You look beautiful, as always."

"Thank you. I didn't know I needed to hear that. Come on in. What brings you to Limoges?"

"You're still a brat, I see," Paul's husband said.

Stash rolled his eyes. "Hello to you too, Arjan. I see Paul's keeping you fit." He grinned at the obnoxiously handsome man Paul had married. "How do you keep so buff? What have you been eating? Steroids and protein shakes?"

"You know I only eat plant-based food, Stash," Arjan said.

The smile Arjan gave him was warm and loving, and he couldn't help feeling jealous. Seeing Arjan was a balm to his thirst for handsome men whose physical attributes he could never dream of attaining.

"I tried that for a while, but it didn't work out," Stash said with a twist to his mouth.

"Why didn't it?" Arjan asked.

"They were so boring. Plus, I love my chocolate mousse too much to completely erase it from my diet. Chocolate's plant-based, right? I'm quite sure it is."

"Right, I remember your addiction to that dessert," Paul

interjected, chuckling at the ridiculous exchange. "Do you have any left in that enormous kitchen of yours?"

Stash laughed. "Of course I do. Come on, let's get inside. When did you land in France?"

"Yesterday," Paul said. "We stayed over at Joel's house. He told us you were hitching up with Eisemann."

"Ugh, now you're all just being rude. Why are you guys always inserting yourselves into my love life? Keep it up, and I won't give you mousse."

"Oh, no, he's threatening us with prohibition," Arjan said. "That means he's serious."

"I am serious. Look, guys, if you came here to snoop around, you can just do an about-face and leave now."

"Stacia?"

Stash closed his eyes and took a deep breath before turning to face Irene.

"Yes, Aunt Irene?"

"Come with me to the study so we can talk."

"We can't, Anthony's there. He's talking to Dad."

Irene's brows lifted. It was a feat, considering how frozen her forehead was from the many Botox injections she had on a regular basis.

"And you left him alone to speak to your father? And here I thought you had more sense than Paul." Irene narrowed her eyes and turned to Paul. "Come, I don't trust Adrien with Anthony. If this were company business, I wouldn't be at all concerned, but he's sent us here to investigate Stash's relationship with Eisemann."

"Ah, damn, Uncle Adrien," Paul said to no one in particular. "Why do you have to complicate things?"

"Wait. Dad was the one who told you to come here?" Stash looked from Irene to Paul to Arjan and back to Irene. "What the hell's he been saying that you three decided to actually do what he said?"

"That's what I'm trying to figure out," Irene said. "If it's just about your love life, I completely understand and support his need to find out everything he can. But he's talking to Eisemann in private."

"Ugh, Dad," Stash grumbled his exasperation, stomped his slippered foot, and ran toward the study.

"Stash, slow down," Paul called out. "You're going to fall."

"He's talking to Ace. Alone. How could I have been so stupid as to trust that old fart," Stash yelled over his shoulder.

"Don't call your father an old fart. That's impolite," Irene said. For an old woman walking with a cane, she sure was agile.

Stash stopped running and turned to face Irene. "You call him an old fart all the time."

Irene raised her brows even higher. Another considerable feat in Stash's opinion. "I can call him whatever I want because I'm older than he is."

"Seriously? We're arguing about what names to call Adrien?" Paul said, finally catching up to them.

"Yes," Stash and Irene said simultaneously.

Stash signaled to the man standing guard at the door when he was a few feet away. The man hurriedly opened the doors just in time for Stash to slide through. Thank God for marble floors and cloth slippers.

"What the hell have you been saying to Anthony, Dad?" Stash demanded, striding over to the desk where he found a wide-eyed Anthony staring at him. "What did he say? Spill it, Ace. I'm not in the mood."

"I told him I wanted a merger," Adrien said.

At the same time, Anthony said, "Your father has pancreatic cancer and has four months to live."

Stash's jaw dropped. He stared at Anthony and blinked. Slowly, he turned to his father's image on the monitor and frowned at him angrily.

"For heaven's sake, Adrien. Haven't you learned your lesson yet? You're still using that sick excuse to get your own way?" Irene said as she entered the library.

"Wait, what do you mean? Wait, wait. Who are you?" Anthony asked, looking at Irene.

"Ace, this is my Aunt Irene. Irene, Anthony Eisemann," Stash said, not taking his glare off his father. He was still too mad, and his father looked positively smug with pride at his trickery.

"Oh, hello," Anthony almost stammered. "Can you please repeat what you said about a sick joke?"

"He told you he had cancer, four months to live?" Irene asked.

"Uh, yes, he did. Are you saying that he's not actually sick?"

Irene stepped in beside Stash and turned an evil eye on Adrien.

To his credit, Adrien's self-confidence crumbled, and he began to stutter out excuses. "Irene, I was just—"

Irene put up a hand to silence him. "You sick old fart. You interfering, old fucking fart!"

"Oh shit, she dropped the F word," Arjan said from behind Stash. "Let's get everybody out. Stash, snap out of it."

Sudden comprehension of what was about to go down between his father and aunt shook Stash out of his temporary paralysis.

"Oh, shit, Ace. Come on." Stash gestured with his hand. "Get out of the room. Now."

"What?"

"Oh, for heaven's sake. It's going to be Armageddon in here. Get out if you want to live."

Anthony ignored Stash. Instead, he stepped up beside Irene, leaned his hands on the table, and peered at Adrien's image in the monitor. "Were you trying to play me, Burcell?"

Anthony spoke softly, but Stash heard him. Apparently, so did Adrien, who closed his mouth, leaned back into the chair he was sitting on, and crossed his arms.

Stash's eyes widened. Things were going downhill and fast.

"Uh, Ace, come with me, please. Let's leave Aunt Irene to deal with Dad," Stash pleaded, watching Anthony's face turn dark.

Anthony's lips tightened to a thin line, but he turned his head and gave Stash a reassuring smile.

Stash was not convinced.

"Stash, please exit the room. I have a lot to say to your father, and I won't be able to do that successfully if you're here."

"Stash, do what Eisemann says," Irene said. She placed her purse on the desk and pointed at a chair. "Before you go, move that so I can see your father's face. This is going to be a long conversation."

Stash went over to the chair, picked it up, and placed it at an angle beside the one Anthony had been sitting on. He avoided looking at the screen but turned a pleading gaze at Anthony.

Anthony smiled and squeezed his shoulder. "It's going to be all right. Don't let anyone disturb us in here, okay?"

Stash sighed and nodded. There was really nothing he could do. Call him a coward, and he would admit to it. If there was one thing he'd learned as Adrien's son, it was to stay out of the way when the big wigs got into combative mode. He was quite sure a battle was about to commence, and he didn't want to be caught in the crossfire. Irene was a fighter, but then so was his dad, and he'd witnessed their fights in the past. It never was pretty. Add in the element of Anthony, and he knew all hell would break loose.

"You want to play, Adrien? Let's play," Anthony drawled out. Stash's eyes widened at the challenge, quickly hurrying out of the room. He came face to face with Paul and Arjan.

"You left Anthony in there?" Paul asked in disbelief. "You actually left your boyfriend in there with them."

"Well, he's a grown man, a CEO. And honestly, I couldn't wait to get out of there, but he was dragging his heals."

"He told you to get out, didn't he?" Arjan smirked. "Oh, to be a fly on that wall."

"That's different. Since when have you ever wanted to be in the middle of a battleground?" Stash poked Arjan on his incredibly muscled bicep.

Arjan flinched and took a step back, rubbing on the spot. "Hey, that hurts, and I've been married to Paul for several years now."

Paul frowned at Arjan. "What does that even mean?"

"He means that he's learned to accept that in our world, there are things talked about and done that a regular person will never get to witness in their lifetime." Stash crossed his arms in front of him, wondering how two men, whose combined IQ score probably reached over four hundred, could be so silly.

"Oh, wow, that's really entitled coming from you, Arjan," Meggie said, coming in from behind them.

Stash looked over his shoulder and frowned. "Why are you here?"

"The guys heard *battleground* and *Armageddon.* You can guess the rest." Meggie smirked.

"It's not funny, Megs." Paul greeted Meggie with a smile. "How are you, Megs?"

"I told you not to call me that name," Meggie said, stomping her foot.

"Oho, there's the little girl I missed," Paul said, pointing at Meggie's errant foot.

"Oh, how I hate you, Paul Howell," Meggie glared.

Paul sighed and bowed his head dramatically. "Then I

guess you don't get to see what I brought you."

Meggie froze. "You got me a surprise?"

"I brought it with me, but I don't think you'll ever get to see it," Paul said with a forlorn expression.

"But why?" Meggie whined and stomped her foot again.

Stash bit the inside of his cheek. Meggie actually whined.

"You said you hated me." Paul pouted, but there was a twinkle in his eyes.

"I hate you, Paul Howell," Meggie claimed again just before she started chasing Paul up and down the corridor.

"She's going to like her present," Arjan said as he walked up to Stash.

"What is it?"

"It's the latest CyNapse phone that Paul developed."

"Ahh," was all that Stash could say.

He watched the two *children* playing a while longer, an indulgent smile on his lips before turning back to Arjan.

"Come on, cook made chocolate raspberry mousse this morning. It should be nice and cold by now."

With a last glance at Meggie and Paul, who had run out into the garden playing tag, Stash hooked his arm through Arjan's and led him to the kitchen. The day had turned out to be an interesting one, but he couldn't wait to get his guests back in their cars and flying out of France.

CHAPTER TWENTY-FOUR

Anthony stretched his arms up to the ceiling and let out a tired, long breath. Two hours. That was how long he had already been battling it out with Adrien Burcell. Now he prepared for round two. He didn't appreciate being played by anyone, even if it happened to be Stash's parent.

Irene Wattenberg sat by his side through the whole meeting. She occasionally passed him notes about how he should deal with Adrien. Most of the time, Anthony ignored the personal details she'd written, but once or twice, he made use of her information.

First, Adrien was disgustingly healthy for his young age of sixty. Second, Adrien had no say whatsoever with regards to a merger. That piece of information had been what surprised Anthony the most. Irene's note was lengthy but extremely informative.

Stash started with thirty-two percent of the overall shares, which he received when he was born. Add in those he'd inherited from his grandfather, Henri, after he turned thirty, he owns a total number of fifty-three percent of the Burcell Group. Adrien's father was a spiteful old man. Everyone hated him. He did it to make a point after Adrien married Stash's mother. Just before he died, Henri turned over all his shares to Stash when he was only twenty. Adrien owns forty-three percent, and the rest belongs to company shareholders.

It took a moment to absorb the details, but when Adrien started insisting on the merger again, Anthony finally found his voice to put a stop to the man's nonsense.

"The merger is non-negotiable, Adrien. Stash will take the helm of Burcell Group when the time comes, and people will accept his control. I'll back him up when or if he needs it, so please stop with the ridiculous demands about a merger."

Adrien looked as if he was about to have a fit. But then he started laughing so hard he had a coughing fit.

"Well, well, my boy. Bravo," Adrien said with glee. He clapped his hands and stood up.

Anthony narrowed his eyes when he saw just how fit the man was . . . and steady on his feet. Adrien bent and put his face so close to the camera that Anthony thought his eyes would cross.

"You've passed the test, my boy. You'll do. Irene, you may inform Stash that he has my approval on Eisemann. Carry on." Adrien promptly ended the video call.

"Incredible," Anthony muttered. He could only shake his head in disbelief.

"He's a lunatic," Irene said beside him, sounding unimpressed.

Anthony leaned back and rested his head on the back of the chair. He felt a little light-headed, probably from holding his breath for most of the two hours conversation. He shook his head again.

"I can't believe he tried to convince me he was dying." He was still at a loss for words. Who would have thought that Adrien Burcell would stoop so low, go to such levels just so he could get the information he needed?

Irene stood up and walked behind him. "Adrien's a tiresome fellow, but he's devoted to his son and would move heaven and earth to protect him. I guess you could say he's driven to these antics because of that. He went through a lot raising Stash." She stopped in front of a painting and examined it. "I guess it's his way of trying to discover if his son had made another mistake or not."

Words failed, so Anthony waited for what else Irene had to say. At his prolonged silence, Irene looked over her shoulder and stared at him.

"He has, you know—introduced men to us who only ended up lusting after his money." She shrugged and picked up her purse. "At the risk of parroting Adrien, I guess you'll do, Eisemann. You certainly made the man laugh. He's a batty old fart, but he's genuine, and you can trust him when it comes to family and the business. Come, let's get out of here." She wrinkled her nose and looked around the room. "I should remind the housekeeper to air this room out."

Anthony didn't move from his position. He was simply too drained. "I'm worth a hundred times more than the entire Burcell Group, and you think I'm after his money? To set the record straight, I'm not."

Irene gestured with her hand. "Did I ask?"

"No, but Burcell certainly implied it, and come on, you can't deny you thought the same thing."

"For your information, young man, Stash is as good as a son to me. I couldn't have children of my own, and after his mother left him, I took on the task to raise him properly, as a Burcell should. It was only right, and I wanted a child. You can't fault me for doubting your intentions. And to quote you, come on. Don't deny you were straight until you met Stash. How was I supposed to think?"

Anthony grunted. "I have no comment on that."

"Ha!" Irene started to laugh, then her expression turned grave. "I don't believe you can switch on sexuality like one would a lightbulb. Arjan taught me a lot of things, even in my old age. You should also know something else about Stash. I doubt he's been able to talk about it, but if you're as serious as you claimed to be earlier, then I think I am the right person to tell you."

"What is it?" What more was there to learn?

"You probably wondered about the tight security," Irene said.

She walked up so close to Anthony's chair that he had no choice but to crane his neck so he could look her in the eyes.

Anthony nodded. "I did ask, and he said something along the lines of the makeup world being full of black-market crimes. That he just wants to make sure he and his products are safe."

Irene's brows raised a notch. "And you believed him?"

"I didn't think much of it, though I won't deny I told him it was a little overkill. I'm not mad at it." Anthony shrugged.

"It's not because of the makeup." Irene's mouth tightened. "You stayed at Joel Byrd's house. In Paris."

"Yes, we did. Eisemann Industries bought out his company, but he's still with us as a creative director. Why?"

"He and Stash were kidnapped when they were children. Stash—then Anastasia—was just twelve years old, and Joel was eleven. Another girl was kidnapped along with them. The FBI got involved, and with the help of Paul's father, were able to find them just in time. Before anything horrifying happened."

Anthony felt as if someone had punched him in the stomach as he gaped up at Irene. He slowly stood as he tried to absorb the enormity of what Irene had just revealed to him.

"He told me they went camping, and that Joel got beat out of his tent by the other boys. That Joel married the other girl."

"Yes, he married her, but not until after he followed Stash—Anastasia—around like a lovesick boy. Imagine his shock when Stash turned out to be just like him. A boy." Irene's mouth pursed. "Fortunately, he was very good about it. He accepted Stash for who he was, didn't ask questions. and for a long time was one of only three friends Stash had."

"Byrd, Meggie, and Miranda." Anthony nodded. It was

clear now what the relationship between the three actually was.

"They were inseparable for a while," Irene said.

Anthony frowned when something didn't add up. "But . . . I asked Meggie about Byrd. She didn't mention anything about a kidnapping."

"Meggie doesn't know. She was away at school when it happened. We instructed her parents and everybody else who was connected to the case, to never tell her what had occurred. Stash refuses to talk about the incident."

Anthony didn't know what to think. He had had a very long day and felt like his head would explode from everything he had to process.

"Does that change your mind about Stash?"

Anthony glared at the woman. "Of course not. It's got nothing to do with us. Let me correct that. It will affect how I understand Stash, but it's not going to change how I feel about him."

"You're probably thinking he's got a lot of baggage, and maybe want to rethink your relationship?"

"That's a far reach, if I may say so, Irene. But no. If one's to speak about baggage, I think Stash and I are about equal."

Anthony didn't want to linger over the topic, so he took one of her hands and hooked it into his arm. "Let's go and find us some of that mousse, shall we?"

"It's passed seven, dinner is overdue," Irene said.

"I'll hunt something down in the dining room," Anthony said as he led them out of the study.

Neither of them spoke as they walked the corridor from where they could hear laughter coming from downstairs. The sound was a welcome relief, erasing the ugliness in the study. Flossy barked in the distance and came running from the bedroom. Without hesitation, Anthony dropped Irene's hand and scooped up the dog into his arms when she reached him. He was fluffing her hair when Irene began to chuckle beside him.

"Now I know why Stash is so serious about you. Truth is, I think you fell for Flossy first."

"Nah, you're wrong." Anthony felt loads better now that he had the dog to absorb all the nastiness away. "It was Stash first, followed a close second by this little lady here."

"I'm curious, so you don't have to answer me if you don't want to. What was it that you saw in Stash that drew you to him? I know you've only ever dated women, so it must have been something profound."

At first, Anthony didn't want to give Irene more arsenal she could use in the future. After thinking it over, he decided that since he already considered Stash as family, he had to see Irene as family as well.

"It was over at Paul's place, in Saint Pierre. Stash was getting out of the pool, and I saw him from my window. At that time, he was wearing this red wig, and all I could think about was my life was going to be complicated."

"And has it? Become complicated?" Irene pressed.

Anthony smiled down at Flossy. "When my father was still alive, he told me that love can mean a lot of joy and happiness, but it can bring about complications that can cause us pain and anger."

"And which is Stash to you?"

"Stash isn't a complication."

"You really do love him, don't you?"

"Yes, you just don't know how much I've come to rely on him." Anthony looked up and met Irene's gaze.

"And he, you." Irene chuckled. "All right, my boy, you've convinced me."

"About what?"

"If you're this brave to take on Stash in your life, I've got your back." Irene began walking again.

"I don't know what to say," Anthony said.

"A thank you will suffice," Irene said, a mischievous gleam twinkling in her eye.

"Thank you," Anthony said. And he meant it.

If there was someone who could best all the bigots and naysayers out there in the world, it would be Irene Wattenberg. As for her weapon? Anthony had to laugh at the thought. People had no idea the type of sword Irene wielded. Her tongue was razor-sharp and would cut anyone to pieces with a few choice words. Her approval or lack thereof could make or break anyone who tried to enter their circles. That was the role of a society doyenne, and she was at the top of her game.

Anthony put Flossy down before continuing down the stairs to the first floor. They turned left to a flagstone hall and into a room Stash called the Grand Salon. It was a warm, relaxing room with polished oak floors and a large granite fireplace that someone had lit. Anthony spotted Stash immediately and greeted him with a smile. Stash jumped when Flossy bounded on to his lap.

"Good evening," Anthony said to the group.

Everyone turned and looked in his direction, then stood when Irene came up beside him. Anthony looked at the two men talking with Stash. He recognized Paul Howell but not the man standing next to him. Judging the way Paul was looking at the man and touching the inside of his thigh, Anthony suspected he was Paul's husband, Arjan. People who'd told him the man was a walking model were right, but he wasn't Anthony's taste. He preferred more feminine, androgynous men who looked like Stash Burcell.

The subject of his thoughts stood up and helped Irene into a chair before meeting his gaze. Stash seemed hesitant, but Anthony solved the problem and went to him. He could feel different sets of eyes watching him, probably wondering how he was going to behave. He ignored them. Aware of the many observers, he gave Stash a reassuring smile before dropping a kiss on his temple. He really wanted to kiss Stash on the mouth, but maybe that would be a little impolite. Anthony glanced at Irene and saw her approving nod.

"How did your talk go?" Stash asked, his gaze searching Anthony's face.

"It went well, actually. Irene helped a lot."

"I gave him notes on how to attack Adrien, but he only used two of them. I was quite impressed with your man, Stash. He didn't even flinch once," Irene said.

Stash licked his lips at the word *flinch*.

Anthony knew he associated it with violence and placed his hand on Stash's shoulder for reassurance.

"Come on, let sit down," Anthony murmured.

"Eisemann, do you know Paul and Arjan?" Irene asked when Anthony and Stash sat on the sofa.

Anthony leaned forward and held out his hand to shake Paul's. "Hello, Paul. It's good to see you again."

"Likewise, Anthony. Allow me to introduce you to my husband." Paul turned to look at the man beside him. "Arjan, meet Anthony Eisemann, Anthony, my husband, Arjan."

"Hello." Anthony shook Arjan's hand.

Anthony flung his arm around Stash's shoulder and pulled slightly so he could feel Stash flush against his side. He kept his expression flat, but Stash's presence was the real reason why he didn't feel nervous. Him, and Flossy, who decided to walk across Stash's lap and lie down on his. He saw Paul's eyes widen at the dog's actions before turning to Arjan and gave him a telling look.

"What happened in there?" Stash asked.

"Allow Anthony to rest his voice, Stash. It was an intense meeting when I was there, so I can only imagine what went on before that." Irene looked at the table. "Don't we have any tea? I'm thirsty."

"Oh, let me call on someone to bring the tea in, Aunt Irene," Arjan said.

To Anthony's surprise, Irene's expression softened when she looked at Arjan. There was love there, and probably another story. But Anthony didn't want to know, not that night. He was too exhausted.

While Arjan talked to housekeeping on the intercom, Irene narrated the conversation she and Anthony had with Adrien. While she was talking, Anthony could see the hurt and surprise flashing across Stash's face. He had been right about Stash and his feelings about people interfering with his life.

"I take it Adrien finally conceded?" Paul asked, sipping on his drink that he'd poured while Irene spoke.

"Well, he had to, in my opinion. Adrien can talk circles around a lot of people, but I think he finally met his match in Eisemann, here. I'm not in the least surprised — Marcus Eisemann was a rigid man, and I would expect he was a strict parent. I wouldn't be surprised if he trained his son himself. Am I right, Anthony?"

Anthony smiled. That was the first time Irene had called him by his name. "Dad wasn't as rigid as you thought him to be. You probably interacted with him in public or when he was working in his capacity as CEO of the company. In truth, he was very tolerant and found ways to protect his sons."

"Then where did you come from?" Irene asked in surprise.

Anthony had to laugh at her confusion but didn't know the right words to give her a proper answer.

Fortunately, Stash came to his rescue. "I think the person you're looking to blame is his nanny, Mrs. Louis."

"The nanny?" Irene's eyes widened. She appeared astounded by the revelation, but then she narrowed her eyes speculatively. "Arjan and Paul's son just turned two years old."

Anthony threw back his head, laughed out loud, only to

stop and throw a warning glare at Irene. "I'm sure Mrs. Louis would be glad to refer you to someone, but no, you can't hire her from under me, Irene. She's my nanny, and she promised she'll supervise my kids when I have them."

"What? You're talking children now? Have you discussed this with Stash?" Paul scoffed.

"Paul!" Arjan snapped. The look on his face said it all.

The sudden silence that descended over the room only enhanced the annoyance that Anthony had been trying to tame for over two hours. Beside him, Stash tensed.

"How dare you?" Stash said through gritted teeth. "You think you're the only one who's entitled to be happy? To have a family? That I, or Anthony, can't have what you're enjoying because I am what I am? A freak?"

Anthony turned his head and immediately swallowed back a curse. Stash was normally pale, but he was even paler now. The glare he directed at Paul was filled with anger, and judging from the tears welling in his eyes, disappointment. A quick glance at Stash's hands showed them balled into fists. Anthony winced and slowly removed his arm from Stash's shoulders and took hold of his hands. One by one, he unfurled each finger only to grimace at the sight of blood on his palms. Each had four crescent-shaped marks that quickly welled up with blood.

"Stash, don't move. I don't know how deep the cuts are. I'll go get something for your hands." Anthony stood up and headed to the kitchen. He thought there was a first aid kit in there.

Anthony hurried out of the salon. Behind him, there was only silence, but that didn't mean Stash wasn't giving Paul the tongue lashing he deserved. The whole day was unbelievable and a revelation that his relationship with Stash would be facing more complications, none of which came from either of them. Why did people always want to judge? To insert themselves into situations they should otherwise not even be involved in?

In the kitchen, he found the first aid kit in one of the overhead cabinets. He hurried back to the salon only to see that Stash was gone.

"Where's Stash?" Anthony asked everybody in the room in general.

"He went upstairs. Said he needed to take a bath," Paul replied, his face hidden in his hands.

Anthony was satisfied to see the regret but decided to glare at Paul anyway.

"Go ahead, Eisemann. Say it. I was stupid, inconsiderate, and an all-around ass."

"You are a fucked-up idiot who doesn't know how to keep his mouth shut and stay out of situations where you don't belong," Arjan said in a harsh tone.

Anthony looked at Paul's husband, and grudgingly, reassessed his first impression of the guy. The man was as handsome as Greek gods could be, and Anthony had thought he was just a face. Apparently not.

"Jan, don't," Paul whined through his hands.

"Don't you Jan me, Paul Howell." Arjan stood up and paced the floor. "I cannot believe you said that to Stash. To Anthony. Why? No, wait, don't answer that. Answer Stash's questions. Do you actually think you're the only one who deserves happiness as a gay man with a gay spouse? Be very careful with your answers, my man."

"Don't be angry at me, Jan," Paul pleaded.

"I am furious, not angry. Furious is a much higher bar than mere anger, here Howell. Now answer the questions."

"No. Both answers are no." Paul looked defeated.

"Then why did you say what you said?"

Anthony whistled softly. Apparently, Arjan was not someone Paul could easily manipulate. That was no arm candy husband he had there. Belatedly, he remembered it was Arjan's name on the patent that had launched an innovative design of one of Paul's products a few years back. It had catapulted CyNapse to the top of the technological world, a position they hadn't come down from since.

"I was just teasing," Paul said. "I know I made a mistake, okay?"

"It was a very bad and stinky joke," Arjan said, but his voice had softened. So had his expression, and Anthony took a step back when he saw it. Right there was what everyone had been talking about when they described the physical impact Arjan Howell had on mere mortals.

"Shut up, both of you." Irene cut in scathingly.

"Yes, Aunt Irene," Paul said.

"Yes. Thank you, Irene," Anthony said. He set the first aid kit on a small table beside the sofa and placed his hands on his hips. "I know where you're coming from, Paul, and you may believe me or not, but family treats family a little differently than social protocols dictate. So, I understand why you said what you said, and I'm a little flattered, to be honest."

"For God's sake, why are you even flattered?" Arjan was incredulous. "He insulted you. Insulted Stash."

Anthony had to smile at Arjan's legitimate concern. "I do feel flattered. Paul felt comfortable enough to tease me like he would members of his family. I'm interpreting that as he's accepted me."

Irene scoffed, gesturing with her hand. "Oh, for God's sake, not you, too."

Anthony glanced at her. "I'm not without my concerns, Irene. Don't take me wrong. I walked out of here knowing the issue was between cousins, between Stash and Paul. I was ready to sock him for upsetting Stash, but I heard what he said. So, that's that."

"Are you not at all upset?" Arjan asked, still looking

baffled.

"Of course I am. Any sane man would be," Anthony said, taking the seat he'd vacated earlier. In the background, he heard Flossy barking and looked up in the direction it was coming from.

"Stash took Flossy with him," Paul said.

Anthony nodded. "Anyway, I'm glad Stash went upstairs for a while. He definitely needed the space."

"You're talking as if you know him well," Irene said, giving Anthony a side-eye.

"I'm not pretending to know him as well as you do. That would just be me boasting. I do know him enough to recognize that he generally feels suffocated from all the security and concern regarding him but has come to accept the situation as part of the norm. After what you told me earlier, I understand why everyone around him acts the way they do." Anthony paused and frowned when Flossy's barking got louder.

"When his father was still alive, Adrien was not allowed to have an executive position in the company. But he had to make ends meet after Stash was born with all the medical bills he had to pay, plus the alimony, he needed money. So he set up a security agency with, of all people, his butler. Jeremy was an army veteran, a combat instructor, and together. The venture was a success," Irene said.

In the distance, Flossy's barking increased in volume.

Paul frowned. "What the hell is going on up there?"

"Flossy's probably heard something and is yapping. Shih Tzus are noisy little dogs." Irene waved a dismissive hand.

No. Something was wrong, Anthony could feel it. He slowly stood up, simultaneously speed dialing Christian, who answered on the first ring.

"Yes, sir?"

"Is everything all right? Flossy's barking, and she's

normally happy and quiet," Anthony said. The barking continued, louder and shriller. "Tell the men upstairs to go check our bedroom. Something is definitely wrong."

Anthony ran as fast as he could with smooth soles on highly buffed wooden floors. He muttered a curse when he slipped but quickly righted himself and continued to run. Behind him, he heard Paul call out his name, but he ignored him. The feeling of dread turned darker until he thought he was going to puke. His mind focused on one thing—Stash.

In the foyer, he saw guards on the second floor run in the direction of the King's Bedroom. A sound he had not expected to hear was that of a pained yelp followed by complete silence. His heart stopped, but it didn't stop him from running faster. He was soon ahead of the men, not caring that he tripped on a step and hit his knee.

He screamed Stash and Flossy's names. Behind him, he could hear more footsteps join his as he entered the bedroom. The door stood open, as though someone had come in and not bothered to close it. That was his first confirmation. Beyond the bed lay Flossy. That was the second confirmation. He knew the diva dog didn't consider the floor good enough and always insisted on sleeping on a pillow on the bed.

Anthony couldn't hear anything that would alarm him, so he went over to check if Flossy was still breathing. He breathed a sigh of relief when he felt her heartbeat and began to look around the room. Everything was where it should be. His gaze rested on the bathroom door, and he took off running toward it. When he turned the doorknob, it refused to give. He searched for something to open it when he saw Meggie and Christian run inside, followed by the other guards. Paul was there, too, but Anthony was too frantic to comment. He tried the door once more, but it remained locked. He grabbed the door jambs and began to kick at the handle.

Somewhere a voice kept yelling Stash's name, maybe it

was him, maybe it was the others—his only aim was to open the door. A final kick and the door swung open. A momentary pause as his mind refused to process the unfolding drama. Then something inside him snapped, and to his horror, he found himself reliving his nightmare, only this time, he was wide awake.

"Get away from him!"

Chapter Twenty-Five

Water lapped over Stash's eyes, entering through his mouth and nose. He shoved frantically, pushing hard against the person who had taken him by surprise and forced him under the water of the tub. He clawed his fingers and raked them down the evil, expressionless face. Blood poured from the wounds his nails created, down his own hands and forearms. It lent a pink hue to the water, but the face never once flinched, never changed its demeanor.

He fought with everything he had, trying to get his head above water as snippets of his past flashed through his mind.

He was confused and scared and had just told his father and Aunt Irene that his penis was growing.

"I decided I don't want to be called Anastasia anymore. Now that I'm a boy, it doesn't feel right." He'd been thinking about it a lot, so he was ready to finally speak his true name.

"What name do you want us to call you, sweetheart?" Irene asked.

"Stash. Just Stash."

"It's beautiful and unique, just like you are. From now on, you are Stash in my heart and mind." Irene smiled gently at him.

"Will I ever be happy?"

"Well, that's really up to you, Stash, whether or not you give yourself a happy ending."

His lungs screamed for air as he continued to struggle against his attacker. Terror filled him, bringing forth the nightmares of his youth. He regretted he'd not told Anthony the whole truth. Even after Anthony had opened up to him, he had still hesitated. He'd told Anthony that he'd gone camping, which was true, but he'd also been kidnapped. It wasn't because he was ashamed of what had happened, but he'd always kept things hidden from the judgment of others.

Anastasia was so excited. Her class planned a weekend field trip to one of the mountain camps that offered the program to private schools for highly privileged children. Adrien had given his consent, and she could barely contain her thrill at the thought of spending an entire weekend without the bodyguards or the servants, who always reported back to her father.

The day started early, with a bunch of kids anxiously waiting for the field trip to begin. For Anastasia and the rest of her classmates, it was their first time riding a school bus. Their homeroom teacher stood at the front, giving them a brief overview of her expectations. Miranda, Anastasia's best friend, sat beside her, and they chatted away. Neither of them listened to their teacher, too excited about the thought of a whole weekend away from home.

Suddenly, for no reason she could imagine, she blacked out.

The next thing Anastasia knew, she woke up in a dark room with Miranda sitting beside her, crying and afraid. She couldn't recall how they got to be there. All she knew was that she was petrified.

Anastasia screamed for help, but no one answered. Miranda had been too scared to move, much less scream, so Anastasia took it upon herself to do it for both of them. Hours passed until her throat became so raw that she could hardly make any sounds at all. Still, no one had come.

She didn't know how long she and Miranda waited in the dark, damp room, but at one point, the door opened, and someone was thrown inside. Before she could think of something to say, the door slammed shut. Then two became three.

The boy introduced himself as Joel Byrd. Anastasia recognized him from school but from a lower grade than hers. She did wonder how he came to be there when the field trip was only supposed to involve Anastasia's class, but she didn't ask.

Hours passed, and Miranda finally stopped crying. Anastasia could hear her soft breathing as she slept beside Joel. She was a bit jealous that Miranda could find solace in sleep while she could not.

Anastasia lost track of what day it was. Her mind started to go crazy, imagining all the horrible things that might happen to them in that dark room. But no one came. The only sign that they were not abandoned was the occasional tray of food slid through a small flap in the door.

Her fear grew by the minute, as well as her embarrassment at having to go potty in one corner of the room. The three of them soon learned not to complain about the smell, especially after they realized voicing their concerns meant getting no food or water for a long time. And hunger only accentuated the stench of human waste.

Anastasia was on the brink of believing she would never be rescued when suddenly, the door opened, and three figures they'd never seen before stepped inside. She, Miranda, and Joel didn't dare move or make a sound. They were too scared of what might happen. When the men picked them up and carried them outside, they still refused to make a sound.

Anastasia froze when she saw her father after what must have been days. Adrien looked tired, grim-faced, red-eyed, and like he'd aged ten years, but he quickly took her into his arms. He didn't comment on how dirty or smelly she was, he simply whispered a promise . . . a binding vow.

"Nothing, no one, will ever hurt you like this again. Ever. Not while I live."

Anastasia hugged her father like the lifeline he was, and for the first time since she'd been taken, she began to cry. She couldn't stop the tears from falling, not even when she was taken to the hospital, or when her father told her they were going home.

After being in the hospital for three weeks, Anastasia finally got to go home. Irene immediately took her into her arms, hugged her close to her chest, and told her how much she'd been missed. It was a balm to her soul.

Anastasia didn't talk about her ordeal to anyone. Not to her father, and not to the police. The psychiatrist assigned to her case advised giving Anastasia time to adjust, and she would talk. But she refused. After a week of silence, Adrien gave strict instructions that no one was to speak about the incident. Everyone, including Irene, had agreed. Anastasia regretted she couldn't talk to her sister-friend about her ordeal, but she reconsidered and thought it best that Meggie never knew about the horror she'd endured from being taken from everything familiar.

Stash's mind snapped back to the fact he was being drowned, and he was beginning to reach his limit. A renewed sense of survival made him refuse to accept what was happening, and with whatever strength he could muster, he began to fight harder. He kicked and clawed until his lungs began to feel as though they were filled with acid and ready to burst from the lack of oxygen. And then, by some miracle, a shadowy figure came out of nowhere. After a brief struggle of their own, the person was able to pull off the assailant. The hands that held him under the water were gone, and he breathed in more water with his relief he was going to be saved.

Weariness overcame him, and he began to sink. Down he went until his back touched the solid surface of the tub. His eyes were wide open, and above him, he could see a circle of light. He tried raised a hand to reach out for it, but he was too weary. Tried pushing up to the surface, but he failed. Exhaustion spread throughout his body, and he finally relented and relaxed into the warm water. Maybe closing his eyes would be the way to go.

Hard hands grabbed his arms and pulled him from the warm abyss, and suddenly, he was cold.

"Stash! Talk to me."

His face was slapped several times, but he didn't fight back. It was Anthony who'd come to save him. His Anthony.

Somehow, he'd known Anthony would be the one. He opened his mouth to respond, but nothing came out. Maybe, if he relaxed, he would finally be able to breathe. To sleep and forget about the nightmare.

The hard pounding in the middle of his back surprised him, shook the weariness from his limbs. He had to open his mouth because something inside him was fighting its way out as the hand continued to strike at his back. He could hear Anthony yelling his name, over and over again, begging him to answer. Like a breaking dam, water shot out of his mouth in what felt like buckets.

On and on, the water kept coming out from his mouth, until finally, he was dry-heaving and shivering. There were voices everywhere, some sobbing, some shouting, some calm and asking questions. But he ignored them all. All he cared about was that he was wrapped in Anthony's arms and beginning to feel warm again. He closed his eyes. Now was the time to sleep.

Dreaming of flying was a wonderful feeling. Stash had always loved flying—it was the landing that kept him on edge. But no matter how terrified he was, he knew he could always open his eyes and see Anthony there, gazing at him, smiling, and just being there for him.

He knew he was in a hospital, but he didn't want to talk to anyone, not the doctors, or the nurses, only Anthony. So before anyone could say anything to him, he would close his eyes and hug Anthony's arm close to his chest. He didn't care if it was against hospital regulations.

Time lost all meaning, but when the time finally became right, Stash opened his eyes. The nightmare hadn't returned, and he felt as though his mind had been cleared of all horror. Beside him, Anthony sat on a chair, reading a book, flipping a page with his right hand while his left arm was extended, holding onto Stash's.

"I want to go home," Stash whispered.

Anthony looked up, and their gazes met. For Stash, seeing those gray eyes was a token to life, but something was wrong with the picture. It took him a moment of silent study until he realized why Anthony looked different. He sat up and pointed an accusatory finger. That his nails were short didn't bother him as much as the fact that Anthony was wearing reading glasses.

"What's that, and since when?"

"Just a few days. I've not been sleeping well and was having blurred vision. I thought I was just tired. Turns out, I needed a prescription." Anthony's voice sounded flat, and his expression didn't look welcoming either.

"There's nothing else wrong with you, is there?" Stash used his elbows to push himself up further up the bed so he could take a closer look at Anthony. After a while, he decided that Anthony with reading glasses was even sexier. Happy at the thought, he nodded and lay back once more.

Not once did Anthony's gaze waver from his. Anthony closed the book he had been reading and placed it on a small table beside his chair.

"How are you feeling?"

"Bored," Stash said wryly. "And grimy. I want to take a shower."

Anthony nodded slowly. "I'll call the nurse."

He twisted to reach for a switch on a wall, but his fingers fell short of touching it when Stash pulled him back.

"Don't," Stash said. "I want to take a shower at home."

"Which home is that, Stash?" Anthony's gaze moved as though he was examining Stash's face.

Stash shrugged. "Where are we?"

"Still in France. Paris, as a matter of fact. The whole family's here, including your *healthy* father."

Stash rolled his eyes. Of course, they wouldn't miss out on his drama. "Where are they now?"

"They stepped out about an hour ago. We've been taking turns watching over you."

"Every time I woke up, I would see you, but I never saw any of them." He clearly remembered opening his eyes several times and seeing Anthony sitting on the same chair, reading a book.

"Rest assured, we were taking turns. Much as I love you, I still have a business to run, we all do, so I wasn't here the entire time."

"But I only saw you," Stash repeated. "And I love you, too."

Anthony didn't speak, and for a moment, Stash thought he was going to say something. Then, to his horror, tears began to fall down Anthony's cheeks. His shoulders began to shake, and his grip on Stash's hand tightened.

"Ace, why are you crying? Come to me, please, sweetie." Stash opened his arms.

Anthony bent and wrapped his arms around Stash. Anthony buried his head in the crook of Stash's neck and took turns breathing in his scent and kissing him there. They stayed like that for long minutes. Not even the crick in Stash's neck or the burning in his back made him want to shift from the uncomfortable angle he was presently in.

"I really thought I'd lost you," Anthony said in a muffled voice. "You swallowed so much water. You had no pulse. You weren't breathing."

"I'm okay now. I promise, I'm okay," Stash reassured. He closed his eyes and pulled Anthony closer. "How long have I been in here?"

"It'll be a month tomorrow."

"I'm so sorry, Ace." Stash couldn't believe all that time had passed, and he'd not even worried.

"Don't be. There's nothing to apologize for."

Anthony shifted and moved out of Stash's arms, but he only took off his jacket, flung it toward the chair, and lay down beside him. Anthony's body next to his was what he had been missing, so he moved until they were flush against each other and laid his head on Anthony's shoulder. He closed his eyes, just for a moment.

When he opened them again, he knew he'd lost time for it was dark outside the window. Anthony still lay beside him.

"Hey, I'm awake again."

Anthony nodded. "I took a nap with you. Did you hear the nurse come in?"

"No."

"She told me to get off, but I used my charm and persuaded her otherwise."

"I just bet you did." Stash chuckled. After a moment, he looked up and met Anthony's gaze. "What was wrong with me? I'm aware I wasn't in a coma, so why is everything a haze?"

"Initially, the doctors thought it best to put you into a medical coma. There was extensive damage to your lungs and organs because of the lack of oxygen. They were afraid you might have suffered brain damage, but their fears were unfounded. The only mystery was that you wouldn't wake up, not even after they'd weaned you off the medications."

"Are you saying they put me to sleep so I could recover?" Stash nodded. He'd read about the medical technique but never imagined he would actually have to go through it. "It must have worked, because I feel better."

"I'm glad you're better." Anthony dragged his hand down Stash's hair and then up again. The repetitive motions made Stash feel sleepy. He fought through the weariness that had come back, realizing he was still weak from the ordeal, but his determination to go back to Limoges didn't waver. Neither did his need to find out what had happened to his attacker.

"Did you get the man who tried to drown me?" Stash said.

Anthony stiffened, but Stash had to know. He had to know what had happened after his rescue.

"Yes, we got him. Plus, one other who disabled your systems."

"There were two of them?" Stash could only recall the one. The man's face flashed before his eyes, and he closed them, willing the image to go away.

"Yes," Anthony said.

There was something in Anthony's voice that pricked at Stash's curiosity. He opened his eyes and poked on Anthony's ribs.

"What aren't you telling me?"

When Anthony still didn't speak, Stash leaned up and peered directly into his eyes. "Who were they, Ace?"

"Lawrence was the one disabling sensors and cameras. That's why security didn't see anyone climb the walls or open the window to our bedroom."

"And the one who tried to drown me? Who was it?"

"It was Gregory."

Stash's mouth dropped open. He couldn't have heard right. "Gregory? What did I ever do to him? I never even met him before our scheduled meeting."

"Apparently, he had been using his position as my personal assistant to find you."

"That still does not explain what his motives were. Did the police ever find out why?"

"Do you know a woman called Melissa Morgan?"

Stash froze. He'd never thought to hear his kidnapper's name after more than fifteen years since she'd died in prison.

"Where did you hear that name from?" Even after all the years, the mere mention of his kidnapper's name caused a heavy sensation in his stomach. His heart began to race, and his vision began to blur.

"Gregory's last name is Morgan. He's Melissa's son."

Stash had heard enough. He felt the cold creep into his stomach, and he couldn't breathe. "Oh God. I'm going to be sick."

Anthony quickly moved out of the way, but Stash was already off the bed and running toward a door he assumed was the bathroom. He was right.

He ducked into the toilet bowl just in time for bile to flow up his throat and out of his mouth. His body began to shiver, and his legs jerked with every heave and cramp. Somewhere, a door slammed shut, and a hand began to rub the middle of his back. The sound of water was soon followed by the feel of a wet towel wiping off the sweat from his face. When there was nothing else to expel, he fell on his side, weakened from the ordeal.

"Come on, Stash, let's get you off the floor," Anthony said.

Stash looked up, expecting to see a look of disgust on Anthony's face. Instead, there was only concern. And were those tears on his cheeks? He held up his arms and was immediately taken into the soft embrace.

"I was so scared, Ace."

"It's all right, Stash. I'm here. Let it all out, I'll be right here."

As if a switch had been flipped, Stash's emotions flew free. He heard his voice yelling into Anthony's chest. Everything he'd bottled up since he'd been kidnapped came out in a torrent of speech that left him out of breath. Anthony's arms never weakened. His body, immovable. He became a lifeline to hold on to, one that would pull him out of the nightmare.

When the tears finally stopped and the words were done, Stash opened his eyes to see that Anthony was sitting on the floor with his back against the bathroom door jamb. His eyes looked puffy and red as if he'd been crying hard, but that didn't matter to Stash. What mattered was that he'd stayed and had kept his arms around Stash.

"Are you done crying?" Anthony asked.

Stash nodded and wiped at his face with his hands.

Anthony let Stash go before standing up. He took a towel hanging on a rack and wet it. He then knelt on the floor and began to wipe Stash's face clean. After a final swipe, he gently poked Stash's nose and followed it up with a kiss on the forehead.

"I think you're going to be all right now," Anthony said.

Stash held up a hand. "Can you help me up?"

Anthony did more than that. To Stash's amazement, Anthony lifted him into his arms and brought him back into the room, where he laid Stash on the bed.

"I must have lost a bit of weight," Stash commented. He looked at his wrists and grimaced at the thinness he saw there. Anthony took both of his hands.

"Don't mind them. It's only to be expected. You were asleep for a long time and surviving on liquids. Once you eat solids again, you'll gain all the weight back. Are you hungry?"

Stash nodded settled against his pillows.

"I'll order up some food. Anything specific you're craving for?" Anthony pulled out his phone. "Christian, can you come in here, please?"

"Yes, thank you." Stash bent his head and studied his short, stubby fingernails. Someone had removed his acrylic nails and filed the natural nails down. The door opened, and he looked up to acknowledge Christian when he walked in.

While Anthony talked to Christian about ordering food for everyone, Stash quietly studied his nails. It felt as though he was looking at a stranger's hands. It was probably illogical, but it had been a long time since he'd had bare nails. After the door closed behind Christian, he looked to Anthony for confirmation.

"So Gregory wanted me to pay for his mother's death?"

Anthony nodded. "He saw you as the reason why she died."

"She died in prison, Ace. She was the one who kidnapped me, Miranda, and Joel. I was twelve, for God's sake. Why is it my fault she died?" There was no anger left inside him, but he still needed to know what he'd supposedly done to deserve such a heinous act of abuse.

"Who knows what a psychopath thinks, or why, but he blamed you. He was probably looking for a woman, and never expected you to be who you are."

"You mean what I am," Stash muttered. His gaze fell on his nails, and quickly closed his hands into a fist to hide them.

"Don't, baby. Don't talk like that."

"I feel like I'm drowning all over again. Why is that?" Stash pounded his fist into his chest and took deep breaths. He welcomed the pain every time he struck himself. At least it confirmed he was alive.

"You've been through a lot."

"And Lawrence? What's happened to him?"

"He's back in prison, and this time I made sure that he never gets out. Not in his lifetime." Anthony breathed out a huff. "He and Gregory were the ones running the scam of selling the shares. Schoffield confessed all after he learned what happened to you. I'm sorry, I had to tell the board why I couldn't be there in person during the meeting, but I was online the whole time it was happening. People understood, and many even congratulated us on our innovative efforts to protect the company. Paul helped me out, just so you know. Through Schoffield, we were able to trace the buyers and have agreements with them to sign the papers the lawyers gave them. All the shares are safely back in my hands."

"Oh, my God, how did those two even meet up?"

"Lawrence had a cellmate called David Zobiansky."

"Who's that?" Stash blinked in confusion.

"Gregory's biological father."

Stash's jaw dropped. "Oh, for fuck's sake."

"I agree."

"Is it finally over?" Stash looked down and hugged himself. The cold, fluttering feeling in his stomach had come back.

"Yes, it's all over."

"I'm going to be sick again," Stash said before jumping out of bed and running toward the bathroom. Anthony rubbed on his back like before, while Stash knelt on the floor, gasping for air.

"I want to go home," Stash repeated.

"If you keep getting sick, they won't release you."

"I just want to go home," Stash insisted. "Do whatever you need to do, just take me home."

Anthony helped Stash brush his teeth and take a shower, but he didn't waste time trying to rush the checkout process. Hospital red tape caused delays until the next morning. Stash's attending physician threatened to continue to delay his checkout by a few more hours unless he agreed to see a psychiatrist. His doctor felt one of the reasons he hadn't woken up on schedule from the medically induced coma was psychological rather than pathological. After discussing it at length with Anthony and Adrien, Stash finally accepted that it might be helpful.

"We could always have him flown in if it's necessary," Anthony declared, after Irene worried the psychiatrist was too far away.

At first, Anthony insisted Stash not to go back to the chateau, but Stash remained adamant.

"It's my home, Ace. True, it's been violated, but I've already talked to Paul, and he agreed an upgrade was in order."

"Not more men?"

Stash shook his head. "No, technical support. Arjan also suggested I take in some of his specially trained dogs. He's got a whole kennel of them. Arjan said if the dogs had been there, Lawrence and Gregory would have had a hard time."

"Flossy did a fine job giving warning. Thank God she's all right. But talking of kennels, didn't you say you'd converted what used to be the original kennels into a pool and gym room?"

"I don't see that as a problem, I have a lot of space and empty rooms that can be easily converted."

"What about Flossy? Wouldn't she be in danger from the bigger dogs?"

"Adrien promised it'd be fine. He said it's all part of the dogs' training, and there will be a vetting before we finalize on which dogs to guard the perimeters. I trust him."

"If you're sure," Anthony said.

Stash could see Anthony wasn't entirely convinced.

They'd been back in Limoges for close to two weeks and had just finished watching an action movie. Stash enjoyed it, but Anthony had tried to ruin it with a running commentary on the mistakes made by writers and producers.

He startled when Anthony suddenly threw a ball across the room. Flossy barked once and jumped after it. When she caught it between her two front legs, she stuck her butt in the air and growled it into submission. The topic of the guard dogs came up again, and Anthony voiced his fears once more.

"Are we back to that subject again?" Stash sighed. "Look, I'm sure it's going to take a while adjusting, but it's going to be all right. Why are you so against the idea of guard dogs?"

"Are you not worried Flossy might not like the presence of strange dogs?" Anthony frowned and pointed at Flossy. "She's kind of a diva and all. Those dogs are giants compared to her. I'm okay if you're okay." Anthony's frown said otherwise.

"Hey, Flossy's my dog," Stash said, reaching out to pat Anthony's hand.

"She's been mine for over two months and sleeps at the top of my head. I worry."

For a moment, Stash couldn't get past the mental image of a Shih Tzu sleeping atop Anthony's head. He shook his head to clear it or risk laughing at his lover.

"Thief," Stash said instead.

"Hey, we all sleep on the same bed."

"Okay, okay, give it a rest. Jeez. Anything else?" That time, Stash couldn't stop himself from laughing.

"Yeah. Marry me."

Stash thought his head would keep spinning from how he whipped it around to gape at Anthony.

"Say what again?"

"Marry me," Anthony repeated.

"I am not." Stash folded his arms over his chest.

"Why?"

"Your proposal isn't at all romantic. Not even a pip of romance went in there. There's zero attempt to romance. I want the dim lights, the flowers. The ring."

Anthony sighed and took out his phone. "In short, you want the movie-style proposal. I guess I can do that."

Stash craned his neck as he tried to see what Anthony was typing on his phone. "What are you doing?"

"I'm making a schedule for the next proposal." After studying whatever was on his phone, Anthony looked up and met his gaze. "How's a week from Saturday?"

"Why take so long?"

"Because of the schedules."

"What schedules?"

"I need a flash mob." Anthony frowned at his phone. He tapped several times more before looking up again. "There won't be champagne or any alcohol, we both don't drink, so what do you want?"

Stash decided to play along. "Just iced tea?"

"Good." Anthony looked serious as he continued to study his phone. "How about snacks? You'll want snacks for the mob."

Stash lost patience. "Why are we talking about a mob? For God's sake, just propose to me right now and forget about the mob."

"I already did. You didn't like it," Anthony said, not bothering to look up.

"Anthony," Stash said, lengthening the name in a mock growl.

"If you insist." Anthony put away the phone and stood up. He went around the room and started turning off the lights and lamps, leaving the glow from the fireplace.

"Oh, that's nice." Stash leaned back into the throw pillows.

"Hold on," Anthony said. He reached into his pants pocket and took out a black jewelry box.

Stash placed his hand over his chest. Whatever game Anthony was playing, he liked it . . . a lot. "Oh my, you really did mean to ask me to marry me, didn't you?"

"I have never been more serious in my life. Now, here goes." He took a deep breath, got down on one knee, and extended his arm holding the box. "Stash, my love, my warrior, my prince. Will you marry me, and save me from a life of misery?"

Stash flounced off the sofa and walked over to a buffet table set against a window. He popped a macaroon into his mouth as he poured iced tea into a glass.

"What are you doing? I'm still on my knee here," Anthony groused.

Stash looked over his shoulder, and indeed, Anthony was on one knee, looking confused and frustrated. He chewed on the macaroon and put the pitcher back on the table.

"I needed a drink."

"You know, when someone says something like that, it usually means whiskey, or bourbon, or cognac. Not iced tea."

"I don't drink alcohol, it messes with my behavior, and I don't like not being in control. Want some?" He raised his glass to Anthony.

"Yes, please. Put lots of ice in it, thank you very much." Anthony rose to his feet, brushed off his knees, and sat on the sofa once more. "Why are you so irritable? I'm proposing to you, and you're getting upset."

"I have a headache." Stash pouted. "I don't like getting headaches. And to be frank, that was a mockery of a proposal."

"Come here." Anthony put the box on the coffee table in front of him and held out his arms.

Stash brightened and hurried to stand between Anthony's legs.

"Lie down on me on your back. Come on," Anthony said encouragingly. He patted at his chest. "A little higher so I can give you a massage."

Stash put the glass of iced tea beside the box, positioned himself on top of Anthony, closed his eyes, and hummed contentedly. He hadn't been lying. Already the sun was too bright, and in his peripheral vision, the rainbow light flickered. The migraine aura had started as soon as he'd woken up that morning. He had taken a pill for it and knew it wouldn't help much, but at least he could avoid the nausea and eventual vomiting.

"Thank you, yes." Stash moaned in satisfaction at the gentle, kneading motions over his scalp.

"What's got you bothered so much?" Anthony asked in a soft tone.

"I don't believe in superstitions," Stash murmured. He

closed his eyes and relaxed under Anthony's touch.

"What are you talking about now?"

"Well, at last count, that was three."

Anthony chuckled. "You're talking in riddles."

"Shut up. You have absolutely no right to have such a sexy laugh." Stash opened his eyes and grinned up at Anthony.

"I have a sexy laugh?"

"Uhm . . ." Stash purred low in his throat, stretched up his arms, and wound them around Anthony's neck. "I want to go shopping."

"No you don't. You're just bored, sweets."

"I want you to come with me. We can take the plane and fly to Paris."

"I wouldn't mind, but I don't think you should make plans for now. Also, think about the carbon footprint. If people found out, we'd be canceled on social. Let's just have quality time together while we're here and say yes to my proposal of marriage."

Stash gently slapped Anthony's bicep. "Why do you have to make me feel guilty?"

"Speaking of ideas," Anthony shifted and pulled out his phone. "Christian, have Genevieve and Jade arrived yet?" He listened for a moment and then continued. "Ask them if they could be ready in an hour."

Stash frowned up at Anthony. "Ace? What's going on?" A thought occurred, and his expression brightened. "Are you surprising me with something?"

Anthony looked down at him and gently placed a finger over Stash's lips. That only made Stash sit up higher and shift his position so he could fully face Anthony.

"Ask Meggie where they can set up," Anthony said once more into the phone.

"What have you been doing?" Stash whispered.

"How would you like to have a spa day, baby?"

Stash squealed and climbed on top of Anthony and started raining kisses over his face. "Thank you, thank you, thank you." He emphasized each word with a kiss.

Anthony chuckled and cupped Stash's face. "You're welcome. Now, will you just say yes, and marry me?"

"Ace?"

"Yes, Stash?"

"I love you."

Anthony raised his brows. "What else?"

"Yes, I'll marry you." Stash rolled his eyes, but he was so happy he felt his face might crack from how broad he was smiling.

"See, it's not that complicated." Anthony's eyes sparkled with emotion. "I love you, too."

Stash closed his eyes when Anthony took his lips in a kiss. It was sweet, unhurried, and cemented his conviction. No matter what complications came their way, he and Anthony were the co-authors to their own lives. Together, they would create their own version of a happily ever after, which they'd unwittingly started with one little note.

Other Books by Jo Tannah

Compelled
Winter Roses
Grass Stains and Flip Flops
Around the Block (Divorced Divas Collection, 2019)
His Christmas Valentine
His Gentle Incubus (Scorched Souls Collection)
The Knockers (Love At Stake Anthology)
A Calling Bird (Twelve Days of Christmas Collection, 2019)

Tales from the Archipelago:
    Kilig
    The Secrets He Keeps

Taboo Series:
    Taboo
    A Taboo Christmas
    Taboo Pleasures
    Christmas Unwrapped
    The Summer Knows

Hidden Series:
    Hidden Evils
    Hidden Dimensions
    Hidden Fates

Rise of the Symbionts:
    Royal Guardian

Royal Consort
Royal Symbionts
Tarragon

CyNapse Security, Inc.:
    Objectified
    Kaleidoscope

The Adventures of Marcus Kildud:
    The Hunt

Chronicles of the Serai:
    Heart Held Hostage

The Phantom Hunters:
    Waylaid

With Ann Mickan:
    Lemonade Stand
    A Lemon Flavoured Christmas

With Lynn Michaels:
    Unchained (Love At Stake Anthology)

Free Stories:
    Sock It To Me
    Tell Him

About the Author

I grew up listening to folk tales my father and nannies told either to entertain us children or send home a message. These narratives I kept with me, and finally, I wrote them down in a journal way back when I kept one. Going through junk led to a long-forgotten box, and in it was the journal. Reading the stories of romance, science fiction, and horror that I had taken the time to put to paper brought to light that these were tales I had never met in my readings.

The tales I write are fictional, but all of them are based on what I grew up with and still dream about. That they have an M/M twist is simply for my pleasure. And I hope yours as well.

Twitter: @JoTannah
Instagram: https://www.instagram.com/jo_tannah/
Facebook: https://www.facebook.com/profile.php?id=100012354600386
Website: http://jotannah.com
Email: jotannah1@gmail.com